■ □ ■ □ ■

TWORKI

Writings from an Unbound Europe

▪ ▫ ▪ ▫ ▪

MAREK BIEŃCZYK

TWORKI

Translated from the Polish
by Benjamin Paloff

NORTHWESTERN UNIVERSITY PRESS

EVANSTON, ILLINOIS

Northwestern University Press
www.nupress.northwestern.edu

Printed in the United States of America

10 9 8 7 6 5 4 3 2 1

Library of Congress Cataloging-in-Publication Data

Bienczyk, Marek.
[Tworki. English]
Tworki / Marek Bienczyk ; translated from the Polish by Benjamin Paloff.
p. cm. — (Writings from an unbound Europe)
ISBN-13: 978-0-8101-2475-2 (cloth : alk. paper)
ISBN-10: 0-8101-2475-0 (cloth : alk. paper)
ISBN-13: 978-0-8101-2476-9 (pbk. : alk. paper)
ISBN-10: 0-8101-2476-9 (pbk. : alk. paper)
1. Psychiatric hospitals—Poland—Fiction. I. Paloff, Benjamin. II. Title. III. Series.
PG7161.I319T913 2008
891.8'538—dc22
2007043987

∞ The paper used in this publication meets the minimum requirements of the American National Standard for Information Sciences—Permanence of Paper for Printed Library Materials, ANSI Z39.48-1992.

■ □ ■ □ ■

CONTENTS

■ □ ■ □ ■

TRANSLATOR'S NOTE

Marek Bieńczyk's *Tworki* takes its title from a small village just southwest of Warsaw that is home to a large psychiatric hospital. The name occupies a place in the Polish imagination comparable to New York's Bellevue Hospital or London's Bethlem Royal Hospital, from which the word *bedlam* is derived.

The novel's characters are known variously by their given names and diminutives. Jerzy (YEZH-ee), the protagonist, is frequently called Jurek (YOU-rek), and even more frequently the text teases him with the kind of nonsense nickname one might hear in such nursery rhymes as "Georgie Porgie, Puddin' and Pie." Danka, his cousin, is sometimes called Danusia (da-NOOSH-a). Other names appearing in the text sound in Polish much as they do in English.

The translator wishes to thank the author and Iga Noszczyk for their many valuable suggestions and clarifications of the Polish text.

TWORKI

■ □ ■ □ ■

CHAPTER ONE

AS THOUGH DREAMED TOWARD BREAK OF DAY, AS THOUGH FROM THE river's very sources, these words came into the world. Yes, in the beginning there was the letter, none too pretty, the tall, clenched letters refusing themselves space, refusing the sentences sails. One might have said, these words are in no hurry to get to the period; and someone else, something's holding them back, but all together now; and I would have said for sure, they'd still like to turn back, to retreat, but now it's too late. At last we should offer them an opportunity to fill out the whole line, a full breath from margin to margin now that it's all over, or that it doesn't matter:

Dear Jurek!

Be good to Janka, and don't think ill of me. I loved you very much. You're a really great guy.

Strange how things work out! Seems like it's the way it had to be! Say hi to everybody I got to know and love through you, especially to your mother. And give *him* another kiss from me: he was everything to me. Fare thee well.

S.

P.S. Be happy!

S.

Jurek read the page twice, squinting suspiciously the way all nearsighted people do, and slipped it into the long-languishing novel, behind the page about the wished-for bell signaling the end of the Polish lesson, and he flew out of the room as though burned. Downstairs at the door he ran into Antiplato, who gently declared, "Even to our heads it spreads," but Jurek didn't so much as wave and, skipping over the puddles, he ran up to Janka, the embodiment of the first words of the letter, who was already sorrowful but not yet crying.

If Jurek Incorrect-Who-Looks-Like-a-Car-Wreck had then had time and opportunity to ponder the letter as precisely as he had picked apart a poet's drama on his written final exam four years earlier, and even then it was all about darkness and gloom, maybe he would have turned his attention to the four narrow posts of the exclamation points. Why had S., to be called Sonia hereafter, as she had been back then, why had she in so conclusive a moment, as she was choking on the words under her ballpoint, as the crooks of her hand crawled as though with ants and her mouth trembled like disturbed water, why had she not dispensed with her two signatures, one after the other, so even in the very middle of the page? Why had she remembered the punctuation? Why had she remained true to the epistolary form of the address line followed by a paragraph on a new line, and why with a graphic sign had she reinforced her well-wishing for the addressee and her sentences of a twelfth-grade—and even humanistic, in the Greek sense—nature? Strange how things work out!—she imprinted hard into the page, as though Sophocles were leading the way, and she backed up her words with an exclamation point, the way the chorus provides commentary in a tragedy. Seems like it's the way it had to be!—she redoubled the statement with an exclamation point, giving fate leave to go, in a royal fashion, performing a low *chapeau bas,* as was wholly apropos.

I'll answer these and other questions many times; when it comes down to it, I'm nearly out of alibis. Maybe she availed herself of these exclamation points because she was already reading about this destiny somewhere. She knew something of it; she'd heard, for example, that it touches all the people named here and still living. But she understood that it pretty much fell to her, that it was she who was caught in a web or safety net, that destiny winked at her with its many little eyes. And, walking away, she had indicated in that graphic manner that she consented, and with her whole self concentrated in a shout—humbly and boldly, with menace and composure—she hit the road like many before her. And in the traditional manner, in the form—permitted to humanity—of a postscript, openly and with a full heart, she wished a better future to those who would remain here. Which is why I think I can ride along those exclamation points, as though on rails, along narrow paths, by a magical line, into those neighborhoods; that through a gymnastic effort I can take them right up to Sonia's square room, right beside Jurek, ever out of breath, and Janka, who is now in tears; slip over onto that side there, near the tick-tocking ticks of Sonia's watch, her black neckerchief with the white polka dots, her flowery dress; that I can follow these rails like a sleepwalker from the high roofs of the blockhouses to the drooping eaves of the hospital pavilions and annexes. For, after all, I've heard and read a bit in my time, and someday, if only there remains strength enough in my vision and in my fingertips to hit the keys, I'll add a few slender slashes, with a ball as round as the Earth at their bases, in farewell.

■ □ ■ □ ■

CHAPTER TWO

FOR JUREK UNSURE-EK THIS WHOLE STORY HAD ALSO BEGUN WITH an exclamation point. "Good salary!" the announcement affirmed grandiloquently. "Free room and board on premises!!" it added on the last line. On the preceding lines the hospital administration had said it was looking for a young man with references and with a good knowledge of the language that had once been essential to the world, and to Europe always, just ask Goethe.

"Good salary," his mother repeated emphatically, leaning over the tabloid. "Your father found his first job in an announcement, too. Too bad," she sighed, "not this one here."

"Free room and board on premises!" Jurek chimed in, biting at the wholegrain bread he himself had stood in line for. "I know how to keep books, I'm great at multiplying figures, and I know which way the wind blows."

"You could come for lunch every Sunday, since it's close," his mother added, briskly slicing more bread.

So the following day Jurek sent an application, *bitte,* with a CV as brief as the history of independent Poland, written on the Continental Wanderer–Werke AG Chemnitz typewriter that belonged to the mother of Olek, his friend from school and soccer. Jurek attached a certificate from the supply office where he'd worked before, for he'd diligently carried out all the duties entrusted to him to the absolute satisfaction of Górecki, the director, and after a moment's thought, Jurek paperclipped an already somewhat crumpled letter of appreciation from the Social Aid Committee, sent in due time to those who considered it a civic honor to help ease the suffering in the capital, worsened by the events of the war, and to those who selflessly contributed what they could to the relief efforts. On Monday he received a summons for an interview, which was already scheduled for Tuesday.

"Tomorrow's Tuesday, so it's off to Tworki," Jurek giggled. "Mama will iron me the white shirt that Dad got for Christmas."

He spent the entire evening in front of his textbook, refreshing his memory all the way up to the past perfect of *gehen,* used only with *sein.* The following day, after a second breakfast, hurriedly devouring what was already the last slice of bread, he filled his briefcase with his credentials and a small volume of poetry, an identity card separating the pages he'd read from those he hadn't yet read, kissed his mother on both her wet cheeks and, when she turned away to hide her tears, took a shortcut through the window on his way to the tram stop.

It was a short trip to the station, and Jurek didn't take his book out; the tram quickly passed the little church on Sowinski Street, where Father Wojtek was sitting on the bench again, reading Schiller's ballads in the original, the golden letters on the cover of his book catching the rays of the sun, ripe as it is at the end of March. A lot of people got on at the first stop downtown, and Jurek gave up his seat to an elderly woman with a wrap of meat, squeezed through to the exit, and was the first, even before the tram braked, to jump out at Zawisza Square.

The rails of the commuter train were a bit wider, there were more free places and doubles next to the single seats, and not everyone from the tram got on, since the commuter train moved with an unsettling punctuality. First he passed the gray tenements, and a moment later he passed only trees, fields mowed for the purpose of planting, the city increasingly remote, crammed against the horizon. A few more stops, a few more verses in his book, a long, green fence farther to the left, and on the right a pond with no boats, but there's a fisherman, and Jurek kept riding. *These verses are really great,* Jurek thought. *In the countenance of silent stars my soul kneels down to prayer/and with mouth gone pale, almost out of breath . . . Only I'm not crazy about the pale mouth, and I'd prefer another color for the soul, particularly on the lips.* In the meantime the brakes had given out a miserable squeak, so the ID goes quickly back into the book, after the poem about the soul's confession, and the book into the briefcase with a thump, the briefcase under his arm, and down the steps he goes, careful not to let his glasses fall as they had three-quarters of an hour earlier while he was jumping from the fast-moving tram.

This is what you wanted. You're here, Jurek thought, frozen before the gate on the other side of the tracks. *To Tworki on Tuesday, here's the platform, and there's the gate.* Pretty dreary all around, under the shelter a beggar played a wistful sonata on a violin, and a guard, like a green smudge and ominously at ease, watched over the gate, and Jurek thought, *It's good that at least it's a short distance to the commuter train, not such a long way to visit home, and the poplars along the wall grow just the same as they do under the window in Ulrychów, though with a bit more foreboding. Maybe go where they lead,* it occurred to him. *Every three meters a new trunk and a new step right up to the bluish distance, and why not get going, since the night is young and so are we?*

"I'm here about the job," he mumbled to the yawning green smudge, with its brown holster on a belt and a pistol in hand. "There was an announcement in the *New Courier,* and here's my summons."

Sleepy and bored, the smudge tossed a glance at the paper, seemed to remember something—maybe the time it had been an usher at the Parsifal Cinema—nodded, and rather politely let him through, and in this way Jurek found himself inside. He went through the gate drawn back with a squeak and started the clock on his new exploits. When he knocked on the door indicated by the guard's gun barrel, the fiftieth second had elapsed from the start of his count; when he came out with papers in hand and a little key hanging from his ring finger, the nineteenth minute had elapsed, to hell with the seconds.

He stepped out onto the path in front of the administrative building. It was tidily graveled, with whitewashed, semicircular borders at its edges. Tall trees, already a little bit green, cast their shadows along one side, and there was nary a feathery ornament in the clear sky today, no glow or smoke dissipating into, let us say, nothingness.

The salary is more on the order of these bushes, he reminded himself, looking at the shrubs beneath the maples. *They deceived me with an exclamation point and conned my most kind-hearted mother with punctuation and style, and the pay won't soon suffice for shoes, let alone for leather ones. That soup you smell all around, that's not from young leeks, either, or from fresh carrots, and if there's meat for the entrée, then who knows whether it's really from the slaughterhouse.* But then again, this place is strangely warm, a safe center like a valley among mountains, and soon, with April, it would be thoroughly shaded by that vegetation beloved of poets, if it drinks to the roots and gives its sprigs free reign. Moreover, the papers here make certain guarantees, smeared *sehr gut* by stamps, and perhaps they get up late, since it struck twelve a while ago, and on the paths there's a lazy procession of pajamas, vertically striped according to the latest fashion, though billowy by tradition and yellowed in the central places of the body.

Feeling a little out of his element in his father's dark suit, which elegantly matched the cream color of the coat thrown over his shoulder, he set off on a stroll through greenery breathing warmth. He spotted a forest over one wall, and over the other the train tracks, poor little houses, and a horse on a tether. He observed a racing trio of cats, maddened by March and striped like the pajamas, and then socks, underpants, and scarves drying on the bars of the windows, sad and exposing their cleanest sides to view as if begging for a change of ownership. From the barrack, with its two chimneys that smoked into the blue, some doubled-up geezer was trudging toward Jurek, arduously pulling the leather straps of a heavy and creaking cart. Jurek didn't so much as glance at the sky, where what is best and in the best condition ascends, and now four rusty and sloshing buckets stood before his eyes. Therein were gathered everything that had been thrown away by a man worthy of better fare and prettier colors. Quartered potatoes and broken bones swam in the pink, opaque depths, ever softer crusts of bread exposed their mold to the world, and a yellow deposit collected in fatty bubbles, the last trace of flavor. The geezer moved along, the stuffiness receded, and Jurek thought that maybe he'd survive this war after all.

His quarters had been promised to him within the hour; now half remained: three poems, add to that a moment of reverie, he figured, and the time would fly by somehow. Having sat down on the edge of a bench, not pressing his back to the carved heart shot through with an arrow, he drew from his briefcase the slender volume, a lemonade, and a yellow apple from who knows where, surely from Madame Zofia, his neighbor, by way of his mother's invisible hand—his dear mother, his poor mother, without his father, who'd suffered and toiled for a year now among the foreigners.

Perhaps on that very same bench, in any case on the fourth one to the left from the main building, I sat yesterday, though now the bench is made of iron, and I with my computer, twenty-five by twenty centimeters and with three hours of charge, they call it a Pentium Texas 2000—I call it a Warsaw 4 Ever. And I'll sit there again in a week, which will be a Tuesday, and on the following Tuesday as well. The bench will be empty, a day with no visitors, the garbage cans gaping with blackness, and beyond the gate the clatter of the commuter train moving closer then farther away, a refrain without verses, an electric memento of return, soon maybe even electronic, and in a couple of years surely an air-cushioned monorail, but you'll still have to have a ticket. And sitting like that, one foot on the other in little sandals and striped socks, waiting like a late traveler for the end of the world, I will tell the willing as well as the passersby, those flying off the train or those waiting for its arrival, the continuation of this story and its actual, unlikely conclusion, its ultimate denouement, its so-called that's that.

On that same bench, now wooden once again, a pair of pajamas sat down next to Jurek, hunched over his book. The pajamas looked like the others all around, with piebald striped socks, and timidly declared, "Hard will be scattered, and straight smeared."

Jurek hunched over more and nestled into his little volume. "Your mouth, young lady, is ravenous for kisses, / It dreams of nymphs afeared of their own cares."

He heard a whisper, quiet, gentle, over his head. "So what is that you're reading?"

Without a word, Jurek showed him the cover. "Poems," he explained. "Selected."

The pajamas grimaced slightly. "If you'll allow me, I'm Antiplato. Beautiful weather today, as one finds this time of year. Soon it'll be spring in full bloom. End quote."

Jurek mumbled a few syllables of his own, gave every assurance that the pleasure was his, and sank into his reading.

"Your mouth, young lady, is ravenous for kisses,
It dreams of nymphs afeared of their own cares . . .
As yet unconscious of men's mouths and promises,
It senses new delights will take it unawares . . ."

Antiplato recited this aloud rhythmically and winced harder still. "They don't write like that anymore. They don't write like that anymore in Tworki. That's how they wrote before Tworki. Do you know what Tworki is?"

"How's that? But we're here," Jurek said and, irritated, slammed the book shut. *But he's a nut,* he thought. *A nuthouse, nuts, crazy in the coconut, and not right in the head, but then again, there are the maples and eternal oaks, the salary, board, not to mention the soup, and then the housing. You could go nuts.* That cheerful young lady dressed up like a bookkeeper—is she nuts as well? With black oversleeves on top, but then all pajamas underneath?

"Pardon me, miss," he asked the whistling passerby over his neighbor's shoulder, "but do you know how to get to Pavilion C?"

"Follow me, please," the stranger answered, smiling radiantly at Antiplato, who suddenly turned red. "I'm going there now."

And there she was, a tall young woman, a woman in bloom, with her right hip sweeping the space that had just been given back by her left, surrendering now this, now the other foot to being shod from behind by his gaze, so that it was Jurek doing the shoeing. Half the heel of her shoe was cork, and above the shoes there was skin so denuded, stockingless, and the first cotton flowers of her skirt, there where one heralded the knee, the selfish kneecap—coochee coochee, to tickle it thus from behind—while still higher mini paradises were concealed in a full carpet of flowers, spring in full bloom, for there were roses and anemones, and maybe also carnations ascending and descending by turns there, in the spot where kids receive their spankings, and thus Jurek's present bumbling, since even in Arcadia one could find a few stones in the end, and maybe they also even had these stupid office oversleeves, like black premonitions at the garden's edge, like funereal shrouds donned by both nature and culture, and it was a good thing that her fingers emerged out of that blackness, swarthy and long, deftly translating her whistling into the language of gestures, counting the measures to the chirping melody, and ordering us to forget all allowances and, with sudden *allegretto* intensified by a *molto vivace,* they guided Jurek's gaze upward to where the conductor's shoulder, at that second raised, was directing the kettle drums to beat and the strings to rush into a finale that flowed into billowy, glimmering, strawberry-blond waves, the image of which Jurek took with him on the last train that evening as "a Niagara of hair" to rhyme with "faithful compare," jotting his words on the little poetry volume's cover. In the moment, though, he tracked the waves with his dumb gawk all the way to their manifold, bicolored roots, separated on the left side by a part and kind of just reined in over the ears by a purple-hued hair band, which toward the back of the head was losing its mastery over that storm of bright silk, but which suited her face—swarthy for sure, but perhaps quite pretty, and, turned back for a moment, smiling radiantly and checking whether Jurek was headed to Pavilion C, since that's just where she was going, that's just where she was going.

How might I present myself? Jurek pondered as he approached the massive wooden door. *What's the right thing to say, and should I start modestly with my first name, or should I spread the whole thing out right from the start—sadly with no noble "-ski" at its none-too-pretty end? Is half better, or the whole lesser? Fast either way, and before we get to those stairs. And what's that we hear?*

"You must be Jerzy," Jurek hears. "You're new to our administration. You'll start tomorrow, and you'll live in that empty room. You'll be on the second floor. Might I show you the way?"

"And you must be Beatrice. You have beautiful, dark eyes and a radiant smile. You're my guide among the paths and pavilions, and you wish everyone well. Hence everyone brings you flowers and writes you poems."

A brief giggle, many stairs. On the second floor something scraped and buzzed metallically, whined quietly, as though kneeling, shuffling, and finally it grated twice. That was Jurek, ever so nearsighted, opening the door in the half dark. He noticed four cream-colored walls, and his premonitions did not disappoint: he had been thinking of a single wide bed with a red-and-blue checkered blanket, and there were two beds, narrow, with white identification tags on the iron frames and blankets the color of unripe strawberries. He'd dreamt of a desk in front of the window, and beyond the window of an eternal oak, and there the oak stood.

What more could he have asked for? Certainly not that picture of snow over the bed, with a penguin playing the role of the dastardly villain, and not this young woman next to him in a flowery dress and half-heeled slippers, who said, "My name's Sonia. We'll be doing the accounts together. I have a similar room, but you can't see it from here because it's in Pavilion B. And the picture in my room has palms and an empty boat on a beach."

"So-nia," Jurek repeated disyllabically, and the first rhyme that came to mind had rich green leaves and soft pink petals. "Sonia. Such a pretty name. Just a little funny to address you formally as Miss Sonia."

"Now I have to go down to the laundry on the first floor: the sheets have disappeared again. And then I can show you the grounds and offices . . . if you'd like . . . So I'll see you momentarily in the foyer."

"I'd like to, I can, and I must," Jurek calculated, quietly closing the door. "I am, I have, I'm sitting, I'm standing, I'm thinking, I'm wanting, I know. Knockout."

He looked more carefully around the room. The aforementioned walls, the desk, the bed, and that oak outside the window have already been remarked upon, but a dark wardrobe to the right of the door has not. Also beyond the window, if only for the time being, the silhouettes of two white lab coats passed each other on the path and shook hands perfunctorily, and a cat, fortunately also white, surprised that a bird was flitting about, while in Jurek's heart there was a picture of a desert and a paradisiacal oasis on its edge, in the country there was constant war, the world brutal despite the kitty. Brutal, black, and evil.

"Whom, where, what, and how?" Jurek wondered, sitting on the desk, his back to the window. Snug as a bug in a rug, and there's a rug here, too, and a stove with cream tiles, right in the corner next to the wardrobe. Is that where you can still have normal questions, when everything's raging, one thing against the other, man against man? Better to ask narrowly, for example, whether Sonia's already finished counting the sheets in the laundry downstairs, whether she's already in the foyer commanding her flowers to sway and her oversleeves to gleam.

She gleamed with a smile, too, when Jurek proposed getting to know each other over lemonade, assuming that that was the best they could find.

"Mister . . . will you be going often, sir . . . Jurek, to Warsaw, will you be going often?" she asked once they'd stepped onto the path behind the laundry. "I hardly ever get out there. I don't like that city; at least here there are so many trees and so much greenery in the springtime, and at night you can even go look out at the sky and the stars. A little like at my sea."

Her sea, as she immediately explained, was at one time also our sea: her waves had washed our beaches in an area mapped out by both sides and internationally ratified; her ambers had belonged to our state, potentially in the sand and concretely in brooches and necklaces, though her native city hadn't been ours at all; her city was—Jurek amused himself—like a maiden to be married off, like a taxi or rickshaw with no passenger, like a poor little snail, right up until the battleship's opening salvos.

"Oh, that's why Sonia's eyes are wide, actually like seashells, and that's where Sonia's charming syntax comes from, with the verb sometimes at the end, and the slight accent."

"Slight?" Sonia said, laughing, and pointed out that they were turning to the path on the right. "The worst may be my *r*."

Perhaps it really was too throaty for such a lovely neck, which became clear as Sonia was showing Jurek the farm, with its already-Germanic chickens and fowl mostly for the hospital's use, and with a cow, black with slightly claret spots, and clearer as she led Jurek around the various recesses, where the wall made switchbacks and where, on a little patch, roses and *Rosen* would soon bloom in their conflicted company, such as it was. It was a strange *r*, and perhaps all of Sonia was strange, for Jurek had started to think more about the immediate future—probably too immediate—than about eternity, because he was talking even more than he was thinking.

"As we are walking here together, ma'am, well . . . with you, Sonia, I'm getting the feeling now and then that this place and I are meant for each other. That a lot of unusual things are waiting for me here. Because I already feel so good here with you, ma'am—Sonia, I mean."

Next they inspected the kitchen, which had, according to Jurek's mumbling, a hellish cauldron for certain sins, and then they saw the dayroom, which was closed at that time, like—in Jurek's estimation—the majority of women's hearts, and they returned to the central path, passing groups of pajamas strolling lazily in the full sun. They passed the bench, empty once again, and yet already so memorable, passed the boiler room, with its heap of coal next to the entrance, and they reached the administrative building, to the right of the gate if you're coming in, or to the left if you're fleeing. They entered a large room on the first floor, and Sonia carefully closed the door.

"Honnette, the director, has his office right across," she said in a lowered voice. "A real humanitarian, he spends all day reading. He came from Freiburg, in Schwarzwald. Very fat, and his Adam's apple is always bouncing, which is supposed to be a mark of good character. Sometimes they come to see him, the ones in black—two in particular—but nothing happens. You can also deal with the one who hired you—that's Kaltz. He's from Weimar, doesn't speak a word of Polish, and it's worth getting in good with him . . . surely you have good German?"

Jurek answered in the affirmative by lowering his eyelids, round behind their thick glasses, like seashells—sadly of the freshwater variety—and, following Sonia's graciousness, approached the nearest desk.

"This is where our typist, Bronka, sits. A splendid girl, good worker, she types with both hands, all ten fingers, more than five pages an hour, even. Very nice, a little shy, and sad. She has two lovely black braids."

"I probably shouldn't yank them," Jurek mumbled, and stood next to the second desk.

"This is where I sit, over here. Fela Jabłkowska, the head secretary—watch out for her. Here's Quick, from Heidelberg, withdrawn, precise, but not too smart and totally harmless."

No employees had yet been assigned to the last three desks. Sonia sat Jurek down to try out the first one that was free, unfortunately right behind Jabłkowska's, leaving the remaining two for an as yet unknown pair, probably to be hired soon because, just as the front was growing, there were more and more people coming to Tworki for the soup at the appointed hour and the insane portion of bread in the morning, when the cock crowed.

Meanwhile, Jurek was looking over the files, albums, and pencils arranged evenly in their case, the abacus with black and yellow beads, and the typewriter with only Gothic type. He cautiously touched its metal casing, gently shifted the roller, and all of a sudden fired away at the keyboard, breaking the silence with a loud click clack cluck, imprinting black on white in the scattered type demanded by the zeitgeist: "In the office there's Fela and Bronka, but I'm a slave to Miss Sonia." Sonia leaned over; Niagara poured its waters over his shoulder.

After their group reading, Jurek obligingly crumpled the paper and tossed it deftly into the wastebasket, though custom demanded that it be burned, and he answered her blushing with blushing and an understanding smile at the watch she pointed to.

"I have to run," Sonia said. "It's almost five already."

Jurek, still obliging, let Sonia through the first door and the second, stepping to the side, torso slightly bowed, heart rather in the throat, in his mouth a half-sweet "You're very welcome." And then there were just quick steps forward, for one set the exit, for the other the gravel path, until the slender silhouette disappeared—though to where he did not know, for it was hard to see through the grating, and the metal bit painfully into his cheeks, yes, the metal was biting into his cheeks.

Behind Jurek's back the Warsaw train came to a screeching halt, let out a handful of people, and took in even fewer, but not the man in his early years, with thick glasses and a worn-out briefcase in which there lay a little book, the apple already gone. This particular somebody happened to be walking around the neighborhood, cautiously adjusting his footing around the puddles left by yesterday's downpour, over the lane by the tracks, as though it had been for him that they'd put down these crossbeams of wood that smelled of pitch and these shiny rails leading through Komorów, Nowa Wieś, Kanie Helenowskie, Podkowa, and Malinówek to nowhere, until finally there appeared the first clean glades and crystal water and grasses without unnecessary markings, to say nothing of the quiet sky lashed with only the crowns of the trees, and, what's more, the blue.

Even here, not so far from the hospital walls, it's not bad, a meadow quiet as though after a flood, a little bridge as unyielding as faith and green as hope, and a little river running under it, not too big, transparent, with little fish as signs of God's love, but made smaller by whatever its name, Utrata—"Loss"—subtracted from its lovely sum. If only arms yet perspired together on the river and in the meadow, in the heat of the late afternoon and in the morning dew, and fingertips still pressed together, and if only dark eyes still gleamed at blue and the wind blew women's hair into the mouths of men speaking in verse, and yes, absolutely, rhyming out a stanza about a strange yet beautiful dream, though we sometimes just call it long, or we just say *c'est la vie.* What more will there be, what more will happen, and what will come of this youth, Jurek Impure-ek? How long, which way, with whom, and for whom will what's written take place, will what comes be written?

But that's the last of the Komorów line rumbling like the *z* dashing in the rear guard of the alphabet, so there's no longer any reason to stick around here, Jurek a-Blurr-ek, because the train's not going any farther than that, nothing but questions to think up or write down, because the letters in our alphabet are numbered, and they're cutting back on the trains, so let's hurry back from the stream to the platform and exchange the scenic view for the window, and in half an hour we'll already be in Warsaw—just enough time for Jurek to break into a poetic description of Sonia, cram his little volume hurriedly into his briefcase, his pencil into his pocket, and, still running, leap out into the grayness at the edge of day and an existence of evening prohibitions. The tram brought Jurek home, the written portrait of Sonia to the halfway point, and the expedition to a happy conclusion.

Of course, his mother was still waiting, with an open window on the first floor and tears in her eyes, the holy trinity of too-late returns, the retrieval of what had been lost, the nearsighted son risen from the ashes, but in a moment the tears will already have been furtively wiped away, dinner served, the auspicious news of employment commented on in words thanking heaven for earth, and then, after a second helping of carrot bread, and after another helping of fragrant cereal, Jurek might hole up in his corner where his chair stood, the little desk, the books, and on the desktop his second apple of the day sat and waited like built-up temptation, and then he might take out some letter paper, the best, from before the war, and describe in a long letter to Danka the complete—though surely not quite complete—course of recent events.

■ □ ■ □ ■

CHAPTER THREE

THIS IS HOW IT WAS WITH DANKA. ONE DAY JUREK LEFT HOME AFTER lunch, as carefree as a young count, and went to see his aunt Irena in Solec to help carry the coal, for since his uncle was carried like a sack of potatoes into that other world the poor thing had been left with no one, and though she had pluck, she didn't always manage men's work. And with coal—well, well, well, how many times must one run up the stairs, and the basement is so deep. So then Jurek lugged the coal, washed his hands of the black work, prayed with his aunt before a photograph of his uncle with a black ribbon, and then Irena set out black-currant liqueur and, so as not to let his fingers rest, asked Jurek to write such and such a letter to her niece in Ozorków because it is hard, after all, for an old heart to set thoughts straight, and then again to be silent for too long is a shame and a disgrace. Jurek gathered all his aunt's recent news, from her sciatica to the pain in her side, her thanks for thinking of her and for the currants for compote, and her wishes for Danka's success in her first professional job behind a desk, and he put all of it in verse and, when his aunt at first cracked up and then grimaced slightly and scratched her gray head, rewrote the whole thing without rhyme, but in exchange needed permission to put in his own postscript.

> Dear Marquise, my brief addendum like an invitation to dance. I'm twenty-one, love and respect my aunt Irena, am interested also in

poetry and books, but of you, Marquise, I know but little. Would you like to dance a waltz with me?

Nine days later the dear viscount—what the hell was the *vis* for?—learned that Danka from Ozorków had the same interest, love, and respect but was nineteen and would prefer never to exchange photographs so as to remain behind a veil of mystery; she also thought a great deal about flowers and quiet retreats, believed as well that life is beautiful and strange, and her cat's name is Amicis, like the heart. To which Jurek wrote back that in this beautiful and strange thing what's most important is love, and the worst thing is loneliness, especially in such difficult times as now, and having obtained confirmation that friendship does indeed count the most, he could, with the calm of a distance runner, launch into a chronicle of daily events and thoughts, minted once a week, exchanged once a week for a provincial chronicle, fresh and charming like a quiet cabin among the cornflowers, like Amicis on the windowsill.

In keeping with Danka's request, Jurek sent no photographs, but with all haste he described more or less what he looked like. "I'll give a few personal details about myself," he announced in his next letter, without beating around the bush.

And so the first thing is that I was born (my biggest mistake in life thus far). In daylight—or, strictly speaking, nightlight, since it was actually at night that I issued my first triumphant cry—I beheld Warsaw. The calendar at that historic moment indicated the date as the sixteenth of May, 1921. In Warsaw I was raised and grew up, and maybe this is why I love and adore it so. I spent my childhood, as the poet says, idyllically, angelically. When I was two years old I acquired the company of a brother, who was given the name Witek. Then preschool. Three years of carefree fun. I ate porridge with milk and . . . I was happy. And time passed, the years flew by. I finished primary school and started to make my way to the long-desired middle school. Now the world already seemed to me big, wonderful, huge. I started to read, a lot, passionately. I count the four years I spent in middle school among the most lovely in my life. After finishing middle school I passed the exam for the high school of management. And at last, after two years of study, the graduation exam, never forgotten, not even in the lush life of the student, rich in adventure. Now it seemed to me that the whole world belonged to me, that everything was there for the taking. The moment I submitted my papers to the college of trade, that memorable September had arrived. War! That word roused all of us young people. It ignited our enthusiasm and rapture. The fatherland in danger! What terrible pain that awakening was, overwhelming us to the bottom of our souls. An awakening all the more painful because it was unexpected.

Jurek added the last words sharply, then just greetings and a big hug for Amicis.

■ □ ■ □ ■

CHAPTER FOUR

WHILE DANKA WAS READING ABOUT THE TRAIN THAT TOOK JUREK TO his new digs out of town, about the little river beyond the fence like the blue Danube in a land of gray people, about the room with the penguin and the guard at ease next to the poplars, which were at attention, Jurek No-Longer-a-Cur-ek, but *homo officus* and errand boy, for three days heard the commuter train only from a distance, during which time he didn't look into the stream, and for three days he punched figures into a table and wrote in our language whatever they happened to *sprechen* at him. At this time, for us at *that* time, next to the desk belonging to Bronka and Jabłkowska's secretary, Jurek placed his body, suspended like all the others between payment and perdition, but now quite well situated for the war, closer to the occasional German mark and the ephemera of a zloty than to that victorious gravitation six feet under.

Because even that Kaltz, his immediate superior, accepted Jurek by acknowledging his agreeable presence before his German mug when they had to go buy more to eat, then buy it for less, and eventually buy more for less at the cheesehouse in Pruszków. Jurek chatted on the side with Żwirek, the director, and from the supervisor's platform the latter reminded the gathered workers of the fable about the fox and the raven, because there was that Polish saying about how nutcases will smile at anything, even cheese, so let's give our nutcases more to smile at. For the time being, there were six extra kilos of rich cheese for a good start and the distant finish.

Things went even better for Jurek at the neighboring slaughterhouse. He was standing behind rolls of hose with an already pale Kaltz and watching as Mr. Staś was dragging a Polish cow through the open gateway. With her rump stiffly raised, she cut her last form of existence against the forest background, like the body of a violin turned on its side, until she finally stopped under the bright vault of the hall. And that may well have been her heaven, if one could make out the starry constellations in the hooks gleaming above her. Mr. Janek waited for the cow to freeze up for a minute, to lower her cries to silence, and bashed her on the head with a mallet, and with a single stroke of the knife Mr. Karol, the first-chair violin, made an inertly prostrate thing of what had heretofore been standing and mooing; the sky came down and swept the bundle to its heights. Kaltz, staring upward, finally fainted. Like the sweetest little *mädchen,* he lay his head on Jurek's shoulder and transferred the burden of his body to him—set him down now, he'll be all right, now he's coming to. When Kaltz opened his eyes, he saw above him two soft Slavic pupils behind thick glasses, and he lapped up the water flowing to him from a mustard pot as though from a fountain. At last the forest was locked behind the gate, the hose bleached the entire scene in long streams, the truck loaded up with a mountain of beef, not just the bony stuff, and Kaltz quietly, so that his chauffeur would not hear, thanked Jurek and patted him on the shoulder. On the way back, he was also pleased with how Jurek Allure-ek, A-Flounder-in-Fact, flattened himself next to Kaltz on the floor of the truck and later pledged to conceal from the world how Kaltz had forayed under the seat at the first sound of bandit fire—or, just between us, Herr Jerzy, the farting from a muffler as holey as Swiss cheese, Krupp and Daimler be damned.

Also, the commander in chief, Honnette, beautifully biconsonantal and double-chinned, kindly took Jurek into his office for a short conversation about his first job as a bookkeeper, when Honnette was all of twenty-one years old, and about life as a big, fat director. He told Jurek how important our studies are for our existence, especially in Freiburg, and how great a role a German family plays, from one's wife to one's grandchildren, now growing up for the glory of the future of a new Europe, and that he was pleased with this Polish pipsqueak and his accent, similar to his grandfather's in Alsace, where, a long time ago, for the sake of convenience, he wore short trousers on suspenders and the sun burned right into his knees, and for the gullet there gleamed tasty white grapes and bright cabbage that was the lightest of any that grows far and wide. If we were to sum up the preceding and add Bronka's quiet laughter over Jurek's poems, as well as the chuckles of several of the loons amenable to Jurek's presence on the Elysian paths of the *inside,* it would be difficult to define Jurek's initial situation other than as—and this is a quote from his subsequent letter to Danka, where he changed the word *farting* to *blasting*—"not bad, promising, at times rather carefree."

And what about Sonia?

Wednesday came after Tuesday, a rain-spattered blues day. On the first floor in Ulrychów the alarm clock was merely ticking, but Jurek's brow was already burning with travel fever. The porridge pot boiled, the aroma pervaded, but the worst thing was the shirt, because it was the very same one for the second time, like one life after another, and you can't stop noticing it from morning to night.

Either this beige one, or a tie, Jurek raged over his coffee, which smelled just black enough and tasted weak. *Nothing fits you, shithead. And even I have to get my father's hand-me-downs. My father's shirt, my father's suit, my father's lousy eyesight, even the same curve over the forehead as my father. And I'll be soaked by the rain.*

His mother wiped his glasses with felt, placed them on Jurek's nose, and smiled, remembering her own youth at the Café Ratuszowa in the Saxon Garden, with that garret room nearby, while the Battle of Warsaw, the "Miracle on the Vistula," was getting underway, not just on the ground, but in her bed as well. Actually, Jurek took after his father, Jan, her husband, whenever Jurek would lay his hand on his high forehead and conceal a smile in his eyes, when he would turn his head that funny way and the down shone white over his ears. So just a moment longer, a little more porridge to finish off carefully, and the Miracle on the Vistula was finally over. Over the beige shirt there flashed a coffee-colored neckerchief, the bright brown jacket hugged his tight shoulders, the belt caught hold of its mark, a light coat enveloped the whole, and it's better not to mention the shoes because, after all, they're barely making ends meet at home, since at home the gingerbread was made from carrots, the butter from memories, but the soles tapped out memories of their own as Jurek flashed before the window with his mother's face glued to the pane, and as he leapt up toward the tram stop as if to seize the day. His mother's red umbrella, because his father had unfortunately lost his black one before they'd rounded him up, quickly lowered its flaps, weighed down by a stream of rain, and rose up just at the sight of the late number seven tram. Jurek's back dried on the tram, and the most important part—the cuffs of his pants—dried out on the train.

But what about Sonia?

The day after Tuesday, a rain-spattered blues day. It had been coming down since five in the morning. Sonia jumped out of bed at six, well, fine, she dragged herself out of bed at six thirty. It was still pretty dark in her room, and she stood in her nightshirt like a radiant apparition before a modest breakfast. On her desk, yesterday's roll was waiting, carefully wrapped in paper, and rutabaga marmalade shone red on the saucer, but no, first Sonia washed herself in the shower at the end of the hall, where our gaze is not permitted, and we can but hear the slap of her slippers and the rustle of her castaway dressing gown. But something had to have happened there, because she returned with her head wet, though Saturday was a long way off and she didn't have much vinegar. Now she was drying her hair with a green towel, and she made such a to-do that the roll jumped up and the glass rang against the spoon. It's a shame that so few are suited to frizzy hair, just as land is unsuited to Niagara, because, after all, there is no way that flowery dress from yesterday will do, and now certainly not the gray skirt that matches the gray jacket like twin mice; maybe the little black skirt and the white shirt would be best, but what is this, school? Anyway, why air out the wardrobe, and it was already quite decided yesterday, before she fell asleep, that Sonia would spend the day in blue and yellow; if only it would stop raining, that slim man would again look warmly and speak so funnily, waving his big, friendly hands, and everything wouldn't be so very wrinkled.

It was. Sonia quickly pulled the iron she'd taken from the laundry out from under the bed. In a light arc the little roll had landed on the quilt between the suit and the blouse, and Sonia's catlike tongue removed the marmalade from her skirt before Mr. Jan, summoned through the window from the groundskeeper's cabin next door and sent to the boiler room, flew joyfully in with what looked like a fervent spirit at the bottom of a pail. The entire room heated up as Sonia ironed her favorite dress, and the sky grew light so that she could now whistle and look at herself in the mirror.

It's not like you haven't already been through this before, her double surely said, tittering stupidly, *and all the same, that gentleman caller didn't call, and the day drowned in champagne chilled before its time, and the new earrings tumbled ferociously to the bottom of the aquarium, but what could you expect, he was so handsome, tall, and American, like, unfortunately, no one else in this rotten country.* Her lipstick left a trace on the glass of tea, and it blended with the roll, enough that Sonia choked and returned obediently to the mirror to repaint, to recolor, that which had done the devouring, had received the wetting, or that had wanted to, depending.

Mr. Jan was waiting patiently by the exit and messing around with something in the broken lock. Five minutes of conversation about what was new in Tworki—about how Goethe had let Bismarck have it in the mouth because Bismarck had nabbed another one of his cigarettes, about Cleopatra, who left the pavilion again yesterday without panties on, and about where Kaltz had spent the night, and what they said yesterday on Radio London—Sonia incorporated it all into the pleasure of morning comings and goings, the usual bows and brief exchanges of complements for courtesies on the main path. This time Rubens praised the colors of her dress and her well-postured feet, thanks to the excellent work of her knees, and Dürer also praised her makeup, which had been applied more carefully than usual. She thanked them by smiling and wishing them a good day, and especially a good lunch, and she arrived at the entrance gate by way of successive greetings and heartfelt hellos.

On the Tworki platform the puddles reflected what was already a nearly clear sky, and the umbrella admitted the last tiny drops onto its red sea. Other than Jurek, no one jumped off, or even got off, the train, and it was as quiet as before a concert. Actually, after a moment, something yelped and whimpered beneath the shelter, and that same beggar as yesterday was already playing his violin, especially on the lower strings. *Things don't look so bad,* Jurek thought, *a red umbrella, a sonata, a shirt with no tie—if only she's waiting for me.*

She was waiting, hard as it is to picture—though Jurek did, before falling asleep. She was waiting right next to the entrance gate, chatting with the guard, who was finally at attention, like a pine before it's chopped down.

"But what an umbrella!" she said as she burst out laughing. "Good thing it's not raining anymore."

"A red umbrella, a sonata . . ." Jurek started vigorously, but he quickly fell silent under the guard's blue-eyed gaze.

"This is Johann," she said. "Just imagine, before the war he lived in Baden-Baden."

After the first Baden, Johann smiled mildly and took two steps back, as prescribed.

They went in. Jurek clanged amiably on the bars and waited for Sonia to turn around.

"And destiny had it . . ." he said quietly, and looked straight into her astonished eyes, "that I would be a bookkeeper."

"We still have a quarter hour. Come on, I'll show you something."

They passed the administration building and ran onto a path along the wall. Behind the sixth birch Sonia suddenly turned to the left and flitted between the tall juniper bushes. Jurek was still running when a swing started back and forth. There, high up near the tops of the trees, her light brown soles became dark, and Sonia's blue-and-yellow dress became rather more bold and colorful than well-made. Coming down, she refracted her colors in the nearsighted man's lenses, and on the way back, her brown soles passed under Jurek's nose like impatient microphones on long, slender legs. So Jurek said, "It'll be warm again today, despite the morning rain. Such lovely weather this year. It's as hot as July. There hasn't been such a vibrant blue sky for ages."

The swing shot up toward that vibrant blue and hung there for a quarter of a second so that Sonia could seem unattainable, which is to say, quite feminine. The kissing would best begin from the ear and the neck and then move downward with the swing, to a point somewhere a half-meter above the ground. For now one might recall this or that about a soaring swan and a beauty, whom you couldn't seize or slow down unless she wanted you to.

"I don't want to boast, but we're really having a beautiful end of March this year," Jurek said, at the very bottom, and ineffectually crumpled his hat. "To say nothing of the swans."

Sonia leaned far out, stretched her neck, rocked her head independently of the swing, and gathered the next bit of momentum, with her left hand holding her dress over that which hadn't come into Jurek's mind but rather had crossed it. *Well, I don't know if I'll catch her, because she's not on the ground*—that's somehow how he sensed it all at first—*she's swinging too high and is maybe too swarthy for my white complexion.* Now, with greater calm, he put on his hat and buttoned his coat next to the birch, white's advocate.

But even so, light and pale, he didn't look bad against the curve of its trunk, if one were looking at him from above, then from below, and again from above. He thrust his hands into his pockets, and his belt buckle was located exactly in his middle, dividing him into equal halves, like the caesura in a good verse. Along the right side, where Jurek ended and rhymed, his coat ran all the way down to the very cuffs of his trousers. In this broad perspective, the cuffs, about which one could say much, spilled ever so wide over the thin and none-too-leathered shoes. But the main thing is that they broke: their wave was swashbuckling, and the tailor had figured them to the centimeter for an exaggeration that dazzled with its announcement of girth hidden beneath material made to measure. Higher up, four buttons above the buckle, the half-raised collar split per the norm into two offshoots, shielding a rather irresolute chin from the standing forest and the suspended woman, though it was freshly sprinkled with eau de cologne, the mouth pressed lightly shut, a bit too narrow for an American mouth, a larger-sized nose, ears much bigger, at the same time right for the hat, that alone being decidedly darker than the birch. As a gangster, by the look of him, Jerzy had already killed more than once before; as a Rudolf Valentino, he maybe didn't have many on his conscience; but as himself, in his own person, he was now only as big and important as those who saw him took him to be.

"You look good from up here," Sonia said, jumping lightly onto the footpath and looking him over carefully. "That coat fits you great, and the hat's really first-class. And how do you like my garden plot? Actually, as far as a garden plot, it's just this swing here and that little bench under the birches. I come here often when I have a moment free. Before going to work, too, because I get up very early. Just don't laugh. Promise me you won't laugh?"

It would have been more honest and suitable to do so on his knees, but in the end he promised from the bench.

"Because you know, Jurek, I really love to ride the swing. Since I was a child. On the sea, a garden with a little house we had. You could swing very high—my dad set up special, thick ropes."

"And why are you so fond of the swing?" Jurek asked, the little finger of his right hand resting on Sonia's elbow.

"I like . . . it's hard to say. I'm here, and then suddenly I'm there, higher up. And here again. And there again. No need to walk. Because I know . . ."

"Where did this swing come from?" His finger straightened, but just slightly.

"One of the patients set it up . . . the one who was with you yesterday . . . he wrote this poem about people on a swing and read it to me, really strange, but he said it was definitely a poem. So one thing led to another. The hardest part was with the ladder; fortunately, Rubens helped him bring it over and took good care that he didn't fall. I didn't know if I should laugh or cry, because he was holding the ladder so tightly and repeating, 'Just a second, you moron, you're gonna fall, just a minute, you moron, you're gonna fall.' "

Meanwhile, Jurek had grown serious. "Have you ever thought about how little room there is in this world for kindness? How rare a phenomenon it is to find a person among people? A person with a soul? And the soul's the heart and the mind. Especially, Sonia, the heart. The heart."

Sonia nodded and focused on Jurek's cuffs. They broke wonderfully, totally American, even when he was sitting like that with one leg on the other and gathering the first rays of sunlight in his thick glasses.

"How few possess one or the other. And yet here this team of two factors, working in harmony with each other, provides what we call spiritual culture, creates a truly great and magnificent unity. The watchword of such unity is to forget oneself and not to lose oneself. To forget yourself means to discover your own axis, which lies beyond you, and around which our lives move and turn. And not to lose oneself, meaning to be true to yourself on the fundamental line of your life, is to be true to those ideals that one should . . . oh . . . oh . . . uh . . . uh . . . uphold."

Sonia nodded again.

"But don't worry away your first workday," she added after a moment, and she scrunched her nose, making a funny face such that the dimples in her cheeks filled in for a moment and, just a moment later, were once again charmingly suited to her face, as dreaming and aspiration and, for the time being, silence were suited to Jurek's. Jurek finally smiled, too, and placed a second finger on Sonia's elbow.

"The first day of work, the second day of elation. Sonia releases waves of sensation. You know, that's how I'd like to talk about everything, to say that much about everything right from the beginning."

Sonia burst out laughing and looked, quite as she had yesterday, at her watch.

"We have to go," Jurek blurted first, sighing. "It's definitely time to go."

A few minutes later, Sonia led Jurek to all the appropriate places, subjecting those who were radiant from the morning and from the morning weary to an attentive gaze and good-morning curtsies, as happens among the working class, and then sat at her desk with the first account, which was admittedly no simple matter to Jurek. And when lunchtime suddenly arrived like an awaited monsoon, repasting the hungry with wet barley soup and little potatoes damp with sauce and what was ostensibly half a cutlet, she placed a mountain of cafeteria trays before Jurek, explained the system of how one did better to take from the bottom of the pot, and she herself poured him the first course right up to the brim, the distribution of the second being left to him who was interested, increasingly thankful, also surprised, ever infatuated, and terribly young.

When, after the first quitting time, which was announced by the ding-dong of the clock and the violent slamming of Quick's German briefcase, Mr. Surprised and Infatuated stepped hesitantly out in front of the building, right into a patch of sun, squinting his eyes physically and psychologically, and Sonia was already waiting next to the gate, which was slightly ajar, like the inside of a metaphor. *She and I,* he thought, *like two wheels speeding into the open space of time, she and I like an eternity let out of work, an anonymous heroic duo, happily linked in the last line of a sonnet.*

"If you want," Sonia said, "I can show you around the neighborhood, since it's such a lovely day," and she took the first step, too fast for fresh similes. They walked toward Pruszków along a cobbled road, among low houses that all looked alike, and Jurek's open coat puffed out with courage mustered from the wind.

"The poet was right," he uttered at the dress waving before him, here yellow, there blue. "He was right when he said that women know how to awaken our most uplifting feelings, that they are the invisible springs behind deeds that require an unusual exertion of will. In particular . . ."

Sonia turned sharply to the left, toward Komorów, and onto a narrow trail that ran through dormant orchards. For a moment they were walking single file, Sonia, followed by what Jurek was saying, and at the end, Jurek himself, until there finally opened before them, near Kopry, a still-sunny glade.

"Now this is lovely," Jurek gasped, catching his breath, whereas Sonia was already breathing normally. "And you, with this background."

Sonia stood before the juniper and looked toward the slowly darkening horizon. Her strawberry-blond Niagara lost its luster in the diminishing light, though it gained an indispensable firmness of form around her fluid eyes, which were fixed on the most distant distance.

"I wish I could describe this. Or, even better, paint it. To do your portrait. A dark green juniper and your figure."

"I love to paint, too. But I like drawing with crayon even more."

"If I were a painter, I would only paint people. Their portraits. And how they stand. But I only barely passed in drawing. Even with the borders in my notebook I didn't do so well. My dear mother had to help me because the lines didn't stay straight, but curved down."

"Why only people?" Sonia asked, and from the crack in her voice it seemed to Jurek an important question, and he felt it deep inside.

"I don't know. Then something good happens. Faces are so rich . . . sort of endless. So that it's a shame if they don't last. That's why I never skip over descriptions when I'm reading. And bodies in clothes are so meticulous and would so like to be eternal. Like me, now, with you on this meadow."

They made a slow circuit around the clearing, and Sonia pointed out how they would reach the tracks through the forest. The train whistle spread out in a triple echo and flickered among the trees like a half visible, magical thread. "And going to the cinema is something I also really love," Sonia said straight into Jurek's downcast eyes. "Most of all I love how they do things in America."

"When the war's over, we'll go see a new movie every day. What do you say?"

"Oh yes, let's."

Again Sonia scrunched her nose comically, and now she indicated which cross-country trail they'd take back to Tworki. Jurek held his ground, that's not the direction and no way, and for a long time he wouldn't give in, when Sonia, laughing, dragged him by the sleeve until something in his coat finally started to tear in warning. They were walking quickly again, Sonia first as always, and Jurek taking big steps to keep up and, as though they were now coming out of the cinema, to suggest something more. The first lights already glowed in the pavilions, and Sonia explained which cafeteria door led to dinner. Again she poured that same soup onto his tray and laughed when he blew excitedly on every spoonful—*that, dear Sonia, is the wind of history*—and when he had savored his first helping she quickly ran to arrange for seconds.

Sonia is the way the world could be, Jurek thought with every mouthful, devoured by a method of sucking in and chewing for a long time, at times too loudly for the world but generally good for the internal plumbing. *Sonia's the way,* he repeated to himself through the leaner days that followed, because there was no half cutlet and the soup had been watered down, but invariably he fed on the difference between Sonia's charming being, between Sonia's beautiful form, and that unconscionable tangle of latitudes and longitudes. If only he could bring the world closer to Sonia, pluck the best from it, like groats from the barley, like that lump in the sauce; so he dreamed, looking at his own visage in the cafeteria tray, bread-polished—*after the French manner, dear Sonia, despite their damned Maginot Line*—if only he could draw the world's four corners around her desk, while she was waiting by the gate, while she was leading people around the buildings and calling to them with a smile, and why not? Well fine, then, and as soon as things were going so well both in the office and in supply, coolly among our own, on good terms among the foreigners, the week now done, Jurek grasped his pen and, in his beautifully calligraphic handwriting, proudly extended an invitation for Sunday, for an early spring picnic in the hope of encountering a better *imago mundi* in a dress to rival all things primary, including Jurek's pals from primary school, all of them magnificent, to wit: Olek a.k.a. the Barrel, Stefek a.k.a. Piper, Jurek's brother Witek a.k.a. Blackbird, and Heniek a.k.a. the Letter, who was a poor shot, but who always read books to the end, and, like Jurek a.k.a. the Syllable, didn't skip the descriptive passages.

▪ ▫ ▪ ▫ ▪

CHAPTER FIVE

"FIRST LOVE, DANUSIA," JUREK WROTE ON SATURDAY EVENING AFTER not finding Sonia at her garden plot, or anywhere, so he just chose his shirt for tomorrow, changed his sneakers, and pondered a long time over the tie.

> First love, beloved theme of songwriters, feuilletonists, and those who gift humanity with their immortal, monumental works of art, conceals much sentiment within itself, at times a childish naïveté, the memory of which is preserved a long time in the heart. Almost every one of us passes through a season of so-called first love. Then the whole world seems beautiful, flowers are more fragrant, the air we breathe has a different aroma. The shadow of an oak is enough to arouse longing and warm, tender thoughts. Our former blood no longer runs in our veins but boils in them rapidly, day and night, a singing, foaming torrent. The days pass by like a procession of tittering girls, every one of them carries a basket filled to the brim with joy. Oh, bid thee welcome, you enchanted days of first love.

Actually, Jurek's torrent foamed at night, in full view of the penguin, but early Sunday morning found him already shaved, washed, and even wearing a tie. The shadow of the oak beneath the window was again enough to arouse, and Jurek, having set himself to courage, went by perhaps too slow a step, as toward his nighttime thoughts, to Pavilion B. Tap-tap may have been his knocking, and the throaty, "It's mc, Jurek," his self-announcing, but Sonia barely heard the shuffling and the whisper. She answered all the same; her dressing gown was sky blue with a low neckline, and the swan was ascending again. She looked at her watch when Jurek said something about going to the morning Mass as a pair, and with the Holy Spirit that would even make a trio in the little Tworki chapel, but the circles under her eyes, like the oak's shadow, said that today it would be better to pray alone.

They met just near the entrance. Jurek's pals, the Magnificents, had arrived at eleven by the commuter rail; they'd flashed through the gate with the crowd of visitors, and against the norm for Resistance fighters, they allowed the guard to keep his weapon. After all, the sun was shining neutrally, amenable to all skins and tones, and Jurek was waiting with yesterday's compote next to someone in a blue-and-yellow dress, judiciously distributing the seeds into marmalade jars, and at the stream, as promised in a letter to the boys, there trembled a little meadow thirsty for its first kicks and last-minute saves, that the ball not fall into the water, and their best years not flow away with the current. "For the boys, dear Sonia, are first-rate players"—thus a minute ago Jurek imparted his wisdom about the Magnificents more or less together with the compote—"the boys shoot and kick like nobody's business, better than the Gestapo at someone lying down, and what's more, Olek can shoot a header with that hard noggin of his like nary an Einstein. In his time, in ours as well, the leading striker of Warsaw and the Polonia Blackshirts, and even a future contender for the Polish national team, if Poland hadn't depended so much on its corridor, and this modest little taunt, Sonia, will go to you, that is, to the sea. Besides that, Olek's very tall and very slim. Small facial features, a light gait, free, unaffected. Always smartly dressed, always polite, composed right to the end. It seems that nothing could ever knock him off his balance. Resourceful in life, with an innately sharp mind, he does fine under all conditions, finds a way out of every situation. He enjoys, as my friend, great favor among the ladies. But in his relations with them he does not move beyond the bounds of common courtesy, for which some have characterized him as conceited, which, believe me, Sonia, is unwarranted. In the end, it is I who knows him best. Since our earliest childhood, he and I have been joined by the constant and unbreakable bond of true friendship."

On seeing Jurek, the Magnificents waved joyfully, and into Jurek's hands, graciously outstretched in greeting, they threw the ball, which was not canvas but real leather, and when it fell, there fell to Jurek's pricked-up ears—and so what if they were red?—several jokes assuredly suited to the place, the situation, and the poet's buttery fingers, if only Sonia's silhouette had not been right there, Sonia's form right there, Sonia's shapes right there, and her smile, her smile. Introductions were made, names exchanged, the a.k.a.'s kept under wraps, Jurek's room was looked over, with complements on the penguin and the oak outside the window, and finally, with a slow step, all thoughts on the sunny Sunday, the people were directed, clearing themselves a passage among several chatty Napoleons by the gate, straight to the river.

And they were together, and they were a group of six as they tried to spy freshwater fish from the footbridge, and they released little branches and twigs into the current—whose would win?—and they were six as they worked their arms, as though possessed, to encourage the mill to work and to ascend like birds before the grinding, and they were six as they returned along the opposite bank for the dividing of the roll, too bad there was no ham, but still there was plenty of rich cheese, which will not be savored today by any Napoleon or Newton, and they were still six while spinning tales about the miracles of gastronomy in times of peace, beginning with what was unanimously the first miracle, namely and tastily that of salmon on a bed of spring vegetables and in Lanckoroński sauce with a bit of jerez of Algarve, the work of Sonia's grandmother, God rest her soul, and add a glass of Mosel wine, and for the last miracle, an onion omelet with bacon as done by Frères Jurek and Witek; yet they were only five as the soccer ball rolled into the middle of the meadow, just five when it came time to roll up their trouser legs, to adjust their glasses—that was Jurek—or to spit briskly—that was the rest of them—and to show the strength of the Polish offense, as well as of the Polish defense.

She who was sixth leaned rather comfortably against a tree, clinked one mug against the other, and the match got underway, toward a goal of birch stumps, between Olek on one side and, on the other, what remained of the world, which was truly the best of all possible. And as many stars as there are in the sky, that's how many times the ball was passed and returned, and as many grains as there are in a field of wheat, that's how many times the ball was juggled and dribbled, blocked, and hit on the volley, as much chaff as there were fouls. Now Olek takes the ball, actually he flicked it up with his left leg, tossed it up, caught it on his out-thrust chest, and as it was already falling back to earth, he raised it with a clever blow from his knee, tossed it over Witek's head, which was in the clouds, and now under the ball, shifted sideways, though without hitting Staszek's back-turned torso—strikingly similar to Lot's wife—he blocked the dispatch better than Achilles himself. With the ball on his leg he ran up to Heniek, though in theory he could have walked up, feinted to the left, made of Heniek an odalisque laid out on his side, Heniek's calf charmingly bared, and drove farther at breakneck speed—just not *his* neck, anyone's guess who's, and Sonia guessed at once: definitely Saint Jerzy, Saint George fighting the terrible dragon since Sunday morning, and now unfortunately felled by the dragon's body check, contrary to the legend, and now he's vanquished and on the ground, during which time the ball rolled, according to the custom of whatever number war you please, into the very light of the goal, there where one finds the advantage of some and the misery of others.

One to zero is still not so great, that's just the first pebble in the courtyard, the first downward stroke in the heavenly status quo of a tie, because there's no point in dreaming of victory now; one to zero is just the lightning before the downpour, so let's call for rain, men, let's cleanse the gardens, let's restore the status quo, and all together, men: Heniek to Witek, Witek to Stefek, Stefek quickly to Jurek, Jurek—well, that's a tough one—to Olek, let's take him down, boys, and let the beautiful woman cool her heels. So the men—boys, rather, to the beautiful woman—did what they could, could what they did, courageously defending the goal with a traditional swarm, extending the game to the wing and over the dips beyond the glade, making wickedly long crosses, kicks, and bum's rushes, though ever too late, for the score loomed ominously like the Bug River over Brok, like the Utrata in springtime over Tworki, for Olek Hardshin, Olek Cleverhead, Olek Worthyleg, and if necessary, hand and elbow, Olek the Capital and Blackshirt Club Player went mad, and in his madness he put all his talent out there, his entire future, and the sum of his experience in the First League and in how to impress women. A blind man would have noticed, so maybe Jurek would have also, that this game wasn't rolling to any goal, that one of these guys is killing two birds with one stone, even in the bleachers there's laughter, awe, applause, and all-too-healthy blushing. And it's lovely that Jurek fought to the end on his own meadow of Thermopylae, having forgotten about clean pants, that he pressed forward, seized up, broke free, twisted, turned, jumped back, blocked, passed into the air and toward the ground, always lifted his glasses like a fallen stone, though he knew that nothing would come of it, that he wouldn't turn the score around, and that he might pray, at best, for halftime.

Someone—most likely time, that feeble referee—was listening to his prayers, and Jurek stretched out on his coat contentedly in the repose of the everlasting now. The gentlemen next to him were drinking compote and discreetly spitting the seeds at their thumbs as a mark of good luck, Sonia was exposing her neck to the sun, and the sun went along with it, and the men were telling Sonia about the goals Olek shot in the championship against Cracovia, and fortune was smiling in the heated air.

But how can one be fortunate here? How can one be truly happy and grant oneself that happiness when one's mouth has just spat out the last of the seeds, the last jokes have faded on the wind, and halftime is declared over? While Sonia was straightening her hair and repainting her lips discreetly in the clubhouse, the teammates ran out onto the meadow. Jurek glanced desperately at Olek, who had already passed the ball, and then Jurek glanced at his legs, which were as awkward as a verse, this time with no caesura, and then he, Jurek Procureek, glanced at his thoughts, as unlucky as a thirteen-syllable line. But let's face it, this fellow Olek, a striker by profession and in private the dearest friend from grade school, looked great, and he did not bring shame on his beloved city of Warsaw, and especially on Wola, its best district. He had as much sapphire sea in his eyes as a woman could want, and in those arms with their pulsing veins he could carry as many children as might strike his fancy, and one could break more than a few red fingernails yanking at that thick blond hair of his. Plus a strong jaw and a mouth that, if it were to be approached, was worth getting close to, a white shirt wet with as-yet innocent sweat and open on a trial basis, and those shapely, though fleshy, calves (so that what's the point of pants?). *What's the point of any of it?* Jurek thought, and slid so hard under the charging Olek that the latter, hissing, clutched his knee and, with no pleasure, shot a goal, four to one, one to four, what a disgrace. But four dead lions is enough for anyone, so the fan looked at their faces and yawned furtively, at which Olek let the ball roll into the bushes and the other Magnificents lounged about on little stumps and called a much-deserved truce with their own abilities. Jurek searched the ball out behind a juniper, placed it ceremoniously at Sonia's feet, and finally smiled.

Half lying, half sitting, facing the sun, the conversation started anew. And the talk was of girls in windows when soldiers are marching, about little crimson poulaines, about Greta and Rudolph as a couple and on their own—though they were better as a couple—about the magic mountains and the white peaks, and about the seaside peninsula as seen from bay and sea, as it was known only to Sonia, and about sand purer than tears, about the cutters coming back from fishing, about the yellow sunflowers that greeted them, and thus also about the little white house, about vacations on the Swider River, about how nice it is there, and then a sigh. And in the end, when all the mouths had gone quiet and their coats were wrapped around them, Jurek, at Olek's request, improvised on any old theme. A clearing of the throat, and he declaimed, not for Olek alone, in an alexandrine:

"Dispense with senseless fears, my dear beloved friends,
These syllables may be ill-fated in their number,
Let's lock our arms against tide, in alternating rhymes,
And speak in verses evermore, so Death is left to stammer . . ."

"More!" the Magnificents all cried. "Now something else, Jurek, about Sonia."

Sonia turned red, but she encouraged him with a quiet voice, saying, "Go ahead, Jerzy, give us one about Sonia."

Jerzy nodded seriously, nestled into the collar of his coat, and pondered. Meanwhile Stefek, the acrobat, stood on his head; imitation was Witek's strong suit, so he clucked and barked in a voice not his own; Olek, the prestidigitator, did a trick with matches, in which one catches fire and the other four smoke; Heniek knew only how to wiggle his ears. Sonia laughed at the acrobat, even at Olek when he burned his heels, and she barked in Heniek's ear like the hound of the Baskervilles, and she looked kindly at Witek, and at Jurek, with all her heart, at that moment when he once again cleared his throat. Now, moment, keep going:

"That Pythia was a lady, this we know from Greeks,
Yet I am but a short one, and on top of that a guy,
But one thing I see well, I'll tell you with some cheek,
She will adore him lovingly, until the day she dies."

Amidst the nature there fell the kind of quiet called dead silence, amenable to birds, to the subtle bubbling of the stream, to the second violin of the trees, and to the clatter of the rail line from Podkowa, ever nearer, ever fuller, until everyone's temples were pulsing and the veins in their wrists tingling with excitement. The sun was now dipping westward, poised to return. They walked the trail in pairs. Olek whispered something quietly and at length to Sonia, Witek was next to Jurek and held his tongue in a brotherly fashion, and he grabbed the ball only if it fell from Jurek's hands. *Good thing it's curfew,* Jurek thought, slapping his hand against the ball a good bit harder than he'd kicked it, and raising his feet high, with solemnity, so as not to trudge, God forbid, good God how wonderful it could be on that stream, along the tracks, and, in the evening, in one's room, difficult all the same, and viscount remains a beautiful title, let's just hope we survive the war, let's hope we're not late for our train.

The choo-choo from Podkowa pulled up just as they stepped onto the platform. The Magnificents pressed Sonia's hand for a long time and patted Jurek, author and soccer player, and one of them even kissed him on the cheeks and promised that he'd come back in exactly three weeks, when he returns from you-know-where. Now running, they jumped onto the train, and Olek spryly dragged Heniek aboard because he somehow couldn't scramble up the stairs. The last car slowly faded from Tworki's view until again there appeared the little houses near the tracks, the poplars on watch, until Sonia lowered her eyes to the ground and inspected the same pebble as Jurek.

"How pleasant that was. I think," she said, unexpectedly extending her hand to Jurek, "that you have really magnificent friends." The stone was still lying there, but the man was already squeezing those swarthy fingers, those long, shapely bits of cartilage that lead straight to the wrist, and those carmine fingernails, and then bang—he kissed it all, including her ring.

"I have to go rest up," Sonia said, then smiled almost sadly and looked at her watch. "Thank you."

She disappeared along the path. She disappeared on the path, and Jurek could shamble around the nearby squares to his heart's content until finally, weary and still sweaty and wearing shoes so dusty it was shameful, he sat on a bench. Perhaps he dozed off, because he didn't catch sight of Antiplato right away, who was perched right next to him. He had on those same pajamas as always, with holey socks in worn-out sandals, and, now comfortably seated, he was looking Jurek curiously in the eye.

"How pensive you are today, Accounts Man. And where is the rest of your charming company?"

"Oh my," Jurek bristled, but then he felt that he had to speak with someone.

"Loneliness, eh?"

"Loneliness, which follows people," Jurek said, smiling bitterly and recalling Sonia's gesture, her hand raised pensively to her cheek as Olek scored a goal.

"Hell of a day. They ordered me to wipe it clean," Antiplato muttered. "You see this foolishness, bookkeeper, here on the wall behind us? Like it's me who wrote it. Idiots! A band of cretins. And it doesn't want to come off with just water, I'll have to use some kind of soap or something. It'll do me in outright."

"MY SPEECH WILL BE SHORT, GET THE FUCK OUT MY COURT," Jurek said, sounding out the syllables, having turned his head reluctantly. "That's probably one of Voltaire's little pranks."

"Definitely. I myself saw him hiding the paint under the palliasse. And they think it was me, because it's like I'm the only one in Tworki who writes. How dumb is that? Just imagine. The first and most important thing being that I do not write in rhyme. And when I do write, it generally doesn't nip at or concern anyone, because I don't speak so directly about anything . . . 'With lack of a universal referent the uprooted axis of the earth / That is, the earth's bust without the mother's breast to the edge of daylight, to the edge of daylight / Anthropos on the settled swing draws out a scattered song, a scattered song . . .' Thus begins my latest work. It, too, will be about loneliness and about love," Antiplato said, giggling. "About loneliness, love, and abandonment. And about how what's written here now is always already torn out from somewhere and is only an echo. And that dots are white whales in the unifying sea of the arch-human and fated."

"Sorry?"

"The work is titled 'A Write.' "

"Aha," Jurek said, sighing with relief. "I'll tell you honestly that I don't especially like the title, either."

"Maybe I'll still change it," Antiplato muttered, turning red as a lobster. "And what don't you like about it then?"

"Well, what does it actually mean? 'A Read'—that I understand: a lousy novel without deep thought, with no ambition, either for quick reading on a train or at the resort or even at the clinic, but 'A Write'? 'An Oddity' is more like it, sir," Jurek said, breaking into loud laughter.

" 'A Write,' Accounts Man, because existence has become a disestablished and uninspired sentence, twisted and indebted. A callback without a call, the echo of an echo that slips away, slips away. You get it?"

"Not quite. Not at all."

"You see, Mr. Count-and-Deliver, if only I couldn't hear it anymore, then I'd get better."

"Hear what, then?"

"What, Deskman, you don't hear it?"

"No," Jurek snarled.

"You don't hear the terrible voice screaming all around the horizon, the voice commonly called an echo?"

"No. Not at all. And I'm not catching any of this. And that's why no one is going to understand a title like that, and there's no point in dreaming—no one will buy the book and read it, if they publish it at all, ha ha—but in a poem with such a voice at the beginning, there's no way, to be honest, to know what it's about, and it holds no water. And no one says 'with lack,' but rather 'because it was lacking,' or 'considering the lack,' or ultimately 'from lack of,' 'lacking,' or finally, as they said in Old Polish, 'for lack of.' For example: 'Lacking, from lack of, for lack of friends he started writing poems.' "

"What will you, Mr. Supply-Man Pup, teach me? I could be your father!" Antiplato said, growling. "No sir, Mr. Suckling, it's none of your beeswax. And after all, Jerzy-Not-So-Freshy, what's the point of casting a shadow on this earth?" Antiplato muttered again and stood, now quite irate and completely red in the face. "And what happened to all the cheese at breakfast this morning? It's almost nighttime, I bid you adieu."

He walked away in a hurry, sinking his gaze into his little sandals and muttering something angrily under his breath. Nearby, the last train whistled and puffed with relief as though it finally had Sunday off its mind, and actually nothing more would happen this day except for Jurek writing a letter to Danusia, Olek inspecting the ceiling over his bed until the rosy dawn, the snoring of Witek and Stefek, and perhaps Sonia taking a late walk, and Sonia's late walk again to the stream.

A letter is a mysterious thing. An envelope and a white piece of paper covered in black scribbles. Not so many, but then . . . such an enormous number. A letter can knock the soul into the abyss of despair or kindle it with the bright, burning flame of joy and cure the heart with the most wonderful medicine: hope. When I open an envelope and remove your letter, all blackness and sadness drains from my eyes . . . You asked me the last time whether I am a "conqueror" of ladies' hearts. Indeed, in my life I've already conquered many and often—admittedly not the hearts of women, but common balls (I don't know which of these two is more difficult), and it seems that in this sport I've achieved results that are not half bad. Whereas I haven't actually tried to conquer the little hearts of girls, because it is my opinion that one must shepherd such things with a heaping dose of know-how, because a little heart can easily fall to the ground, crack hard, and break apart. Actually, a certain friend of mine maintains categorically that the hearts of women are many times harder than the hardest balls (do not try to deny it). But, on the other hand, wise nature knows the true art of gluing together the feeble wreckage of the broken hearts of man—especially, Danusia, when a merciful someone is willing to help her in this cause.

You write me, Danusia, that against the prevailing current you do not fall in love and that you do not even know how it's done. I did not know that one needed special know-how and broad expertise to love somebody. That's only human, and it will come when you least expect it. It seems to you that no one could interest you anymore, that one needs a strong will for that. And, at the same time, not. Suddenly someone will appear before your eyes . . . on the tram, in a store, on the path . . . and that's it. You'll see that this is the person for you. And then he takes root in your heart for life, until death. And right at that moment everything starts to make sense: You've reached your goal: to live for someone, to live for a person. One person can give you more than all of them together. He will never be truly happy who, even in the work he has undertaken, attains his intended goal, who has dedicated his life to a certain idea, unless he has by his side someone—the one—close by, who knows how, dear Danusia, in moments of doubt and resentment, to give him a good word, to calm his exhausted nerves and breathe new strength into his further endeavors.

Night had fallen in Ozorków as well, Danusia was already asleep, ivy shone discreetly by the windowsill, and a couple of dogs on the road were howling at the man in the moon.

■ □ ■ □ ■

CHAPTER SIX

TIME PASSED, AND FINALLY THE MOON, A COUPLE OF HOURS OLDER, abandoned the blue horizon, and the first rays of sunlight illuminated the *Arbeitskommando* of nature, and the dew glistened in good order, a new week had begun like seven years of famine. Thin little soups arduously marked the subsequent afternoons, and little cutlets, the progeny of the most lamentable cuts of meat, came to yet another arrangement with the miserable salad, and even the transparent compote turned itself into a consumptive. There was also somehow less of Sonia, she was somehow fading from Jurek's abacus, she vanished at quitting time like a diamond in water, she smiled more seldom than usual and hardly at all at Kaltz when he brought her successive biscuits, and she even flitted along the lanes so quickly that the nutcases turned pensively after her.

Boredom befell Jurek, still enamored and now hopeless. He drove with sad Kaltz to the farmsteads beyond Pruszków for potatoes and carrots, and nothing happened along the way, all he had to count was the price of laundry, the letter from Danka was late, and to make things worse, the action of the book he'd brought from Ulrychów was set in a school just before the starting bell. And surely nothing would have interrupted the grayness of the days of that week and the painstaking labor of his reading (a professor of Polish had just entered the classroom with a grim expression) if not for the appearance of—at the neighboring, heretofore empty, desk, next to the nearby cafeteria tray, next to that same wardrobe and on the second bed—of a bipedal and thoughtful, though partially lost in thought, somewhat older, also in a cream-colored coat, as well as glasses, not to mention blue-eyed, Marcel, Marcie to his friends, or even Marcelek, on the payroll Brochwicz, with a *c* and *h,* as in *challah* or *Chanukah.* Marcel Brochwicz! Ho ho ho! An accountant from the heavens! Hired from a subsequent job announcement and the best of four competitors! A two-handed typist, champion of the paragraph, an artisan of paper clip jewelry. A master at detecting forgeries and looking digits in the face, an enemy to alteration of the balance sheet and diarrheic expenditure. Barely had he managed to extend his hand to Jurek—in the book it was five in the afternoon, too, very meat-and-potatoes that endless last lesson—barely had he performed a polite *chapeau bas* before the penguin when he'd already taken a peek under the mattress, knocked around on the floor under the bed, judged the distance from the window to the ground, and recited all the pseudonyms of the author of the book Jurek was reading. But in the final account, as is often the case among accountants, not much separated him from Jurek except that he naively sought a second carrot and a third potato in his soup and he regularly fed the cat, Virtuoso, who lived in the first-floor laundry room. Just like Jurek, he'd elected to go to business school before the war, rooted for the Polonia Soccer Club, preferred Westerns to the Professor Wilczur movies, and liked to spend his evenings with a book, especially with the mysteries of Paris. Just like Jurek, he went to bed at eleven, and like him, if he didn't oversleep, he cleaned his shoes in the morning, including the nonleather ones, and sought Sonia's company, and, with an identically hurried step, he stepped aside for Jabłkowska, the secretary. Before bedtime, Marcel wanted to speak with his predecessor as much as Jurek wanted to speak with him, the newcomer, and in their conversations, long into the night, they compared the past of the Polish people with their present, which was like comparing the color of a parrot to dun Virtuoso, and when Jurek recited, Marcel sang the same text to a Bizet melody. Because it was thin toward the back, Marcel combed his hair similar to the way Jurek did, and he cursed like a sailor as he fumbled with the key in the dark foyer. And finally, with the same longing, he thought of Sunday, pressing his shirts and cuffed pants alongside Jurek. Flannel with flannel and cuff on cuff. However, on the second Sunday there arose a single, essential, beautiful difference: Marcel Brochwicz had a wife.

It was another warm Sunday morning. Pink mists rose languidly far above the Helenów Forest like fanciful aerial garters. Sparrows perched under the eaves of the groundskeeper's shed, and the air smelled of pines wet with dew and, as though in anticipation, of perfume from the city. The doors of the commuter train parted noiselessly, and hosts of passengers flowed silently onto the platform. And then, on the threshold, stood Anna. Anna Brochwicz, the last one out, stood on the threshold like a Madonna in a chestnut frame, like the entire Renaissance in symbolic abbreviation. The war had been ugly, thus Anna's neck was all the more beautiful, and let us invoke all the bridges of the world to mark its passage toward a neckline denuded like the heart of the Savior. The war had been terrible, hence Anna's hand seemed so beautiful holding the first flower of spring in an innocent hue, the beautiful hand and Anna's fingers pressed to her waist like five slender synonyms. The war had been savage, and thus Anna's bright, shapely dress with a cheerful frill along the edge, the delicate texture of the material, and the vigilance of the silver buttons on guard. For the difficult times Anna had chosen pastel lipstick in a violet shade, straight hair—thick, pinned at the back—and timidity on her face, the best makeup. And so proudly was she standing in the museum of the early day, invisibly signed in the lower right-hand corner, and so proudly did she remain, Anna, wife of Marcel, lady with a little yellow flower, frozen despite herself in the pose of a queen, until the admonitory bells finally heralded the train's departure a second later; in half that time she stepped onto the platform of our modest little Tworki station. Please remove yourself from temptation, starry-eyed angel in slightly worn-out slippers.

Under the second poplar by the gate something lunged and was held back: impatience met tact, man as always with woman.

"Wait. Let them greet one another," Sonia whispered, her hand still—oh, still—on Jurek's sleeve. "Don't you see what's going on?"

Now Jurek did see. Marcel calmly slid his lean form out from under the first poplar and set it motionless three meters in front of the platform, sinking his hand into his pocket. His eyes discerned the horizon, the peppermint in his mouth suddenly turned over, his temples stuck to his hat. The earth clung to his feet, his face grew dark like the sun on Sunset Boulevard. Marcel Brochwicz was ready to meet his wife.

The wave of she who had arrived in good health broke its hurried course on the rock of Marcel's body and, having merged her currents with his, sloshed through the gate, carrying a great deal of kielbasa and Polish compote to these Robinson Crusoes of insanity. The platform emptied out, though there was no longer a platform but a ferry of happiness and the weightlessness of the times. May NASA someday remark upon it, may every observatory spy that wonderful vacuum around two beings suddenly independent of the law of gravity, free from the soil by the side of the road, from common lumbering and atmospheric pressures. Screenwriters might also use it, if only they have no fear of gaps in the action and an exaggerated rapprochement, and if they can manage to hold their breath as Jurek and Sonia did. Marcel was still not moving, Marcel's wife was also not moving. They stood there, but more than that they were watching, watching, but more than that they were waiting. They were still separated by ten days of solitude, ten hourglasses placed continuously on end, a ton of sand in the face, which now hurried to unfurl an amorous khamsin. And suddenly it happened. There was no longer room in the pocket for his hand, nor room in her hand for the flower. Anna stretched out her arm, Marcel threw off his hat. Marcel soared, Anna ran up to him, her shoulders encircled and stifled the lost time. They were together again, fate to fate, nose to nose, fake identification to forged *Kennkarte.* And they confirmed that they were really there, touching each other's hair, their cheeks, a long time and persistently, until tears came to the lady behind the second poplar, the gentleman was blubbering audibly, during which time, on the concrete rug of the platform in Tworki, they were nestling into each other. Now let's have a wide shot: the brown hat and the yellow flower.

Marcel led Anna to the receiving line.

"This is my wife, Ania. And this is Sonia and Jurek," Marcel said, introducing those present, ever present, and smiled widely for the first time since he'd gotten the job.

They shook hands, Jurek even bowed, and before they went to sip some compote they chatted by the tree about this and that, and first of all about Operation Arsenal. Anna spoke slowly and had beautiful enunciation, and listening to the others she opened her eyes widely, and when they passed through the gate, she turned around, touched her cheek with her hand, and gazed at length into the cloudless sky. And that's how Jurek remembered her best.

They inspected the workspaces, Marcel's desk—with its pencils so sharp that woe unto you, numbers, plot your course for zero—and they saw the penguin like a holy icon over the bed, and they hiked out to the Utrata. By the first little bridge it was confirmed that Anna was a teacher, by the second, that she taught music to children, and by the mill her defenses broke down and she drew a small, beige recorder from her handbag. They sat on boulders by the side of the road and squeezed onto Marcel's cream-colored coat because Jurek didn't want to take off his.

Anna twisted off the cap, blew inside a couple of times, and let her gaze float into the sky through seven holes for seven sounds, for the harmony of the spheres, for notes gathering that which is fragmented in us, too quiet and torn. The solemn silence whitewashed the entire district, and a moment later the first notes jotted their own timid story tremulously on the white, tremolo on nothing. They reminded Marcel of his childhood in a small town before he left for the capital for his education, and they said that maybe it wasn't worth those years at business school—so much effort, and even his thesis published for the benefit of the Ministry—that maybe it would have been better to get away, even without his diploma, as Anna had wanted, right after they had met at Julian's name-day party on Karolkowa Street, when her muslin dress shone like the afternoon sun and felt like a rough orange to the touch. But they also told him that things had been so good for them here, as when he and Anna sang Bach cantatas in the chorus at the Church of the Visitations and later walked down New World Street, which was just within reach, right there, and how they'd sipped Viennese coffee right in the Café Ziemiańska, and once they even drank at the Adria Club and danced with officers and ladies on the parquet floor until daybreak, and then they sat for a long time in the bathtub in that apartment on Elektoralna Street, that tiny little apartment they had on Elektoralna.

Anna's increasingly heavy notes spoke to Sonia of a strange longing at the tips of her fingers, and about a yellow and blue ball that flew from the garden and perched on a branch in the brook; it rocked and swayed under the force of the current and, from under a shadowy pocket of air, it winked at little Sonia with its two alternating colors; it rocked and swayed, it was so light and distant, now blue, now yellow, and in the water it revealed its true form, blurred, colorful, semicircular, illuminated; it rocked and swayed, and Sonia left it there swaying in the brook, and at home she told her mother, because her father had gone a-plotting somewhere again, that her ball had up and vanished but that she didn't want a new one. As *re* to *mi* and as *ti* to *do,* so it was ball to ball, and now the new notes were still speaking to Sonia and telling her how many goals can be shot on this meadow with a single soccer ball when one is in good form, and the shots are there for the taking, and about how that fine striker might never encounter her true defense.

Ania's music reminded Jurek first that Sonia was sitting next to him and that he had had bad luck with pretty ladies because, though they existed, in the end there weren't really very many of them, and the melody seemed to be taking him by the arm, charging full force toward a finale of closing notes, after which real life would begin, but then it spun him a tale about the summer resort in Urle, upon which his entire middle-school class had descended, he and Olek always in the same section, to take their lessons in the fresh air and to drink extra glasses of milk straight from a Podlasie cow, and in the evenings, when they had already slogged through and lost three rounds of bridge with Professors Dyrda and Kamiński, he went to the brook and stared into the water, which flowed in a swift, inky line, like hope that passes before your eyes, fills your throat, and sweeps into the future, signed and certain to be delivered.

La ti do went suddenly silent, scared off by Marcel's voice. For Marcel had taken a deep breath and released a strong, melodious, and colorful tenor from his very diaphragm. For an instant it was a brisk sound, modulated and ascending, but a moment later, from over the flute, a soprano joined it like a quiet wave, and both voices settled into long words. First they sang in strange octaves about the suffering of the sons of man and the inconsolable tears of mothers, about beauty and truth, about when everyone would be brothers, and then they sang in our native style about sandy roads, about soldiers' honor, and finally about brunettes, blondes, and all you girls out there.

Jurek asked for a few more songs from the fashionable repertoire, especially about a certain emotion that means never having to say you're sorry. Finally Anna and Marcel grew tired and glanced uncertainly around them.

"You really sing beautifully. Better than on the radio. More clearly than on the gramophone," Jurek said, actually nodding with excitement, and Sonia, a blonde in theory, kept clapping. "And what you just *sprechened,* even that sounded good. Music refines our manners. Your voices are so well matched, like a husband and wife, you should sing us something every day. Music and poetry, that's all that matters."

"And Jurek recites beautifully," Marcel said to Anna, and Sonia agreed. "Dear Jurek, do give us a little poem, please."

Jerzy consented right away. He grabbed everyone by the arm so that they all rose from the rock, gathered in a circle, and stood in a tight huddle. And then he whispered among the temples touching each other and the tangle of hair:

"A little bit of tragedy, a bit of awful parody,
A peak—and an abyss,
A little whiff of wormwood-scent, and then a smell more flowery,
And that's what loving is."

Two hands clapped Jurek on the back, and one stroked his head. The circle disintegrated into two pairs, and both looked great, though perhaps Marcel and Anna were better, so tightly did they nestle into one another, and so much did they whisper into each other's cheeks as they were returning to the domain of the penguin. Jurek and Sonia slowed their pace, stopped in the shadow of the oak, and smiled at each other, slightly embarrassed.

"They love each other very much," Sonia said. "So much that it makes you wish for everything."

Now, Jurek thought, *it's now or never.* The first leaves on the oak already knew what wind was, the gravel on the path held fast with all its might.

"Sonia, I also . . ."

Sonia quickly cast her eyes at her watch. "Excuse me, Jerzy, but I have to go home," she said, somehow sadly. "We've had another lovely Sunday."

"Come on, I'll take you," the little whiff of wormwood-scent said on Jerzy's behalf.

"Really, do you want to? Okay, but just for a bit," the more flowery scent consented.

They passed a group of pajamas debating on the bench beside the lawn, and Sonia walked so close to Jurek that her shoulder rubbed against his.

"Why don't they live together?" Sonia asked. "And don't they have any children?"

"They got married barely half a year before the war. Then they had some problems with the apartment. Anna lives with acquaintances; it seems that there was no room for two."

"They shouldn't be apart like that."

"Tell that to the penguin," Jurek replied quickly, and Sonia gave him a strange look. "You remember that Olek is coming in a week? Hopefully without the ball."

Sonia looked at him more strangely still.

"No, I didn't remember. Yes, I remember. I have a moment—maybe you could come in for tea?"

Something swayed in the light, shook excessively, and bent over, a certain sea parted, glaciers took on new crevasses, and sure, Jurek agreed to have some tea. With one swift motion Sonia turned the key, pushed the door with her body so that it might open wider, tossed her nightshirt under her pillow with lightning speed, and invited Jurek in.

An empty little boat settled into the picture in the shade of a palm, and it was for Sonia what the penguin was for Jurek: it was apt, rocking even, a bit shadowy in the middle. On her desk there was also an empty vase, and the hairpins tossed about on the desktop traced a road to nowhere. There were pretty little pink pebbles gathered at the corner of the desk, and right next to them a drawing of a house with a garden, unfinished, for there were no steps down from the porch, and one banister was missing. By the sea, begun with a thin stroke somewhere on the horizon, Jurek surmised that the house was no invention and that the garden was also real.

"You miss it?"

"Yes. But you know, I never told you that when I was quite little we lived in different cities. Dad changed jobs, and it was only in those last years that we moved to the sea. But Gdańsk is such a lovely city. Not like Pruszków."

"Why did you leave?"

"Why indeed! In Pruszków there's only one cinema," Sonia said, laughing, and went to the washbasin to pour water into her mug. A moment later she was standing with her back to Jurek, and Jurek thought about the turning of a card in solitaire, how it tells one's fortune for the evening or for one's whole life. The jack of clubs revealed, the debt's return is sealed. The ten of diamonds turned, a journey soon is earned. The worst is the ace of spades because it means that the blonde takes everything. But generally, when everything is so clear, can one, can one still dream of the queen of hearts? Now she'll turn on her heel, she'll be quiet, and she'll be flushed, and the only thing dividing us will be the two cylinders of these thick glasses. The water filled to the brim of the mug. Jurek removed his glasses and touched Sonia's back lightly. She turned around quickly, the mug shook but didn't spill, and she said, "You know, I still haven't told anyone about myself. I'm glad you're here. I don't have any friends here, Jurek. Only you."

What was there to do, Jerzy-over-the-Hedgy? One must drink what has been offered, though it be bittersweet to swallow, one must swallow that tea in the glass with the clinking spoon until the clink finally dies away, the dregs show that they were once leaves, and that the abyss need not be so terrible, once it fades to brown and is slurped while still warm. What was there to do, Jurek Insure-ek? One must hold a moment's solemn silence, not understanding too much of all this, envying Olek, and being a little sorry for oneself, and when the moment has passed, smile, get up, and say, "If that's the way it has to be, then we'll just stay friends."

The paths had cleared by now; all the nutcases had run off to dinner in the hope of a full portion of cheese, and Jurek could calmly choose his favorite bench on the main lawn. He felt a sudden desire to express himself in a poem about Sonia's—or all women's—situation, but he had no luck finding an appropriate rhyme for *doldrums,* or even for *doldrum.* "My heart, it is so ill," he wrote, trying a different opening, "for it's gnawed upon by worms." But the masculine rhymes gave him even more resistance: *worms—germs,* yes, very good, *worms—herms,* great, even better. But finally he managed to concentrate, to inspire the words within him, and carefully rhymed words on a scrap of paper: *wretchedness* with *homelessness, sadly* with *badly,* and *so friendly* with *on Sunday.*

As he wrote this, nibbling on his pencil, he spotted Marcel and Anna in the distance. They seemed locked in an affectionate embrace, and then to shift slightly, in the very center of the world. The main path, which they walked to the gate, split Tworki into two equal parts, leaving the pavilions, the little houses, and the trails on one side or on the other, dividing the lawns, trees, and sidewalks in half. If this couple were to disappear, perhaps Tworki would also disintegrate along what remained of their steps, yet they were still there, and their silhouettes, darkening into evening, were held close by the buildings and paths. The horizon traced the advancing circle of twilight above the station; they were standing at the gate, and the guard, most likely Johann, saluted them jokingly and maybe also a little solemnly. They froze for a moment, turned around, and their faces lit up like the most prominent points in space; the scene stuck in Jurek's eyes, and they disappeared behind the kiosk on the platform. Jurek stood and went unhurriedly to his room, which was still warm.

■ □ ■ □ ■

CHAPTER SEVEN

HE WILL HAVE MORE OF THOSE LITTLE SCENES WITH HIS MOTHER. The one from the following Sunday, from the arrival of the train, as full as the duodenum at midday, maybe would not have been so acute and prominent in his memory—the choo-choo calmly pulled up and braked with a squeak; Mama was the first one off the train and, without even looking around her with any kind of curiosity, walked right up to Jurek, gave her hand to Sonia with a smile, as if she had known her for ages, and handed him her mesh bag, and we know that what's in the bag has a shell and is hard-boiled—if only he hadn't been so nervous, so pale, then red, then pale again, and as for the sweat that shone pearly on Sonia's face, if only it hadn't glistened on Sonia's saddened face, if only her cheeks hadn't been scrunched downward. He hadn't arrived, he hadn't come, though he'd said precisely that he would, Jurek had led Sonia to believe so, but he had not gotten off the train that Sunday, and who knows whether that was the last Sunday there would be, and he had not darkened the door, not tread the earth or thrown leather to the air. He won't whistle like a blackbird in flight, nor will he glance that way, askance, stretch out his six-foot-two frame of *Übermensch,* or even six-foot-even, or offer his hand by the footbridge. Where's the mop of blond hair like a white Rheingau wine, where are the blue eyes like the waters of the Spree, the nose as sure as Dürer's line, and where are the other *membra disiecta,* everything in the best American style? Heaven was silent, and Jurek didn't know either.

Mama knew a bit. Witek, who ran over to Mama's yesterday afternoon, knew more. Guteck, the *Untersturmführer,* was even better oriented, while Zweibel, the *Bauer,* and his Mrs. *Bauer,* knew best of all. If these things lent themselves to telling, if they spoke more clearly and less apprehensively, one might also be able to learn something from the tarpaulin on the Sauer truck, from the barred window of the train car, from the plank bed in the barn, the piece of straw pricking the heart.

For while Olek was lucky in goals, he didn't come off so well in that roundup, and it was not with the joy of victory that he had raised his hands high. Witek, who had been with him on the same tram, had a better nose and jumped out onto the other side of the street, where the gate took in more and let them farther in. From the loge on the second-floor stairs he could then admire the overture of the truck's tailgate, Olek's solo as he jumped inside under the surge of extras, and the development of the plot up as far as the crossroads. Stefek, the son of a railway man, soon told about Olek's first attempt to escape from the waiting room of the station, where those who had been rounded up were crammed together, and Olek himself could speak of the tasty milk—not only cow's, but goat's—and about the pork fat in the soup in a letter that reached Mama in Ulrychów two weeks later, and that Jurek, not without some *Schadenfreude,* read to Sonia right after breakfast (sadly, Sonia, without Austrian milk), and a second time for dessert after lunch, the cafeteria trays empty.

"Beloved Jurek!" Olek, a.k.a. the Barrel, de facto Farmhand Al, started the letter, on a piece of paper torn too violently from a notebook.

> I'm in a village at the Zweibels', who have a large estate in the mountains near the city of Innsbruck. There's still a lot of snow in the forest above the field here. The meals are good. And now I'll describe what my day looks like. I get up at dawn, half a glass of milk (cow's or goat's), two decent slabs of bread, and then right to work because there's a lot to be done. I have a break at two. I get a rich soup and my fill of potatoes and fat, and again it's to the pigs and cows, or to the field, and just so, right into the evening. Quitting time's at seven in the evening. But today's Sunday, and before noon I even kicked

the ball around with three farmhands. I was very sorry you weren't here, the two of us would have shown them a thing or two! It could have turned out a lot worse because the transport from the station went first to the factories. But among the transport guards there was a guy by the name of Guteck, and he helped me get here. He used to play soccer for Fortuna Berlin. Because I'd lost my shoe back in Warsaw and then I say to the guy next to me that now I'll have to play barefoot, just like Leonidas in the championships with Poland, and this Guteck looked at me and says, "Six to five, now that was a game!"

I hope that things turned out alright for Witek, because I didn't see him anywhere along the way. I've already written to my mom, but please, Jurek, do go to her on Wilcza and console her so that she doesn't worry. You're really good at that sort of thing. And I have one more request for you. That Sunday in Tworki was so nice, and I keep thinking about our visit. Could you, Jurek, give Sonia my compliments and greetings and tell her how nice it was for me to meet her in Tworki? You're good at that, too, and you know what a clod I am toward a pen. I'm very angry with myself that it's all turned out this way, but don't worry about me, and I'm waiting for your letters. I really miss our Warsaw. Say hi to everyone and kiss them for me.

Your Olek

Jurek greeted everyone and kissed just a few of them, but twice, not counting the one that was from him, and would have gladly read Sonia the letter a third time, but sadly she refused.

Still, the following Sunday he succeeded in persuading Sonia to visit his mother in Ulrychów to listen to the gramophone and to show her the neighborhood, his books, his collection of photographs since 1930, and his class pictures, especially the one with him on the same bench as Olek—at that time, Sonia, you still hadn't carved out Jurek's heart—as well as ones from their school vacations together in Brok, where there flows the River Bug, which is how Poles say *God,* though they spell it a little differently. And of course the memorial photo from when the certificates of graduation, i.e. maturity, were distributed to the pupils of the General Sowiński High School, despite their Latin being so poor that they could barely decline *puella,* their stubbornly saying *Konrad* instead of *Gustaw* when discussing Mickiewicz's *Forefather's Eve,* and their preference of gerunds to active verbs.

Having looked over Jurek's "room" in the kitchen corner, the "porch" on the window ledge, and the "sitting room" on the sofa bed, the young Tworkians bowed their heads inquisitively over albums from times when ice cream was tastier than all of lunch, a slingshot more important than falling panties, and a bell sweeter than silence. In the pictures Olek was absolutely unlike the tall, blond soccer player and fighter, and he did not yet have anything American about him, whereas Jurek wore the same rather round glasses and stubbornly furrowed his brow while reckoning with his figures, which once again were not working out. But they were as little different from one another as Frick and Frack, they peeped at each other kindly on that bench or on the soccer pitch, like a royal cup-bearer and the court clerk.

And yet, Jurek recalled, there were feuds and fights over the bigger share of the bench and space in the frame. Already by the lesson on Fredro's *Revenge* Olek had doodled a Jew over half a page in Jurek's exercise book, eternally sullying Jurek's beautiful, clean calligraphy and scribbling away any semblance of pedagogical order.

"Speaking of humor in *Revenge,* we posed the following question," Sonia read aloud, giggling and following the black ink blots, vast as longing, with her finger in Jurek's orderly, rather pedantic notebook. "Is Fredro's humor cavalier, good-natured, well-intentioned, but his comedy merely on the surface? We answered this question in the negative and posed a second question on the basis of the first: does comedy aim to ridicule certain classes, and if so, which ones? The answer to the second question is as follows: Fredro's comedy is a satire of drunkenness, hot temper, lack of education, the squabbles of the nobility, mooching, insolent boasts, and lying. The satire is characteristic of comedies in which the humor arises not from internal situations but from the incongruity of certain types of characters."

"Precisely," Jurek said, and he sighed heavily.

"Speaking of drama, we forgot to mention that a play must have stageability if it is to be presented on the stage," Sonia continued. "In a play the number of acts does not exceed five. Additionally, each act is divided into individual scenes. So that we might see *Revenge* in a critical light, the teacher read us a critique of *Revenge* written by Professor Sarnowski."

"It's supposed to be Tarnowski," Jurek said.

"Tarnowski," Sonia said, correcting herself, stifling her laughter. "Before that, however, we delineated our view of criticism. Criticism is an appraisal of negative and positive characteristics."

"About art," Jurek added.

"About art," Sonia said, then read to the end, and both started to laugh.

Mama brought in some tea, cut the gingerbread, and things could not have been better.

"Let's list our negative and positive characteristics," Jurek proposed. "Art criticism for Sunday tea. Would someone like to go first?"

"You, Jurek, are a lazybones," Mama said. "You were supposed to bring the coal in from the cellar, but you didn't. You're a slob: look at what's going on in your wardrobe. You're a glutton: you've already eaten your third piece of gingerbread, and Sonia's just finished her first."

"No, no," Sonia quickly protested. "Jurek is quite gallant and always knows how to carry a good conversation. Jurek is sociable and very funny, and nicer than anybody. He's very well-read, unusually intelligent, and willing to help. He's also very decent."

"And my negative characteristics?" asked Mr. Gallant and Well-Read, maybe not so Funny.

Sonia thought this over seriously, for she looked at the ceiling and out the window for a long time. "No, there are none . . . really, I don't see any. Just that Jurek is . . . not American enough. But please, whatever that could mean, don't ask."

"And Sonia is really kind and really cheerful. When she's in a good mood, a stream of volcanic, vivid words flows from her mouth in an uninterrupted chain, right to the zenith. She has a heart of gold. She dresses with grace and an exceptional sense of color. Any well-read man can appreciate that. Just as her smile evokes the whitest pearls, and her eyes the shiniest little diamonds. In fact, Sonia has only one negative characteristic."

"What's that?" Mama and Sonia asked simultaneously, but Mama was louder.

“She’s fallen for someone else,” Jurek announced triumphantly and glanced around the room with satisfaction.

Sonia quickly bent over Jurek’s little exercise book before Mama could ask why in the name of the Miracle on the Vistula does he always suffer a Disaster on the Utrata, why is it so rare that his narrow shoulders, round eyes, and large ears celebrate triumph, why is it that what he offers is hardly ever wanted or taken?

“In this class we worked on a short report called ‘The Linde Dictionary.’ Samuel Bogumił Linde, of German origin, did a commendable service to Polish literature. This individual decided to gather all Polish words into one tome, to explain and elucidate them. The dictionary had this charm”—Sonia started laughing—“this charm, that therein the author quoted authors from various centuries, citing their poems in which they say something about the given word. So that every expression was worked over such that there was really no longer anything left to add. In the dictionary one can detect a certain German accent.”

“Just as with Sonia,” Jurek said, snorting.

“Be quiet. A German accent, and too few words from dialects, but we must forgive Linde, who, not being a native Pole, could not learn the secrets of the Polish language.”

“That’s exactly what I can forgive in Sonia,” Jurek said, snorting again.

“Be quiet. In today’s class we worked on a short report called ‘The Encyclopedists.’ First we were informed about what an encyclopedia is. An encyclopedia is a sequence of bound volumes marked by letters of the alphabet. Under each of the letters one finds various explanations of knowledge from various fields of the sciences. It’s all mixed up”—Sonia took a breath—“and makes for a certain chaos. At the very beginning of the text we moved through a description of Diderot, a man of letters. Diderot was broad-shouldered, his face had a high brow and vivid eyes.”

“Very American,” Jurek said, tittering.

“Be quiet. Diderot’s work required great endurance combined with confidence and strength of character, and this man of the quill had all that and achieved what he wanted. He dedicated almost his entire life to his Sisyphean task.”

“End of scene on the sofa bed,” Jurek said, now very theatrically, and he winked from behind his glasses, though no one noticed. "Act Two: the fateful stroll around the neighborhood."

They drank another tea and then, to warm up, two vodkas, and Sonia put on Mama's thick sweater, for it had unexpectedly turned as cold as kissing an iceberg. And if they were to have the good fortune of keeping the thermometer in the minuses, when you could see your breath, if the Quaternary Period were once again to settle down over Wola and over all the Polish lands, if everything were to become clean as crystal and halt entirely, then the long worms of the trains would freeze forever in transparent little boxes and would never move again, as would the sheepdogs that look up to man, and the rows of people lined up against the wall would not fall, nor would the silhouettes dashing for the gates, and pens would freeze on an unfinished letter, and on the village green, next to the pillars that once suggested the posts of a goal, two thoughtful figures muffled in wool sweaters with white cloudlets by their mouths would grow into the earth like pedicels, eternally young.

And an aficionado of comic books might read in those cloudlets: "Sonia, this is where we kicked the ball around throughout our school days. I remember our first game with the older class like it was yesterday. Olek scored the first goal—off my assist, actually—and played a sensational game. And it was after that game that we sat on the same bench for the rest of school. And when we took class trips to the River Bug, we always slept in the same bunk bed, he on the top bunk, I on the bottom. And see over there, behind those maples on the right? That was our Indian camp, the wigwams stood by the bushes, and that big oak was the whipping post."

"Whipping?"

"You know, like in a dime novel . . . we'd tie whoever was playing Old Shatterhand to the tree, and from fifteen meters out we threw pine cones or, better yet, apple cores at him . . . Once I got Olek in the eye, because I was an Apache then. He paid me back sincerely when it was my turn."

"What, you got it in the eye, too?"

"On my glasses, my ear, my nose, and on my new sweater from my mom, straight from her knitting needles, similar to the one you have on now. And over here, to this shack in the corner, we came after the match to have tasty lemonade for one grosz. Now it's all boarded up. On even-numbered days Olek paid, on odd I paid. Unless we both had empty pockets, as is often the case when it comes to the sons of tram drivers. Anyway, after payday we'd go for a doughnut, and sometimes even for two. And now I will show Sonia to the pond, because in those days some important things took place there."

On the pond the native knights harassed those of the Teutonic Order, the Lithuanians wouldn't stay in line, and the law was upheld most often by the well-read sheriff. The sheriff was drowned but once, but Olek had to save him several times, for evil, unfortunately, succeeded in triumphing over good, and the bandits from the second class in beating honest Jerzy or, rather, the gallant knight McGeorge. From time to time the bandits' pursuit of that noble and, dear Sonia, quite American custodian of the law left the little streets of Ulrych City-on-Pond and, surmounting the rocky mountains of the garbage cans, carried forth into the depths of Wola, where one world ended and another world began, heralded by figures dressed in black and by the lacrimosa of the eyes over the onion stalls. Then the persecuted McGeorge mixed with the crowd and celebrated the victory of his no-longer-trampled heels, at the expense of feeling alien and lost. A feeling now inaccessible, except perhaps if one were to squeeze through what's left of that first wall, now visible out there, in the distance, the work of Schmidt and Münstermann, and then to conquer the second wall bird- or looter-style, or to hide cleverly in the smokescreen that's been billowing there profusely for these last fine days.

Jurek also showed Sonia his school building, with ever that same hole in the fence out back, the veritable gates of freedom during chemistry lessons, which Jurek couldn't stand, or Polish, which Olek would have none of, and a bit farther on, the memorable place where Olek of Ulrychów, with fists, elbows, and a cunning kick to the belly, defeated Maciek of Jelonki himself, the thug, aggressor, and all-round King Kong of those neighborhoods. But later Jurek fell silent because Sonia had stopped asking questions, Sonia had turned sad, Sonia was leaning against a tree. Thus yet another little crystal for eternity because of the great silence and the unusual calm in the air, because maybe Jurek would best remember her like that. First the blue-gray sky, the smoke-filled sky over a Warsaw trembling from cold, lower down the already green crown of trees, open buds, low, underneath the ever-wider boughs, and even lower down the straight trunk, slightly coarse, right down to the veil of bright hair, today tied with a red ribbon, down to that picture of a smooth forehead, the brow slightly furrowed so that the eyes might squint properly, misty and staring into the distance; mist, so that she's gone, Sonia's gone, all the more because under the shapely profile of her nose her lips were slightly parted in a veritable half-smile at her own thoughts, dancing somewhere in the neighborhood of her temples, but in fact perhaps a little lower, where her polo sweater rose from her breathing. And then there is just, though it is infinitely much, her hands stuck into her pants pockets, her legs squeezed together and farther and farther away from the tree so that she could pin herself against the trunk and lean hard against her back, and now on the very bottom, on the edge of the little crystal, her feet joined in miserable little shoes turned in toward one another at the tips, nestled into one another, as though all of Sonia wanted nothing but Sonia and now was left with no one but Sonia.

And when they finally started on their way back, because Mama was waiting with lunch, and when Jurek, now quite hungry, was going on about the familiar charm of that beautiful expression, that "waiting with . . ."—warm and kind like the soup would be a moment later, the second helping, and then another right after that—Sonia suddenly slipped in under his arm, so childishly and so awkwardly that Jurek thought of the penguin in his room, but then Sonia's arm grew more serious, hardened, and Jurek, an Atlas burdened with the world, felt her beautiful weight all the way to the kitchen, with its steamy window and the smell of carrots, and he also felt through his sweater, the thick needlework notwithstanding, the light motion of her fingers giving him signs he did not understand because maybe he was too weak in the Esperanto of gestures and generally in any language through which one might wish to convey despair.

"What's this all about? What is the meaning of life?" Sonia suddenly asked once they had entered the dark foyer. "Tell me, what will become of us, where is man heading, what determines all this?"

They leaned together against the wall, again with their arms intertwined, and kept silent for a long time. And what Jurek said, he said softly: "I often think that we're all being controlled by some inexorable hand of destiny, and that a person, at the dawn of his life, already has a set course, maybe once and for all. You know, not long ago I was reading this book . . ."

"Yes?"

"For some this line is straight, clear. For others, twisty and steep. And what we call a surprise, an accident, in the parlance of our time, is essentially determined in advance, sketched out. Like in mythic Greek tragedy, where with such genuine enormity a mysterious, inexorable Fatum emerges that controls the heroes' fate, making them a kind of tool in the hand of this higher order of the world."

With compote, naturally, everything lightened up, and the sun even shone through the bluish clouds. For how can one shiver with cold, wallow in pensiveness, when everything in the glass is so pink and volatile, one thing sinking to the bottom, another drifting around the top, a memory of the overripe as ethereal as a mote, as comic as a pit spat into one's fist, spoon, or right onto one's saucer. The last seed to fall with a matriarchal clack was Mama's, so Jurek could tell that now Mama was going to tell fortunes, to read their individual stories as written in hands of solitaire and in their lifelines. Sonia learned from the cards that her birthday is on the twenty-fifth of May, and she agreed to the letter, and also that it would be her twenty-first; that her auspicious months are March and July, and that she should beware of December; that her money is in fact holding up, and that love, like a faithful river, will wind around her life if Sonia follows her heart and isn't taken in by the insincerity of hazel eyes. On Sonia's right hand it was written that her colors are yellow and sky blue, and that she should keep an emerald on her to protect her from digestive ailments. From her left hand she learned that she should drink more compote, for Mama was smiling maternally and ran to the larder for a new jarful. They drank unanimously that you must remember this, a kiss is just a kiss, and to what one is not to do with a baby and the bathwater, and Jurek told the latest joke about a certain painter of mild manner, wouldn't you know, and then the beautiful ladies here gathered found a few things of their own to discuss over their compote: the sea and its fish, sweaters and jerseys. Jurek, as Mama's son and Sonia's friend, who was now discussed rather than criticized, stepped out to the other room and rather scribed than wrote a letter to Olek.

In it he told of the preprandial visit to the yards and squares of their shared "schoolboy Arcadia, or the paradise of childhood," about Sonia's smile, now sad, now joyful, about her lively interest in every detail and place shown her by her magnificent guide, about the competent explanations of that "stubbled Beatrice," explaining why Beatrice and why stubbled. Jurek also recalled a great deal about the kind of longing triggered by Olek's unexpected departure. "You left a great void when you vanished," he assured him, and then he provided a digest of their youthful existence against the backdrop of universal history, for "it has fallen to us to live in difficult times." Yet this man of the quill closed with the following words: "Beloved Olek, in a couple of weeks, the twenty-fifth of May, it will be Sonia's birthday. I hasten to assure you that your letter and its well-wishing will bring her indescribable joy. You do know how ladies love to receive letters. Please, do not neglect this opportunity, and put down a few sentences, though I know how difficult it is for you behind the pen (apropos of which, that is, in connection with what I just said, one does not say 'toward a pen'—perhaps it's an Americanism). She is most certainly waiting for your letter, believe me."

Jurek kept at it for long enough, though Mama and Sonia kept at it longer about fish, smoked and stuffed, with particular praise for carp, about bookkeeping using Polish and foreign—truth be known, more accurate—techniques, about the wedding at the Town Hall Café, and thus also about how the groom was now laboring far away. Then they played thousands and rummy, because unfortunately they were lacking a fourth, because the fourths, both the groom and Olek, were abroad, and today Witek is lugging coal at his aunt's. It got to be too late to go back, and soon they went to bed, Sonia in the room where Jurek usually was, Jurek where the kitchen table usually was. They slept hard until the earth had done its share, turning on its axis like a coquettish ballerina, and then daybreak presented itself obsequiously at the feet of both employees.

When they had gone, having been roused for cereal and the rest of the gingerbread, the sun had already dispersed yesterday's cold and once again heralded the coming of May.

■ □ ■ □ ■

CHAPTER EIGHT

NEVER CAST A CLOUT TILL MAY IS OUT, OR SO THEY SAY. SONIA WAS there, Olek wasn't, Marcel was there, his wife never with him but back in Warsaw, and there was Jurek, but neither hide nor hair of Janka.

But Janka was already on her way. The train poked along, the train smoked and sometimes whistled in Ulrychów and in the kitchen, and for the last hour in the room there was quiet snoring, and only Janka's wide-open eyes spoke of her true exhaustion and about her nightmare, which was no dream. She was seen from above, as if they'd undergone their own Assumption, by two identical pigskin briefcases, the purchase and delivery of which her dad had overseen personally, just as he now personally, though not individually, was taking his repose, quite low, in a shallow hole. What was hidden in these briefcases was anyone's guess—right up to the moment when Janka herself wanted to open them, first on the train at the request of two gentlemen in dark green uniforms and speaking a very guttural language, and then, now around the corner from the toilet at the Warsaw station, to two gentlemen dressed in navy blue and babbling familiarly about an idyll on Szucha Boulevard. Discouraged by the thick accounting textbooks and the New Testament concealed beneath a sea of cotton underwear, they withdrew their hands from under the pile of bras and panties and left, cursing under their sauerkraut breaths.

The day was like any other. When the train with Janka arrived in Warsaw, and Jurek and Sonia were waiting for the departure of the commuter line, all the accountants and accountettes had left their homes. In the Tworki office, Kaltz was sharpening one pencil after another and taking erasers from the drawer to eliminate the errors committed by every second accountant and every single writer. On his order, Quick, deftly covering his slack jaw with the very same splayed hand he used to *heil,* placed ledgers with new purchases to be entered on Sonia's desk, and on Jurek's desk he amassed financial accounts, this time with the specification, Herr Jerzy, for three spaces after the decimal, and without the rounding off typical of Slavs.

Janka fastened her jacket, grabbed hold of her briefcases, and, looking around curiously to her left and her right, directed her pace toward the exit. It was warm again, and after she was around the corner she threw her jacket into her open briefcase, having shifted the Bible to the side and crammed the stockings against more stockings. At a very particular address a skip and a jump from the station, there was no longer a certain somebody to be found, and thus she could now walk straight ahead or turn wherever she liked, for it is the freedom of an out-of-towner not to know the districts, to get lost in the capital, and to sweat and glisten in the sun like the grapes and green olives on the Campo dei Fiori. This is why, in memory of her father, Janka went any old place, changing direction after every cross street to cover her tracks, looking around left and right, and praying at the intersections. Finally, weary and thirsty, she sat down at a café to drink, as every accountant does at that time of day, a mug or glass of good tea.

Sonia didn't always add sugar, but Jurek gladly did, especially when Kaltz treated them to the real crystallized thing. Sometimes Jurek offered the extra seasoning of an anecdote, and they were quiet all around and snorted when the tea was drunk and the joke fully understood. Today he gave them a funny little verse about a rook hanging on a crook, after which he plunged with his thoughts into the credit column of a certain someone, for Sonia was smiling at him as well, and the tea was tasty, the morning late. Janka, as an equally satisfied customer, even ordered a second glass, but the innate hospitality of the capital, with a smile on her ruddy face, placed three glasses on the oilcloth, evenly poured and steaming upward like bats toward the belfry, into the bands of blue. Two men, having carelessly hung up their coats, sat down to the glasses and struck up a conversation. It must have been enthralling, for Janka eagerly paid for the tea, four shots of vodka, two portions of herring, or "fishies" as they say in Warsaw, and two—let's get this out of the way—little pickles, and in not so bookkeeperly a fashion, she left these gentlemen the change. Sadly, it was time for her to go, and she moved into the city, now flooded with sunlight, despite a couple of columns of smoke swirling over there behind those houses and that large carousel.

Janka passed the old ladies with their Polish flowers, peeked at the watches in a shop window, stopped for a moment by the carousel, and looked at the manège with its silent little horses. Glancing around curiously to the left and right, she reached a wide boulevard and walked along the tram tracks, counting the stops and comparing the number of the tram cars coming and going, as an attentive bookkeeper does in two columns, like Jurek now collating expenses with revenues and cursing a blue streak from Kaltz to well beyond the second decimal place. Next she could count the benches in that park and the flowers on that lawn, but whatever she counted, it was she that was the unknown quantity, and thus, now quite exhausted, she turned onto a commercial street, halted momentarily before a shop window, and suddenly spotting her face in the pane, a face in which spring had not yet been counted, the wrinkles as yet unaccounted for, and where the eyes always came out victorious over their dark circles, she reached into her inside pocket for the last-hope piece of paper with its scribbled address, not a sure thing, in fact a rather risky place to go. A kind young rickshaw driver carefully placed the briefcases by her legs, and the rickshaw flashed swiftly through the city. The vehicle's little bell rang out cheerfully over the cobblestones, and Jurek's typewriter brightened resoundingly at the end of the line, for everything was finally in glorious harmony, rounded up once again, and plus the driver and passenger could see the hospital.

And now for Janka, not so long a road to him, to the promised land of the cafeteria, to the compote with the potential second helping, and to the oaks casting shadows. Because it had turned out that at the very uncertain address next to the Opacz station, Miss Aniela was truly willing to take you as she found you and was on the take as well. Thus another ten days in a room with a garden view for what was then a reasonable sum, given the colors and smells, and, furthermore, the first May nights reading want ads in the *New Courier* and methods of balance that were at times as obscure as a May night, yet as logical as a one crushed by a two. And yet only a glimmer of happiness in the form of Sonia, who was at Miss Aniela's sewing a new dress of fresh flowers, sort of similar to the daisies in the garden and so beautiful and strange that it was heretofore unknown to all admirers of pure nature and attired women, at best it had been dreamt up by the nutcases in Tworki, and now Miss Aniela pressed it against the hips with a black belt with a silver buckle.

Birthday! Birthday! The unrestrained press of spring toward the big day and the figures to be honored, that they might arrive in all their well-roundedness! The alluring rustle of the colorful material and the flash of the neck with a little pearl on a chain, that the faces all around might break into laughter and stick around, that the glasses might be raised for toasts, that justice, for we are already coming back down to earth, might be done!

"We will throw you a great reception," Jurek declared to Sonia, "of at least a dozen guests, and the majority of them from the city, and Mama, according to the old Polish custom, will come with cake and compote."

The glimmer of happiness, which had come here a couple of stops by the commuter train, thus looked Janka deeply in the eyes and scrutinized her pile of textbooks, and Janka insisted that the dress be shortened by a centimeter, to take it in from the back and raise the belt a bit, and in this way—without any (God forbid) additional frill, Miss Aniela—Janka was invited, registered, and kissed by Sonia on both cheeks, and on the following day employed according to the usual method, which is to say that Sonia whispered into Kaltz's ever pricked-up ear, and thus Honnette's sweeping signature on Kaltz's A4 application.

When, two days later, Janka stood on the threshold of bookkeeping, Marcel's fountain pen scratched harder on the paper, Jurek's chair creaked meaninglessly, and on the ledge, the cat, Virtuoso, yawned. Jurek's eyes squinted behind his thick glasses, and from the threshold into the depths of the room there crept a coffee-with-cream-colored stain, taking on increasingly elaborate forms with each meter. Jurek had already figured out the stockinged, bipedal stand; he now made out the arms, flowing with a felicitous motion from bright sleeves like porcelain handles, begging one to be gentle with the whole; two more steps, and he was struck by the sight of a coffee waist filled to the brim with the 100 percent arabica of a body, and after the subsequent step he could make out the darker vapor trails of her hair rising from the neck, and among them the face of an Aphrodite born out of the mist and bowing coquettishly, now to one side, now to the other.

Now Janka glanced around one last time to the left and the right and stood hesitantly before the empty desk, but Marcel had already risen and Jurek had already leapt up. Sonia made the introductions. She opened by praising the choice of dress, after which everyone, with the combined efforts of the accountants—disregarding Quick, alone in his corner—sat down to some freshly brewed but unsweetened tea. The tea leaves didn't manage to drop to the bottom, and Jurek had already scalded his tongue and steamed up his glasses, and he lost his composure in his own fog. And that's as much as he had to say, together with his traditional little verse about how tea is nice in paradise, given that his next angel brought her well-formed lips to the glasses Jurek proffered, that she took his spare, soft aluminum spoon in her shapely hands, and that which is unsweetened is not bitter, for he, Jurek—think of him as a friend, no formalities here—could drink, and even sip, that tea for many long hours, until more than one spring passes and the truth is out. With the next pouring, the door quietly opened and Kaltz stepped into heaven with a Mars-like expression, as befits the superhuman, and a mouth full of long nouns, but, knocked off kilter by Sonia's gaze, the most fearsome Katyusha in the *gubernia,* worse than the *Banditen* by the highway, he waddled meekly to the *Zucker* and, having sat down among the celebrants, he told some shtick about how a German meets a Pole in hell, and the devil asks . . .

■ □ ■ □ ■

CHAPTER NINE

WHO CAME WITH THE DEVILS OUT OF HELL ONLY HISTORY CAN TELL, but let's not occupy ourselves with the long term, for short is our breath, long the rush of blood within us, for over there not much time now remains before the birthday party on Saturday. Jurek Paper-Pusher-ek assumed the command and general supervision, a scriptwriter *ex machina* in the subtroupe of the theater of the world, the great architect of the celebration. To bring to fruition that which he'd beautifully calligraphed, with subpoints and references, he had enlisted everyone, regardless of their state of mind or their degree of fondness for Sonia. The valiant team of emperors from Pavilion F, under the democratic leadership of Nero, cleared the meadow over the Utrata and, with the gathered stones, assembled a remarkable buffet table. The saints from Pavilion K used letterhead paper to make attractive garlands, which a squad of Martians and one guy from Neptune hung along the lowest boughs of the pines. Vivaldi walked back and forth along the main path puffing out some four-part melody under his breath, and for two days, Rubens, the master, had been revolving around Sonia in stained pajamas and with an enigmatic expression, while Antiplato was holed up somewhere and wasn't showing himself to anyone at all. The beloved cafeteria pledged tin mugs and plates, and Kaltz promised to arrange for genuine knives, long ones, Herr Jerzy, definitely long ones, as well as for as many passes as were needed. One afternoon, right after quitting time, Jerzy went suddenly to Warsaw, was seen twice as he walked toward Pruszków, and in the evenings he locked himself in his room with Marcel, where there were blasts, chants, and playing. On the last night something mysterious whistled under the window, and we'll soon find out what that's about. A great deal of work also awaited Janka at the subsequent fittings of Sonia's dress, which went better and better from day to day despite Miss Aniela's alterations, and during the lengthy meetings with Jurek and Marcel about the final appearance. Moreover, the day was already stretching delightfully at night's expense, the winds were chasing away those incredibly gray clouds, selling admissions tickets only to the cumuli, and Mother Superior Earth and Father Time were quaking ever more anxiously near the Volga River.

On Saturday, the twenty-fifth of May, the first one to wake up was Virtuoso, the cat. He meowed the prescribed three times and licked his muzzle. At that signal, the sun allowed a test ray through the leaves and, when it caught only bark, rolled its heavy sphere from behind the roof. Just then the second-floor window opened with a great boom, and two pairs of nervous eyes hung out. Someone whistled cheerfully, maybe Marcel, and someone hummed, that was Marcel for sure, and someone was chatting away next to him, this being Jerzy, as the sun, our cosmic aspirin, was bringing relief to life and an appropriate setting to the celebration. For the smell of spring these gentlemen bedaubed their cheeks with amber water, for the golden air over the eaves these gentlemen put on genuine cotton jackets and trousers, pressed as best they knew how, for the deep green of the grass they put on socks with a colorful band above the ankle, and for all things still beautiful and not yet squandered, these gentlemen used radiant ribbons as boutonnières. Marcel looked at Jerzy, Jerzy looked at Marcel: *Good God, how I do love him,* thought one. *Merciful Yahweh, how I do love him,* thought the other.

Meanwhile, two pavilions away, a window banged, and the madonnas pulled on their undies and stood eyeball to eyeball with the wardrobe, opened by the draft.

"Well, here we go," Janka called out. "No reason to wait around, because we have to be getting to the office."

There were things to wait around for: for God's mercy and the end of all this, for better times and going back home, or in actual fact, not—Sonia sobbed into a pressed handkerchief—for what's the point of this more or less everything, what's the point of these flowers on a dress and a belt with a silver buckle, and this little phial for Parisian essence, where there is none and maybe won't be any. It was Janka, more ravenous for the future but sensitive to prophesies, who reached for the second handkerchief, and the madonnas hugged, and they whispered something into each other's ears and cried some more, and the tears flowed profusely onto their slips, onto the silent witnesses of what was hidden underneath and in the heart.

But what was there to remain on the surface if not the flowers and aromas, more persistent than gloom, if not heels taller than the stupid earth, and the belt, which had to be properly tightened? The buckle finally reached the last hole, Sonia looked one last time into the mirror, fixed her hair with a deft move, and carefully descended the stairs to receive her morning cup of cereal and slab of bread with marmalade in the cafeteria.

There was thumping, there was bumping, and behind the tree where Jurek was, some tittering. In front of the door, a choir of nutcases in profile formed a tight semicircle, from the tallest singer to the shortest, and at Marcel's signal after he slipped out from the shadows they let out a trial *sol.* It came together fantastically, so Marcel smiled with satisfaction, raised both arms menacingly, froze, and pulled the sky down with a sudden motion. The first syllable, as round and long as any age and all centuries, escaped from throats tensed under their striped collars. Repeated many times, the birthday song arranged itself into a request for a long existence, somewhere around 10 percent of eternity, for a waterproof roof over the head, and a stork on the nest, for four-leaf clovers, for constant sunrise over a lagoon, and for tasty things in one's mouth at a time when it is already singing the good fortune of an everyday day. And additionally for a drink, just in case, with the choir.

Marcel's hands lifted the dumbstruck sky, swung downward once more, and silence fell. Sonia went rouge and pale in turn, yet still paler was Old Man Methuselah, the doyen of Tworki, who had a good memory of Cortez's expeditions and the dawn counterattacks of the Indians. He stepped out of the line with a mug of steaming cereal and a thick slice of bread in his hand, and with foot atremble, he approached the birthday girl, bookkeeper, and Aztec goddess all in one, and furthermore a saint from toe to crown, except insofar as she had a waistline. Having given her what he'd carried with absolute deference, he genuflected and croaked solemnly, before he burst out crying: "Oh, accept this offering and remain with us, Eternal One, and allow us to honor your day!"

Sonia raised the mug with one hand, showed it to everyone, and in a sacerdotal gesture, placed it to her lips; with her other hand she patted the old man on his gray head and curtsied amidst the applause. Then the choir pushed out the brat, Sleep Little Jesus, drowning in his too-big pajamas. The youngest of the bunch but already a complete loon, he ran up to Sonia, kissed her unceremoniously on both cheeks, placed a cornflower garland on her head and, having shouted a loud "hallelujah, hallelujah," and, after a moment's reverie, "Heil Hitler, Frau Buchalter," darted back into line. Everyone broke into jolly laughter, shouted, "What a nutcase," and the semicircle, transformed into a procession with one snap of Marcel's fingers, stood ready to march. Sonia, beaming and whispering "thank you, thank you" to left and right, moved first, and the choir stepped after her to the time of a song about rosemary in the moment of blossoming and oh so lovely. At the doorstep of the administration building, Sonia turned around and thanked everyone once again, cradling the mug and the garland theatrically to her heart. Then Marcel stretched his arms before him, splayed his fingers, and the choir, muttering something unevenly under their breaths, reluctantly dispersed, observed from behind the next tree by Jurek, the supervisor, and by Janka, his liaison officer.

At the sight of Sonia, the typewriters and abacuses in the accounting office started tapping, and one German pencil fell to the floor. They were acting stupid somehow; fortunately, a breathless Janka, Jurek, and Marcel, still waving his arms, ran into the office and kissed Sonia so loudly and so many times that Bronka dared to smile and to compare the dress with a Persian rug, that Jabłkowska wished her all the best, and from the corner some blond guy gasped, "*Ja, gut.*" Our folk winked at each other and, now as employees, started to underline indirect sums and carry into the second column those figures that were necessary to our continued existence from birth unto twilight, and today from seven thirty unto half past one. Because at half past one the pens went into their caps, the pencils into their mustard jars, and Kaltz slipped into the room even more quietly than usual with a paper in his hand: "His Honor the director, Herr Honnette, wishes Miss Sonia all the best on the occasion of her twenty-first birthday, which falls on this day." He was reading even more quietly than he'd come in, and he turned red after having first gone pale. "Much happiness, satisfaction with your work, and a long, successful service for the good of our hospital community. And as a token of recognition for results achieved in the first quarter, you are hereby awarded a one-time monetary bonus in the amount of forty-five zlotys to be paid next month. Signed, His Honor the director, Herr Honnette."

He repeated the amount twice, bowed stiffly, and left before Sonia could thank him and offer him the cookies that had been circling around the desks, amid the snorts and giggles, for a good hour, until finally Quick took one and smacked his lips loudly just as the clock struck quitting time.

Sonia went up to Jurek and Marcel, who were looking impatiently out the window. Jurek preferred that she not say anything, so he himself muttered, "They're supposed to be here any minute. Maybe Mama will bring mail."

Sonia smiled with embarrassment. "What now, since I already have this dress? Will you all come to our place for a drop? I bought two bottles. I won't say from whom."

They knew from whom, because they had their own, because it's lovely to multiply the festive number twenty by two, or even, if the moon has shone favorably, by three percent, and to pour it into glasses, drinking on the meadow to every blade of grass holding us above the ground. But better let Sonia run in for those bottles and come to the Utrata punctually in an hour—why let them go to waste?

She was a couple of minutes late because when she was coming out of the pavilion, Kaltz emerged without a peep like a cat from behind the mound of coal, and he couldn't open his mouth for a long time, even when Sonia poured him a capful. Finally he muttered something about a personal gift on the obvious occasion, poked around in one pocket, found nothing, nor anything in the other, smiled helplessly, and right then, from his back pocket, he took out a small, handsome pigskin wallet. "Maybe it will come in handy for your extra pay," he whispered. "Miss Sonia, I wish you a very fine evening. At a young age, one should have fun."

She was a couple of minutes late, but she stood dumbstruck longer still, staring through the gate of birch trunks and spruce branches at the head of the trail, at those stone decorations in a free-classical style, at the garlands on the pines, at the buffet adorned with leaves and bark. Meanwhile, they'd already toasted her welcome and made a second general toast, and after the third, the real one, a long line, an entire train of good people, came together for the linking of cheeks and the squeezing of Sonia. Sonia looked solemnly into the eyes of the orchestrator's mom when the latter drew her to her breast and placed on the stones a cake inscribed FOR OUR SONIA, with hearts made out of icing. Sonia turned rouge when Stefek kneeled before her after he had already hugged her and kissed her on the hand, Warsaw-style, and discreetly placed in her hand a little cartridge casing with a tiny engraved heart and an inscription, FOR SONIA, FROM THE BOYS. She burst into all-vowel laughter when Heniek and Witek, the next to be carried along the receiving line, pressed kisses onto her face powder and bowed with their hands on their hearts. What color remained of her lipstick was destined for the cheeks of Bronka; Anna, Marcel's wife; and Joasia, Anna's sister, a surprise so that there would be more women for the boys. And Sonia completely broke down crying when, in the end, Janka, Marcel, and Jurek hugged her all around and again screamed, "All the best!" in her ear and for the entire wood.

An even twenty-one matches burned down to their own waistlines and warmed Sonia's hand before she managed, with the next one, to light up the pile of spruce brush and fragrant juniper. Amidst the applause and congratulations, Jurek and Marcel handed everyone a bayonet and a hunk of kielbasa acquired from where we won't say. The people leaned over the fire, and the forest stirred over the people. When the first droplets of grease had fueled the embers and the mouths had gnawed through the skin of the sausages, the boys poured out the fourth and Jurek, having glanced at Sonia and at his watch, announced sonorously:

"Before our hearts are occupied with toasts
And music moves us all to dance,
We'll give our gifts to Sonia, all our best,
Now dearest Tworkians, advance!"

Presently, something on the trail was shuffling and making its way with the difficulty typical of people carrying a cross, even if it happens to be a picture of one and a half meters by two and a half. Finally, Rubens lugged his work into the middle of the meadow and leaned it against the stone table. When he had caught his breath and fixed his crooked pajamas, he pointed to Sonia with one hand and with the other, even more proudly, to the painting.

A miraculous multiplication ensued. Because on the left there stood Sonia, and on the right there stood Sonia. Now there were two Sonias, two mouths for kissing, two necks for adorning, preferably with some jewel, and two noses, thus four nostrils, and two pairs of eyes. The birthday girl newly arrived looked at the birthday girl already present, and she, with disbelief, looked at the rest and at Rubens. The rest laughed and clapped, and the artist proudly sank his gaze into the earth, the inspiration for his art.

For from the earth there had emerged a new Sonia, like a new world after the transformation of the clay. Ever had she been a body, but lighter than thought; ever was she a woman, but now she was an eternal creature. The bare feet and calves grew out of a still-black foundation, but their muscle took from it what was best and most lasting. That's why the nakedness could work its way higher and seize the knees, gracing the utterly plump thighs with radiance and skipping the middle parts, and it let the Creator and our half-formed friends on the meadow in on the edge of a mystery, with one nipple at the end, while still higher it revealed the length of the neck, now and forever accounted for, the mouth moistened with a timid half smile, and finally the entire soul divided between the left and right pupils.

But let us return *in medias res* to the pelt. Yes, Rubens had enshrouded Sonia's waist in something bushy and tawny. The former paws wrapped tightly around the hips and obscured whatever it was they didn't give two figs for in Paradise. The erstwhile torso wound around the abdomen and across Sonia's breast and shoulder and on her back met with an ancient tail, indicating that the entire thing was soft, near at hand, and a tad tongue in cheek. And perhaps this new Sonia wanted something, standing like that on her powerful legs, like maybe to slip the fur off and to see the first woman from perhaps the seventh rib, warm, embarrassed, and ardent. For such was the timid yet eager shade of her smile, such was—next to the eternity of the rest—that particular fur, suggesting that there was no contradiction between them, and that what was hidden beneath it, here and now, could be embraced and taken, even forever.

There was no doubt that the master of the portrait had earned it all: both his name and his long stay in Tworki, a shot filled to the top and a piece of kielbasa, a squeezing of the hand and a heartfelt kiss from Sonia, and another drop, drunk in the usual fashion with the head tilted back—just maybe not that cackling of Stefek's from behind Jurek's back. For a touch of world music, the sounds of an ocarina carried sonorously from behind the bushes, and on the meadow, lightly and airily like spring, the year's first season, Vivaldi stepped out with a flower boutonnière on his pajamas. Having bowed once and twice to Sonia, and without even glancing at the kielbasa, he continued to blow fervently into the instrument, and a melody was unfurled. Given the passing time, he played perhaps too slowly, but given the cycle of eternal return, really quite well, so that nothing would go to waste, a stalk of grain was made into bread, and the storks again wove a nest for a future family. By the time spring was over, verdant and spare, he promised a hot summer and a so-so fall and winter, and when, having made several turns with a stamp of the leg, he recalled the first notes after the last notes, something again moved loudly in the bushes.

"Come out, Antiplato. It's okay now," Vivaldi shouted off script, looking uncertainly at Jurek and the horrible scowl on his face, and before the applause broke out he'd gone, uninvited, to the buffet.

And Antiplato began, after kielbasa and two drops for starters, like every artisan of the word. Sonia nodded with amazement and even caught Jurek by the sleeve, so lovely did the new guest appear today, so proudly did he fill out his pajamas. Combed for the first time since time immemorial, his beard was sculpted into long, gray coils, the thinner part of his hair on his balding skull was divided from the thicker by a dashing part, his potato nose was somehow less shiny, and his pale-blue lips were made crimson to match his new socks in his de-mudded sandals, polished to a shine. At last he swallowed, licked his beard and mustache clean of mustard amidst the friendly laughter, cleared his throat boldly under his clean little collar, and, his legs stretched between the two Sonias, he cast into the suddenly godforsaken silence:

"Our spring has come, and May's in bloom,
Let's praise the world for lack of gloom!
Spring has come. It has come without the stir of icecaps, without the violent crumbling of the fluvial eyes of winter. It has come like a dream of silence and to its bosom the pained earth has been coddled. And in its wake is May, ringing from a distance with a wealth of charms.
Our spring has come, and May's in bloom,
Let's praise the world for lack of gloom!
May—the king of the year, the duke of the twenty-first birthday
May—good weather of souls, relief of pains, livelier tempo of hearts
May—youthfulness, youthfulness . . ."

Antiplato suddenly stammered and started to look nervously at the piece of paper hidden in his hand.

"Immaculately," Jurek said in a whisper.

"Immaculately," Antiplato repeated furiously, then crumpled the paper violently into a ball and tossed it furiously into the bushes. "And to hell with it."

He went up to Sonia, again stood with his legs apart, stroked his beard, and took on a solemn expression. He said, "Antiplato to Sonia, glory and honor. In no great measure does the manifestation differ from chance, from chance. Among equals hence you have no king, the dogs have gone into the forest forever. Not the first one, who barks, but that second one, who barks back. In these woods there is no wilderness. This is a wood of woods, he flees, who hunts, the deer shoots, a boar counts the cartridge. The hunt goes on, but there are no animals, nor will there be. Hence to you, Sonia, to your twenty-one years from the depths of all time do I proffer the most beautiful, most humble tribute. To Sonia, the birthday girl, from Antiplato, glory and honor."

"I don't really understand," Sonia whispered to Jurek, clapping even harder than the others and answering the deep bow of the speaker with a curtsy, "but well spoken and amusing, perhaps."

"Nutcase! A total nutcase. I asked him. Now he's totally lost it," Jurek mumbled and stepped into the middle of the meadow, also clapping and nodding in recognition. He waited a moment and, when all the hands had finally reached for their glasses, summed up what had happened:

"Our art has reached our meadow, to art we're ever true,
Communing with the soul, the word, and music, painting,
These gifts they gave to Sonia, a sweetheart through and through,
These dearest Tworkians, their love most unabating!"

"Moron! A complete idiot!" Antiplato whispered to Rubens and Vivaldi, but he shuffled meekly behind them to the head of the trail, as they were bowing deeply for the last time.

Sonia led her guests ten or more meters off, and on the meadow Marcel had already set up his one-man orchestra of concertina and pedaled mallet striking a board. But before Sonia dances the oberek and a spirited polka, she is held for a few minutes on the trail—Marcel is still tuning his instruments—by the words of yet another Tworkian, and who knows why he was not announced by Jurek though he may have been nearby and he'd certainly been drinking. Allow me, too, dear Sonia, to offer my best and sincerest birthday wishes. For you to be beautiful for a long time still, and then ever lovely, kind, and charming, and to have a fine figure. Non omnis moriar, they say, and they write it on gravestones, but even this bit, to be honest, is a waste. Hence I wish you, and even ask you, to remain here forever, not to move farther than the length of the trail from the gate to the meadow and not to cross the tracks for any price. That you might remain forever at hand like a letter to the pen and like feminine rhymes. If you'd like, like Mephisto I will give you eternal youth, and quite unlike Mephisto, I'll pay for it myself, with my life, my quirks, position, cash, if only you don't leave Tworki and forever tread its gravel paths and smile broadly at its nutcases. And when they start dancing, dance first with Jurek, if at all possible, for he's earned it.

The concertina expanded its lungs: Marcel was ready. Heniek went up to Mama and made a gallant bow. Witek stood next to Anna with his hand—this being Witek—in his pocket. Stefek ran up to Anna's sister, Joasia, and grabbed her hard by the hand, first as a test, cautiously in his thoughts, then whap! Jurek spun around like a top and, on one side, saw a smiling Janka, and, on the other, a laughing Sonia. When he felt breath on his cheeks and smelled the perfume from Sonia's neck, he jumped up like a wheel over a pothole, rolled straight ahead, and stopped next to that very same fragrance, only another one, because it was Janka's neck. A chord rang out, and on the meadow all the couples locked arms, the second chord sounded, and on the meadow Sonia was the odd man out, the third chord played, now forming a prelude, and in the middle of the meadow, Sonia was dying then and there. Then Marcel looked at Jurek, and Jurek peeked at his watch again, raising his arm high. And he shouted piercingly, for he knew how to do that as well:

"May hope now fill our hearts, may love in our hearts ring,
If we must stand and wait, then let us wait for spring!"

A tall silhouette in a coat with an upturned collar emerged from behind the trees on the right side of the meadow. It directed its long gait straight toward Sonia, stopped before her, and asked in a resonant, trained, artificial tone:

"May I request the lady's charm to join me in a dance?
To whirl her, leading, to and fro, and hold her in my hands?"

Sonia nodded and then nodded some more. It half embraced Sonia with its right arm, and the left hand sought out a hand.

Marcel banged away on the keys, and the keys into the crux of what matters and can be repeated with spirit and more than a little heart. The melody was brief but more than roomy enough for the steps, turns, and glances. Others were whirling around, too, dispensing their steps, adding one foot to another, as the waltz demands, and those others also one-two-three rolled, and even, as Witek did a moment ago, stumbled, but only in the middle of the meadow did it sparkle so or was the ground so kicked over. One, two, three, the man circled around Sonia's supple axis, one, two drew her to the side, and three drew her in, and two, three flew with her, and one and one he spun the air, and we can no longer see much, now Sonia, and the glimmer in her eyes, now Olek, and a face smiling more broadly than long and carefully shaven, and the hair ever tied back over Sonia's nape, and again Olek's nape buzzed short, and once again Sonia's eyes, one of them winking perhaps to Olek's whisper, and when Olek suddenly opens his mouth wider, hair slips out from under the ribbon holding it, blows over her neck, and again we can't see anything, and we hear only the one, two, three, one, two, three of the spirited waltz on a dead man's chest.

Yes, Marcel had changed the melody, had perversely carried those treading the earth into a sailor's tango, more wobbly, yet less rotary, closer to the clouds and a breeze of boundlessness, thus Olek's coat strained like a sail from port to port, thus Sonia's dress blew about at full steam, but here Marcel, with this shrewd measure and new chords, ordered them to make for shore, and from the far reaches of unknown waters he headed to a land both beautiful and amicable because it was ours, where the heart is, and the oberek yo-ho-ho and the mazurka ha-ha, and Sonia and Olek like a lady and her gentleman in the courtyard, the pasture, and now in the meadow, in the unparalleled stamping, yes, among the people, yes, the rumbling, for yes, I'm yours, yes, yes, I missed you, yes, I missed you and longed for you, yes, yes, I want to, yes, yes I want to and love you, yes.

But now Marcel, as though he himself were surprised by the song, collapsed the bellows, and when all the couples stopped, and Jurek and Janka ran up silently to light the candles on the birthday cake, suddenly a new, though familiar, melody soared from the bellows into the sky, and Poland—Heniek hummed with Mama—long a province be a nation once again, with Stefek and Witek finishing it off in the bass. At Jurek's signal, all the guests gathered close to the flaming cake, and around the guests daylight still flickered. And at that moment, Jurek swung around, raised the glass Stefek had rushed to pour him, and, looking persistently now into Olek's pale face, now into the lustrous pattern on the cake, said, "A warm May evening. The wind is still sleeping in the dark dens of night; it is not tugging at the trees, not whimpering quietly and mournfully. But as dusk slowly settles, when the shroud of night begins to wrap our Polish land in its dark shroud, far off, somewhere in the distance, you'll catch sight of the wisps of flickering flames—that's where our soldiers have made camp. There they chat quietly, they who have made the greatest sacrifice—their lives for the fatherland. They are at rest, perhaps unknown, about whom the future will say only: regiment, battalion, battery, unit. O Polish soldier, whose only worry, whose sole concern was not hardship, not loss in the ranks, not the bullets and bombs that decimated you, but a sacred mission. You defended yourselves against insane odds, you defended our nation's freedom, and though you fell in the murderous fire of battle, you rescued honor and virtue, which for us Poles has always been, and is, the greatest, most sacred thing. We, whom God has ordained to remain here, continue to stand in defense of the purity of our feelings, and we offer all our sufferings as a sacrifice to the one God. And we believe that if he has stricken us with such a heavy thunderbolt, with burning lightning, then he clearly has confidence in us. That we will lift ourselves up, improved and strong. On this warm May day, on a day most festive for those of us gathered here, the thoughts of all living Poles are on you, Polish soldiers. From your graves, scattered through the battlefields of Norway, Holland, France, through almost all of Europe, may there arise a *great* Poland."

Having placed his emphasis on the last adjective, Jurek went up to Olek and cast himself around his neck. They stood there hugging and squeezing, and Sonia was crying next to them, Mama sobbing, and the boys stared at the tips of their shoes. After a moment Olek kissed Jurek on both cheeks, went up to Sonia, and led her to the stone table. Sonia took a deep breath and held it for a long time in her lungs, as though she were taking it in for good, for her eternal use. When it had already filled the deepest alveolus, reaching her diaphragm, she leaned over the fruit-and-nut cake, three-layered, round, and bright, its twenty-one little flames timidly blinking, and blasted it desperately with wind. All the candles went out, and the cake faded.

"Happy Birthday"—Stefek intoned, and ran up to Olek—"hey man, where did you come from?—to you."

"Happy Birthday to you," everyone corrected, and they joyfully besieged Sonia and Olek, and the man within Olek, and the happiness within that man, as well as the frog in his throat. Happy Birthday to you, may we all live a hundred years, may the cake turn out to be sweet and really to have three different flavors, may that bottle hidden in Mama's mesh bag turn out to be fruit liquor from Aunt Irena, may everyone sit down comfortably, may Sonia seat herself next to Olek, and may Olek answer all the questions rolling to the mouth through little lumps of vanilla cream with real nuts, if one might be so lucky.

"Actually, I told Jurek everything," Olek responded uncertainly. "There was some trouble and adventure, but somehow I managed, time-wise. Jurek will tell it better."

"He beat Burghof, took advantage of their inattention, got on Helga's bicycle, and was gone. Then he rode under the parcels on a freight train till midnight, swam a breaststroke across the Danube, and crossed the Tatra Mountains to Zakopane with a Hungarian courier—no problem, because he'd already been to Budapest, fast across Poland, and now he's home. Just that the damn train broke down in Włochy, and he had to walk half the night, threw himself over the wall, and then he wakes us up." Jurek cut himself some cake and calmly swallowed it. "All thanks to a kicked ball. There was supposed to be a game on Sunday. 'You'll lose without me,' Olek said to Schnitzel. 'After all, you know how well they kick it in Burghof. They've already beaten Dorfhof and crushed Zamthof. And so, Mr. Supervisor, who are you going to put in, Reschke and Waldtke? But they can't even keep up with cows. A waste of these three barrels of beer.' So this Schnitzel, the best midfielder in all of Dubhof, trudged over to the farmer's with Olek and said, 'We're taking him with us, sir. No one can shoot a header like he can. We're going to make cow pies out of Burghof.' Some day I'll write about it. I'm going to call it 'Olek's Escape.' I've already even prepared something for today."

Jurek pulled a piece of paper out of his pocket, tore into the last piece of cake, and calmly swallowed it down. "So it looks more or less like this:

Courageous Olek longed for Warsaw's cobbled streets,
And Helga, much enamored, hid away her bike.
A heavy din arose around the soccer cleats,
He shot a goal and left poor Helga in the Reich.

That's as much as I've done because I had to get some sleep," Jurek said apologetically, and he asked for more cake, but there was none. "That's what it was like, right, Olek?"

Olek nodded, and everything became as clear as an Alpine glacier, as the hair of Helga, waving good-bye for a long time, and the whole was good in its telling, but what manner of birthday present Olek had brought from across the southern border, no one had yet guessed. And after all, everyone was listening about cows and rich milk for chocolates, for Mozart balls and *Mozartbombe,* about green pastures on a cold background of glaciers, about feathers behind ribbons on hats, and about clean water, when the first snows give out and the yodeling begins. Silence fell for especially good effect, and it became dark all around, for Olek had told everyone to close their eyes. The wind stirred and died down, and then quietly, very quietly, a silver, silver, silvery sound rang out. "Tim tam ti ti tam," it jingled, and then another "tu ti dam." A small Alpine bell shivered on Olek's warm fingers and made light of everything, of the four corners of the world, and particularly of the East, of its own euphony, of the twilight after a long day, and of the order of things. And it twinkled now coquettishly, now mysteriously, it was winking at everyone with its totalitarian eye, only not so to Sonia Kubryń. For Sonia still imprisoned the sound within her closed eyelids and the spikes of her lashes, held it under her tongue and even deeper, in her throat, releasing blushes of happiness to her cheeks by turns, and Olek Przybysz raised the little bell over her ear and gently nudged it until Sonia had absorbed all its music, until her body swung and rang out on the inside.

And then everyone danced again in the pairs established by the prose of life and by poetry, which is ascribed to who knows who. The first dance had just concluded, and Heniek started like he'd been burned, because Jurek had quietly approached Sonia after him.

"May I have this dance?" Jurek asked.

She looked at him for a long time. He took off his glasses and stuck them through into his lapel, next to the boutonnière.

"May I have this dance?" he repeated, furrowing his brow slightly.

She rested her right hand on his shoulder and kept quiet.

"May I have this dance?" he asked again. "Would you like to dance with me? May I ask you to dance?"

Jurek may, Sonia did. She kept quiet for a moment longer, looked intently for a moment longer, until all her senses concentrated within her, compounded, and called out for an embrace. Then she hugged him as strongly as she'd kept hugging the birch, the first one on the left from the river, when, after Olek's disappearance, she would come to the meadow and the sun was starting to set. They shuddered slightly because the melody was wistful and Marcel entranced. Jurek swayed appropriately and led Sonia confidently enough, and Sonia laid out her question in line with the *deux pas:* "Why, why all of this? And why for me?"

Jurek had a prepared answer about beauty, which one should acknowledge, feel, and appreciate where it truly exists. More important, however, was the Schubert running along in a quiet phrase and the white of sorrow like a birch trunk, so let Sonia's hands embrace the birch one last time, warmly and strongly, and let the birch hold its tongue, let it shed resinous, furtive tears and wipe its bark in farewell, and we beg you, maestro Marcel, let it forever breathe in the balsam of her strawberry-blonde hair and the blessing of her dark eyes on what she hopes is yet the long road of their lives. Here, the sky overhead, three little clouds, farther on the water ripples softly, and let it be, just be.

"Tell me, tell me," Sonia asked a second time, just before the last act.

But the birch still maintained its bleached-white silence, until finally the notes completely died away, and it became Jurek again, richer for this one and perhaps most beautiful experience, for this ever-so-long—let's hear it for our beloved Marcel—spring dance, and again he became the organizer, calling out sonorously: "The long-awaited change of partners—once more the gentlemen ask the ladies, the ladies ask for lively music."

Witek, the boy from Wola, and when necessary from Targówek, grabbed the concertina, and he banged out a tango as thievish as a prison tattoo, a dragon on the left shoulder, and on his bellybutton a naked lady with a mermaid's tail. Thus, for their common enjoyment, Olek asked Sonia; Marcel, Ania; Stefek, Anna's sister Joasia; Heniek, timidly Bronka; and the dragon himself, Jurek, Miss Janka.

And that's how it remained. The dances passed, and the sunset labored on, and the same feet kept trampling, and the same hands kept greeting. Olek's fingertips counted Sonia's fingers more than once, tested the durability of her wrists, where the blood pours into the hand and one feels the ticking of that which beats higher up, and they also saw that it bends at Sonia's elbow, and they forgot that that's a beautiful place to kiss because it's beautiful there, soft velvet in a bony setting, and that being the case, they turned back to Sonia's hand like the mouth's unhurried herald and wrote out in a delicate slide, which was received as a pleasant tingling, the approaching facts of the night. Marcel and Anna's hands already had a great deal behind them, though lately so little of each other, and on the left their hands were drawn together out of gratitude for what had already been, and on the right, as Witek played about a girl dumped by a cardsharp or about Mack, for whom no one waited, though he had a beautiful knife, they touched their cheeks, for there, in the delicate skin under the eye, a great deal of a person is concentrated, especially when they are faithful to one another and connected by more than a single night's dream. Let's pass over the hands of Bronka and Heniek in silence, because nothing is going to come of that; about Stefek's hands, we know that, fortunately, they weren't all that sweaty, and a week later he brought three pink carnations to a café near the point where Marszałkowska Street runs into Savior Square. But now it would be best to comment upon what was happening with that last pair.

"Jurek, Jurek," Janka whispered when, before each new dance or after the whistle of the train from Podkowa, into her hand, stretched out by another hand, there fell Jurek's lips and once his entire nose. "Jerzy, come now, Jerzy," she said right after the dance, when his lips returned, boisterously parted, to that same hand, or to both. Yes, Jurek bowed, said thank you, and he straightened up, showed his respect, and eyed her down. And it seems Janka looked pretty good, her hand was pretty soft and fragrant in receiving tribute from the softest and only slightly moonshine-chapped part of his face, for Jurek Panther-ek pounced when necessary, and led when he had to, and smiled, and looked warmly without smiling, for under his ruffled hair a thought popped up about a new pair of syllables and an impeccable rhyme: Jan-ka, Jan-ka, he repeated in his head, and he felt it in his stomach and—parental guidance suggested—even lower, Janka in Casablanca, a kiss our *lingua franca* (Witek was singing just then about a plush kitty and a wooden doggy in love at the flea market) and Jurek whispered his favorite dream quote into Janka's ear. "She threw her little arms around his neck"—he started to bring his hand behind Janka's collar—"and she pressed her itty-bitty ears to his ears, pressing them with a kiss in which heavenly sweetness combined with the fire of a thousand hells. Cuddled close to each other, rocking slightly with the measured movement of the tango, intoxicated with happiness, similar to the gods, they dreamed a golden dream of love, which conquers all."

Meanwhile, Witek had already finished because unfortunately the kitty was sold and the little beasts parted ways, and thus the tango came to an end. Dusk had fallen, and they had to put the fire out. The Magnificents ran with the bottles and mugs to the stream, the flames choked, and the birthday passed into its nocturnal stage. Now nothing is burning, it's dark, and we can't see anyone, only over there, where Janka and Jurek stopped in a dancing pose, two silhouettes are hazily coming into view, just from the stream over there. From the stream we detect a faint gleam.

And who else but Jurek could interrupt that dark silence and illuminate the night anew?

"If Nature will withhold its ever-verdant grasses,
And music dies away as dusk obscures the notes,
Let's go to Sonia's room, pour coffee down our throats,
And don't forget to bring your . . . um, yes, your glasses."

That's all right. He'd been as clear as he could and swore under his breath because his words had gone a bit stale in the alcohol of poetry, they'd gotten a little too pickled, but the appeal was heard, and the company, which both we and the river enjoyed, moved single file down the trail of their obligatory returns to Tworki.

Oh, how short the distance from word to word, from celebration to separation, and from dusk to dawn, because it's barely two hours, no more than three, and again a Warsaw day will rise. They sat shoulder to shoulder on the floor and on both beds in Sonia and Janka's room, they tasted real coffee and sipped the rest of the liqueur, and a few green apples were found to boot. Olek continued to recall the Alps and held Sonia's hand, Ania and Joasia sang beautifully about a trout and, together with Mama, about weavers in Łódź. Then everyone hummed quietly like some old brigade, only Janka forgot the second verse. Jurek recited a poem about Pleasant Street, which isn't always pleasant, and Stefek unfortunately told a joke about a certain Miss Fela. And again they drank coffee with a bit of fresh water added. Witek imitated the voices of people and animals, and he was best at doing a rooster and Adenoid Hynkel, oh, that Adenoid Hynkel. Finally Marcel remembered that he'd left a bar of the purest dark chocolate in his room and one more surprise drink, but he did not want to go himself. Thus, under an already-graying sky, they went to change depots, as Stefek put it, and they snickered once again at the sight of the penguin. Sonia and Olek remained at Sonia's for a little longer, because if Jurek and Marcel happen to be staring at you, then you probably don't want to get up from the bed, and the desire for genuine chocolate passes entirely.

An hour passed, and we know only that Olek Przybysz had a scar on his side from when he'd had his appendix removed before graduation, and thick, brownish hair covered his torso. Sonia Kubryń was adorned with a birthmark on her right elbow, one beauty spot plunged past her neckline and another beneath her heart, and she had a very visible, light-blue vein on her left thigh. And we also know that the first ray of sun fell first on Olek's right shoulder and, a moment later, slid over his chest and brushed Sonia's hair, and then her brow, nose, and left cheek, and finally flashed brightly on the tiny silver chain around her neck.

Marcel's surprise was a very thick orange juice, as authentic as could be, but still in its can from the prewar import of the Brothers Schlaubmann, and they drank it with gusto, and it went great with three cubes of chocolate for those present and another two for those who were running late, so again they hummed something while sitting quietly shoulder to shoulder, and when the sun shone through, they decided to greet Sunday in the fresh air. Olek and Sonia, out of breath, joined them right in front of the gate and greeted everyone cheerfully, though the chocolate that had been set aside had vanished somewhere. Sonia's dress looked just as good at twenty-one as when Sonia was twenty, and they walked straight along the trail, having exchanged a morning *guten Morgen* with Johann, the guard, who gave her a pleasant kiss.

■ □ ■ □ ■

CHAPTER TEN

I LOVE JUNE BECAUSE THE DAYS ARE THE LONGEST OF THE YEAR AND also because the blotches on the moon quickly disappear. You can see everything like it's in the palm of your hand, and it's a short way from the hand to the computer keyboard. There goes Olek; he has something stuffed into his jacket pockets and is whistling a tune under his breath. He looks dashing because now that he's in hiding for good he's wearing an American blazer and, so Jurek believes, American briefs as well. He's had Johann light the cigarette he himself has rolled; to Rubens, conversing with a shiny pebble, he says, "Good day"; he conquers the stairs in four bounds and drops in on Jurek without knocking. The only one who spots him is Virtuoso, who first hisses, then cuddles up to him and wants to jump on his lap. Today Marcel is lying in bed and staring motionlessly at the ceiling, Jurek is scribbling something in a little notebook, and all the veins are popping out on his forehead. Olek waits for him to finish writing a line, then says that they've caught code names Parasol and Plover, so they'll be meeting this Sunday at Hangman's, and not at Frog's. Marcel smiles derisively, and Olek hands him two absolutely, truly American cigarettes and watches with a smile as Marcel passes them under his nose, first the one with the filter, then the one with no filter, and lastly both at once. Olek leaves some kind of package under the bed, hears some nutcase nearby, and leaves, saying that he'll be back.

"You'll be back, oh yes, you'll be back," Jurek mumbles, and he lights Marcel's cigarette. But Olek is already on the first floor, then on the path, then in Pavilion B, then on Sonia's shoulders. He draws three apples, green with red flecks, from his pocket, plus a bag of fudge chews, and a glass ball. When you shake the ball, snow falls, but when you put it on a table, a little pink house with a chimney emerges in the fine weather, a little horse with a sleigh waits in front of the house, and a dog yaps happily because the people are going to take a ride and he's going to run after them until the sleigh stops in the forest and a wonderful silence enfolds every living thing. Olek sets one apple down by Janka's head, and she is panting lightly, having dozed off after work, and he and Sonia step out for a walk, giggling at least for the time being. Next to the path, a stone is explaining something to Rubens, and on seeing them, Rubens places his hand over his mouth; Johann gets a fudge chew made from the milk of a Polish cow and salutes cheerfully, as always. There are poppies growing by the train tracks, and Sonia asks Olek not to pick them, so Olek turns back and gives her his arm, and they turn to the right because on the day before yesterday they'd gone to the left.

They pass between the first little houses, among rows of strawberries already ripening, a child running, some fido frolicking about, and they could touch these cherries with their hands. Sonia refuses to wear them as earrings—they're too red—but she gladly sucks the pits.

"Ssuck, ssso, sself," Olek says, laughing.

"What language," Sonia says.

What eyes, Olek thinks.

Farther on, the road goes out into a field and narrows, the wheat comes up to their knees, and the scarecrow looks like Olek's aunt, especially in that hat.

"I'd also like to flit about," Sonia says, looking at the birds. "To soar high and far and have a hollow in the forest." Not far to the forest now, so her lips are near as well, Sonia leans against a pine, and the tree and the woman suit each other well. Olek stretches his arms toward them, and now Sonia makes that beautiful gesture: she spits a pit out of her kisser. She's a bit embarrassed, but she wants to be more embarrassed, but first things first, she thrusts her hand under her mouth, she squints a little and alters her face slightly because she is only twenty-one, but now she has found the pit with her tongue, and she leans her head back and, looking straight into Olek's eyes, she removes the pit with her hand and tosses it back like a superfluous key, then kisses him first.

Back on the path, Rubens has now come to an agreement with the stone and is accosting people, but Janka flashes swiftly by and knocks the conventional three times, and she pauses before the fourth. Jurek opens the door because today Marcel is just lying there and smoking, now the second one with the filter. Janka asks Marcel for advice, because there's something about these revenues she doesn't quite get, and there is nothing about it in the textbook, and Marcel explains it away with one sentence and a wave of the hand. Jurek passes Janka an apple from Olek, but Janka takes out her own, and they eat in silence—let's see who takes the loudest bite—and Marcel keeps smoking, and he blows smoke into the penguin's eye, and he finally smiles, for it is Janka who bites her apple the loudest.

And it is quiet in the forest again, as though there had never been anyone there, so who cares that the moss is dented and a branch broken if toward evening or tomorrow at the latest the hole will have patched itself up and the branch will have sprouted leaves. One might still peek around there, behind that tree, but that ribbon belongs to a fern and that button is a small mushroom. So we'd better go back quickly through the field and diagonally through the wheat, for Sonia and Olek—oh, so sly—are already sitting down by the table with an ashtray crammed with cigarette butts. Marcel is now shuffling the cards, and now in the first deal, four hearts came up, like love, for a square, like two hearts in a mirror, which are fortunately won without a problem by Sonia, because two aces and four powerful trumps have revealed themselves to make a dummy for Olek.

Meanwhile, Marcel has gotten a run of spades on a void of clubs, so bad that he's started fidgeting in his chair and then hissing and looking imploringly at the ceiling, for only there might one find divine mercy when someone so human as Jurek has closed the bidding as high as three, like a beautiful, one-word poem. Janka is surprised because from Jurek's mouth, as subtle as the color of birch, as responsibility and work, the beginning of a naughty phrase has started to fall, but Jurek has in mind only *holy cow*—perhaps very holy—and Olek laughs and Sonia giggles right up until the moment she puts down a simple three of diamonds because she has forgotten to bring down the trump and has led with a club. Olek threatens to return to the Alps, where the bells bring happiness in every number, and Janka, the pupil, doesn't understand anything anymore, especially the difference between the jack of clubs and the knave of clubs, and what they meant by "face card on face card, better stay on guard."

But the real battle of the couples had only just begun. The cards were coming somehow too luckily for those who had already had enough luck in love, so Marcel defended the honor of the accountant and the supplies officer with devilish courage. He blocked the contracts, made clever discards, and when Olek played without a trump, Marcel brought him down with nothing but a clever lead in the shortest suit. Jurek was glad for his partner's talent and their common glory, for the heroic defense of Fort Penguin against an invasion by the Eden Group, in a guest performance by Adam and Eve, and especially for the fact that he himself had played consistently with nothing, game after game. But Janka watched with persistent awe as he counted the points, touching each card with his finger, slapping his jacks on the table as he laid out the dummy, so Jurek doubled and tripled on his favorite meadow of Thermopylae, muttered to himself over the cards, explained to Janka that it wasn't all his fault because he'd only picked up the ace once, and he lurched in his chair, saying with a sigh, "Victory to him who has the heart," as Olek again bid a contract of hearts, and he looked furtively at Sonia's cards until everyone had averted their eyes from shame, and he played from under his middle finger and then from under his little finger, so pitifully crooked, and he counted the trumps, only he forgot about the first trick. He sweated like a polar explorer come home, thought on a lead, but what for? He was playing majestically, panting logically, crossing each bridge as he came to it, and they were yawning in Tworki, but that better life continued to envelop them. Sonia played her card, Olek and Marcel smoked one after another like men, and it was a lucky thing for Jurek that Janka didn't have anyone else to fall in love with.

The last shuffle finally got underway, and Olek was already ahead of the game with Sonia and seventy points to the finish, like seventy years to a whole century of existence, if he manages to play it. And Olek muttered for a cool spade in order to finish it all off. Jurek, of course, countered, and Marcel, to be sure, grimaced, and Sonia, well, for a long time Sonia didn't say anything. Finally she looked hard at Janka, as if she were looking for an invitation in her eyes, carried her gaze past the window, and suddenly burst out like thunder from a clear sky: a slam without a trump. I don't know if I would have made the same call in her place, with what was admittedly a lot of important face cards in the hand but only one ace, and I don't know if I would have been so decisive without the queen of spades in hand, and I don't know if I could have pulled it off, what with the lands infertile and the seas gone dry, but Olek had blue eyes and warm hands, and stubble like velvet standing upright. Olek had blue eyes, and beyond the window there stood a green oak, and someone had to be holding those aces, someone who's young like a god and lofty like the mountains. Unlike Marcel, let's pass over Jurek's counter in silence, let's have a quick but understanding peek at Janka's open mouth, because even she has figured out how a slam works, and let's look right away to the table, where Olek, with an absent smile, is putting down his dummy cards. The superfluous low cards already lined the playing surface, and in Olek's hand there remained five final secrets. The ace and king were a given, the third card from the end was a queen, and the second an ace of clubs. Marcel furrowed his brow, and Jurek lowered his eyes to the floor, where one shoe was scraping the other, announcing their impending defeat and no doubt a stroll soon to come, for, as always, when things are screwed up and cockeyed one looks to the feet, both of them a good distance off from Marcel. And on top, turned over at last, the ace of hearts is declassified, and it sways there for a long time, and for a long time Olek's gaze rolls toward Sonia's smile, and Jurek obligingly lights Marcel's cigarette.

And tobacco ash was already fertilizing the main promenade, on which a new generation of Bonapartes, a few Marie d'Arquiens, and an entire hosts of Lennons, a couple of bald ones among them, will grow up in the future. But for now the accountants are still walking, the bridge players are still walking, and they are as fond of each other as the sun is fond of the west, they're walking right down the middle, first two mixed pairs—ah, very mixed—and Marcel alone behind them, shuffling on his soles and kicking stones, the main heroes of more than a few rebellions.

■ □ ■ □ ■

CHAPTER ELEVEN

BUT I, DEAR MARCEL, DO NOT KNOW HOW TO REBEL AND TO HOLD my tongue about the fates of your heels and your battered soles, and as soon as that utterly lovely June day comes to an end, a day when the strawberries in the Lipskis' garden grew more than a gram and the cards created fascinating arrangements, while Olek kissed his good-byes until tomorrow and his see-you-tomorrow-morning on Sonia's mouth, and while Jurek pressed his lips to his lady's hand, as soon as you next lie down to bed, Marcel, stretching out your now-shoeless feet on the crossbar and lighting what will certainly be the last cigarette of the day, I will ask you through Jurek's mouth, now no longer occupied with other things: "What's going on with you today, Marcel?"

And again, a moment later, "Marcel, what's wrong?"

"You know, Jerzy," Marcel will respond, has already responded, "my name isn't really Marcel—it's Jerzy."

Jurek bit his lip and thought about the corpses of Resistance fighters swinging with chalkboards on their chests.

"And Brochwicz isn't my name, either. Brochwicz is for the Krauts, but it's not really me. And what's hidden in my pants, only the Lord our God knows that."

"I'll call you Marcel," Jurek said hoarsely, because the corpses could be shot as well. "So we don't get mixed up. Marcel is very nice."

"I might have to get out of here tomorrow," Marcel said then, sighing. "You understand, the train brings all kinds, but I don't know how to explain this to you."

Maybe like this: here comes the choo-choo, here it comes from Warsaw after lunch, and there are passengers on the choo-choo, some to Tworki, others to Podkowa. These two guys get off, their speech low, the fatherland Polish, poplars along the fence, willows numbering three. Briskly they go, boots on their feet, toes all snug in their socks. The buildings they pass, the right one they reach, because every nutcase on the path knows where to find Marcel. They stop in the foyer, the walls painted green, a spider eats a fly, the cat arches its back. A door slams upstairs, they run as a pair, just a moment, Mr. Brochwicz, or whatever they call you, just a moment, one second, we have a matter to discuss. We'll come back on Sunday, our itty-bitty hands outstretched, we'll fill our little wallets, till Sunday, Mr. Brochwicz, there's a whole lot of time. And the two are now gone, the path smells of linden, always nicer out of town, when the world is in bloom. There goes the choo-choo now, soon it'll be in Warsaw, excellent herring for dinner, the gang will come thereafter, and a good time will be had by all.

"When were they here?" Jerzy asked with difficulty, and he felt like he'd been raised to the next power, though he was quite uneasy.

"The day before yesterday."

"Yeah, the train brings all kinds," Jurek said, sighing again, and he regretted his youth, these little nonleather shoes on his awkward, flat feet.

"They knocked right on Paradise's door. That's the first thing that popped into my head, that thought. That time doesn't flow here, and that nothing can happen. That we're sitting here behind the oak of good and evil, snug as bugs in a rug."

"The minute I came here, I thought the same thing, exactly the same," Jurek said, sighing heavily again and scrunching up his face weirdly, sort of solemnly, as his eyes went round behind his glasses. "Yes, Marcel, the train takes all kinds. So tomorrow, after work, it'll take us, too. But without your things—we'll squirrel them away. I'll bring them to you later."

What good were Marcel's things to him anyway? What good were those objects of occasional use, for on the following day, beyond the window, the one to the left of the tracks, the eternally kempt shrubs will flash before his eyes, the creeks will show white, and the stalks of wheat will grow like never before in the land of Canaan, for Egyptian scarabs and Polish dung beetles will press forward along the trails, and there, where the grass is tall, goldfinch will again wait with goldfinch for the hot summer. And what good are things, for in the wardrobe next to the sofa bed where Marcel will sleep and wake up in a sweat there yet remained a couple of shirts and socks, and if anything happens, Jurek's mom is a great seamstress and knits 'round the clock.

"At our place we drink tea at least four times a day," Jurek said, and Mama agreed. "And if you get bored with washing glasses, you have books in the sideboard. Just don't laugh at my notes. And don't go out too often, because Mama loves to chat, and she doesn't have anybody to talk to."

"Where could I go?" Marcel said, laughing. "Cast out of Paradise, straight home—really, nothing better could have happened to me, because here it's exactly like our place in Berdichev when I was a kid. I slept in the kitchen there, too; we lived on the first floor, even this sideboard is like the one we had, with that same mirror in the middle. And Jurek, your mom really reminds me of my aunt, my dad's sister. And these cakes!"

"I'll drop by on Sunday. We'll play some bridge; Mama and Witek play no worse than me," Jurek said in farewell, and he jumped out through the window because he heard the tram.

Then it happened to be Thursday, the middle of the week, and as far as days go, rather shabby, but there are exemptions from fate when one has a little help from people. Marcel was now sleeping in Jurek's claret-striped pajamas and on Jurek's sofa bed in the kitchen, and the locks of his dark hair were pressing their curlicues into the pillow. And Mama had already fallen asleep after she'd said her prayers, today twice as long as usual, though still to the same God. But in Tworki there was somehow no snoring: at most there were grunts, sighs, and a couple of solid groans. Everything became clear in the morning. Jurek was lying in Marcel's bed and whistling to himself before work, and nearby, in Jurek's bed, was one of the Graces, and because it was the first time for them both, that's not such a bad description.

The train was driving straight toward the setting sun, like a well-scheduled moth toward a great brightness, when Jerzy, having said his good-byes to Marcel, was returning from Ulrychów to his empty room. In the Helenów Forest, the wind from the day before yesterday had died down, and the vapor trails on the now bluish-pink sky had frozen until morning. Johann straightened up to attention next to his guard box, torn again from his reminiscences about the wooden toy horse at his father's knees, and wished Jurek a good evening, Herr Buchalter, a good and warm evening. Which is why, my dear Jerzy Over-the-Hedgey, hurry it up a bit, all the more because you're being egged on by the history of Europe and an unusual warmth in nature, and the space of the Garden of Eden. Hurry up, but no stumbling on the stone on our main path in Tworki because in a second that coffee-and-cream spot behind the oak is going to melt in colorless unfulfillment and needs will return to the norm, like foxes to a cave.

Like woodpeckers to a hollow: she was standing with her shoulders pinned to the trunk, she kept her hands in the pockets of her skirt, and she knocked the bark with her thick heel, such that one could count from one to a hundred. Jurek stole up on his tiptoes, quietly, because Dürer and Goethe, smoking pipes on a nearby bench, barely turned their heads, and he clung to the tree from the other side. Ninety-six, ninety-seven, and now ninety-eight, he reckoned to himself.

"Ninety-nine," he said aloud.

"A hundred," he heard from the other side. "Have you been there long?"

He'd been there barely two minutes, maybe three, okay, four, but who cares? A half flatfoot and a low arch, and an inner ear focused so as not to wobble and crash out clumsily, out into the open; who cares about time? For in these little shoes—we've already established that they're nonleather, right?—and on these flat, nonmilitary heels, his whole body stood, shook, and waited, and where we find the ribcage, Jurek's little core, right behind the brain stem, all of Jerzy's existence was concentrated there, from dawn to de-formation, from birth to absolute maturity, but always to unfulfillment, always to unfulfillment.

Goethe and Dürer packed their pipes a second time and dragged with delight, exposing their countenances to the evening's warmth and their eyes to the sight of the oak and the people, who had just encompassed it with their arms outstretched before them, and only a hundred years in the growth rings, boughs, and bark separated them. A hundred years like barely a single instant of time in which to stick one's head around from that side, smile to oneself knowingly, and agree that, with regard to the evening, it's extraordinarily warm and worth spending in long conversation together, without disturbing Olek, who today is paying a visit to Sonia.

"Come on, I'll show you something," Jurek said, and he showed the Grace the way. "Maybe Sonia hasn't told you yet. The secret garden plot. In the garden plot a swing, and on the swing, us."

They strolled easily, and behind them, wrapped in the smoke's fragrance, Goethe and Dürer discoursed anew on the illusion of passing and the certainty of new incarnations, and today the whistle of the last train from Podkowa sounded like duration—uninterrupted, attenuated.

Like white unsullied by any pigment, the birch wood led them along its milky way to the gate of the garden plot, with its squat juniper lions on guard. The swing hung there motionless, looked strangely superfluous, like a throne in a republic, and within a moment the Grace was swinging, having first gotten on and pushed cautiously off the ground with just one leg. She shifted before Jurek's eyes, now a bit faster, and he could lean momentarily against the birch and think his way through the duties of words toward the plans of the body. He didn't look bad as, in his quiet way, he followed the swinging Janka with his gaze and stuck his hands in his pockets; there was something in that torso, hard as wood and fresh as the world when everything was still growing and evolving within it. But he'd finally thought it through and said, "Have you ever wondered about how little room there is in this world for kindness? How rare an occurrence a person is among people? A person who might have a soul? And a soul is a head and a heart. Especially, Janka, a heart."

Janka said nothing, both in the air and over the earth, and when he went up to her and gave her a good push, she was afraid to look him in the eyes, rounded off as they were and seeming to invite her to come over, to step into the focusing glass of his lenses.

"Now these two factors working together, hey . . . hah . . . well . . . harmonizing, makes . . ."

"Jurek, you know what?" Janka called back, suddenly braking with her feet. "Maybe . . ."

". . . makes what we call spiritual culture, creates a truly great and magnificent individual," Jurek finished hastily, and he wanted to sit down next to her, suspended and milk-and-coffee colored, but there was no room, so he heaved the swing again. The more she swished, the more the plank board underneath Janka flew away and the crux of the evening lagged behind. Jurek slowed the tempo, held the line steady, and asked like any swing operator, "Maybe that's enough?"

Janka nodded, and Jurek picked up where he'd left off. "Such an individual's motto is to forget about oneself but not to lose oneself. What do you think about that?"

Janka kept somehow pleasantly quiet, so the swing operator, now a gumshoe, again attempted to scramble onto the plank board, but there was no room. The first flashes of moonlight among the birches underscored the reality of the situation. He was standing, she was sitting, and once again, amidst this nature, everything depended on people.

"Listen, where's Marcel?" Janka asked suddenly.

"What do you mean, where?"

"He's been so glum these last few days. I stopped by your room at half past four, and nobody."

"Well, I took him away."

"Where did you take him?" Janka asked, raising her voice, and finally looked at Jurek. In the moonlight he might even have had larger ears, but his hands were also heavier, closer, and warmer on the line.

"He had to leave . . . period. He found better, more interesting work. You know, I don't know what to attribute this to, but for the longest time it's been hard for me to get it together to write even a few words. Could it be that I've become indolent, or is it because the days are all starting to seem the same, one like the next, gray, cobwebbed . . ."

"Listen, where is Marcel? Where did you take that train?" Janka glared into Jurek's face, but instead of his round pupils she saw two pale, bare crescents reflected in his glasses. "I saw you get on. Only he didn't have anything with him. And no good-bye."

". . . cobwebbed in sadness, burdened with the pain of unhappiness. And only the ivy of hope, that—well, stop looking at me like that, I didn't do anything, and don't worry about him, I'm telling you."

"Where is Marcel?" Janka asked calmly and straightened out her dress so that it covered the entire plank.

"Oh, jeez. In a very nice place. I said, snug as a bug. Just let it go . . . As I was saying, to forget oneself means to discover the axis . . ."

"You know where he is?"

"How am I supposed to know? In Warsaw."

"In Ulrychów?"

"Yes."

Janka straightened out her dress again; after all, she didn't need to sully herself on that board like that. The moon moved high up, Jurek a bit lower down.

"Yes, have a seat," Janka said. "There's enough room."

He sat cautiously and put his arm over her shoulder. She snuggled in hard and slipped her hand under his.

"Well, what are things like for this person you're describing?" she asked.

In the clearing of the garden plot the swing swayed rhythmically. Heave-ho, heave-ho, they plunged from tree to tree, heave-ho, heave-ho, they were out of sync and flipped back, just like a wave in the sea.

Like bees to the hive they'd now gathered so much honey in their fingers and fingernails, so much sugar concentrated in their blood, that the overabundance was opening the honeycomb of night, love's museum of wax figures. Janka got down lightly, Jurek jumped down weightlessly, so that the birches felt it in their roots, and they walked, still hugging, still cuddling, toward the path. By the oak one could still detect the smell of a Goethean shag, the benches blinked with the eyes of their bolts, a little horse over the wall whinnied for no reason. On the first floor something slammed, scraped, and scratched, jangled and knocked—that was Jurek in the half dark opening the door to his room, like the portal before a treasure trove.

Like a log into a fire, like salt on bread, like smoke, like a splash, like a silvery dream into a lake, like your hands into mine, close, even closer.

■ □ ■ □ ■

CHAPTER TWELVE

WHAT JUREK WAS WHISTLING TO HIMSELF IN THE MORNING IS HARD to say right off, and it's still hard, even after a few notes. Janka was still sleeping and didn't hear anything. Mr. Jan, sweeping under the window and fishing butts out of the ground, was certain that it was the song about April in Paris and chestnuts in blossom, or rather the one about being in the mood for love. It finally became clear that in actual fact Jurek was whistling about himself, how he was lying on the bed with his arms over his head and his legs drawn up at the knees, but above all about how he felt that life is worth it regardless of the situation, even if it's behind a desk and over a stack of paper, and that hope wraps this day and all others in its cobweb because Jurek wants some, can have some, and will get some.

Yes, that was a beautiful day. The sun had already deluged the main path, and from everywhere, from the side paths, from the lawns and the annexes, masses of pajamas started to flow out onto the beaten gravel. Conversation, greetings; thick slices of bread with beet marmalade wandered unhurriedly to mouths, hovered in the air, dispersed in every direction together with the gesticulation of arms, engrossed or explaining, and rose again for the subsequent cavity. All around, to the left and right, increasingly thick groups formed to converse about today's menu and the new line of the front, and over the whole path there spread an insect-like buzz of syllables. Jurek and Janka, with their still-whole slices in hand, struggled to press through the chatting, billowing breakfast files on the agora.

Welcomed by bows and greetings, they felt themselves to be the first couple on a stage, prima donna and *Überman* playing breakfast. The second couple was pressing through from the direction of Pavilion B, distributing joyful smiles, and was already halfway there. Olek was walking ahead, blazing a trail for Sonia, who with two thick slices in her hand advanced cautiously behind him like a doe behind the hunter. They pushed their way between Rubens and Zorro, who were wrangling ardently over the most fashionable shape of hat; Jurek and Janka had overtaken Newton, who was just then handing an apple to Cleopatra; and they stood face to face with each other.

Night to night. The morning still maintained a touch of night, and that sun, and the warmth of the hand on its own iron bars, on soft mattresses and tensed springs, and morning gently carried them farther down the path toward the desks, beside which Kaltz was already impatiently sharpening pencils. But they weren't in too much of a hurry; they hugged like four allegories and now steamed en masse along the gravel, among the kindly smiles of the pajamas they had to push through and drive back. At the very last moment Antiplato dodged off to the side. He didn't pay them any attention and didn't even turn red at Sonia's apologies; he jiggled strangely as he walked, eyes fixed on his sandals and holey socks, and crooned something indistinctly to an unfamiliar melody. "Hey, jump over the mountains, the shepherd boy drunk, gloomy without his alpenstock," made its way to their ears. "Hey, jump over the mountains." The sandals pulled him farther along on their thick soles, carrying the song away as well, and the allegories exploded in laughter that stretched out in the new silence, like the trail of their passage over the gravel.

Coming ever closer, they are at their great apogee. The first one on the right, Love, waves her free hand in the measure of some melody and briefly straightens out her pastel skirt, which has slipped from under her belt; a smile brightens her face at the sight of her neighbor's eyes, blue and American, her hand fawns for the touch of her neighbor's hand. Next to her strides Serenity, distinguished by his great height and boot size; he slows down deliberately, laughs at each of his few thoughts, and looks forward to tomorrow and tomorrow night, whatever they bring. That hand under his elbow on the other side belongs to Hope. Hope looks around cautiously to the left and right, adds her steps to others more than she herself leads, but she has a lovely face, well rested and quite pretty even without powder, which has run out. Closing the line, their hands and, it happens, ring fingers intertwined, Bliss. He squints his round eyes under the surge of light, also tries to hum something, and the cuffs of his trousers swell out delightfully; he takes care that no one slips out of the line, that it remains even and in rhythm, and from time to time, stone-faced, he deviates suddenly to the left, pulling the line with him with all his strength to the edge of the path, the line returning a moment later amidst panic and giggles, and moving along unhurriedly toward the door of the accounting office, toward the sentence's distant period.

Olek heard the approaching train and said his hasty good-byes, forecasting his return the following evening. Kaltz even smiled at the accountants' common collective bow, and around eleven he brewed the tea himself and distributed the glasses, with spoons ringing for a good afternoon, among the desks. And for their common eating pleasure—because he had finally stopped whirling around the room and glancing timidly at the lowered eyes—he felt around in his pockets, for a long time wasn't able to find anything, and from behind his wallet finally pulled out a bar of—and this was unheard of—milk chocolate. "I received a pay raise," he said quietly to Jurek so that Sonia would hear. "Herr Director—a real humanitarian."

The chocolate was good, and Jurek even smacked his lips when it melted in his mouth, together with the taste of perfume on the neck, the touch of fingers immersed in his hair, and the cry of the night, the cry of the night on the white pillow. Janka was counting something on her abacus, shifting the white and black beads from left to right, from right to left, and only occasionally took a long look past Jurek's head at the open window; Sonia was transferring something assiduously from column to column, and that something was here, too, sitting among them and finishing his tea, duly registered between two peaks in the order of calculation, in the river of existence.

After quitting time they went to the orchard by the tracks to buy strawberries. Sonia and Janka again took Jurek by the hand and went as far as Komorów, amicably picking the green stems, now in unison, and theatrically tossing them back behind them for the new planting. It was somehow so mature and certain, the sweet flesh, the close, warm muscles under the sleeves of a dress, and his strong arms, pressing and leading. And in the early evening the good-byes to the ladies with two gentle handshakes so that nothing belied what the skin remembered or what the heart at least knew. Yet Jurek delayed his return to an empty room and rumpled sheets. He still had to pay a debt of paces to a few paths, a debt of sitting to the bench under the oak, and still a debt of the word to his own needs.

The letter from Danka shone in Jurek's out-going mailbox with a golden flower painted on the envelope, and in the beam of the nightlight it started to glow quite like the twilight before nightfall, like eyes before reading.

> Knock, knock! May I? Will the Lord Viscount receive me in the quiet dusk? I'll sit at your feet and tell you a fairy tale. All right? There were these great, inaccessible woods, and there were distant steppes . . . And a girl lived there. A little girl from the provinces. She had it good. Hundred-year-old trees rocked her to sleep and told her fairy tales about azure lakes, about the distant, bustling world. And she was awakened in the morning by the prayers of songbirds and the whisper of the distant, emerald steppes. Until one day there came a winged boy, and the young lady learned what happiness was. And the happiness miracle lasted a week. One sunny autumn week. And they were happy. They learned the secrets of the boundless forests; quiet kurgans and bent crosses telling legends of glory led them over serpentine roads. And when a silvery gloom enveloped the land, wistful Eastern ballads and cries flowed over the land. But everything must end, and so the tale also had to end. The boy went away, and the young lady had to go away. She went far, to a great city. And sitting here among the walls, she mused about returning to her wilderness. But fate is cruel . . . She learned of people and their evil, and she could no longer return to her land, and she is ever turning her sorrowful eyes in the direction where her beloved things are. Will she ever go back? And now good-night, Viscount, pleasant dreams, and may you dream of me. But not of her from the fairy tale, but of a normal girl who loves laughter and people. And if you want, please—take my heart in your hand, only don't squeeze it, and don't play with it. At most you can lay it down next to you, and it will

whisper fairy tales to you until you fall asleep. And then? It will fly off far away . . . toward its happiness and its destiny!

The brown owl no longer hooted, the beguiling ghosts lying among the kurgans were no longer roused, and Jurek Manure-ek-with-Pencil-Secure-ek was already responding: "Night has fallen." That's how he began.

All around the shadows are becoming a lily-colored mysteriousness. At such a time the face of the moon is as though cut out of silvery silk, the black branches of trees as though from Japanese patterns. I love to watch as the stars chase one another across the sky. Because at such a time everything is so soothing, and clearly it is then that is the best time to think and dream. And on just such a night I heard a knocking at my door. You came in, you had kindness in your eyes, and on your mouth the golden trace of a smile. We were alone—you and I. Only the sickle of the growing moon peeped curiously at our window. You have long since finished your tale, and I still hear the singing of the birds, and I hear the wistful songs of the East . . . The girl will surely return. A smiling blue day will come. A sun beautiful beyond comprehension will descend, will embrace the whole earth in its rays. It will dry all tears with its warmth, it will warm chilly hearts. New life will burst from all bodies and wash over the sparkling shoals of the world in a wave. And the little girl who has forgotten her smile will return to her woods. She won't be alone; she'll go back with her winged boy. The golden brilliance of his eyes has such an effect on her that her heart starts to ring long and uninterrupted within her. And they will be happy. Those wonderful days will return, when they were awakened by the whispers of the emerald steppes and the hundred-year-old trees rocked them to sleep.

Jurek removed his glasses, put his hand on his face, and wiped it in the way he always did before sleep, when he was detaching himself from the day, descending from the world into his own darkness. The cheeks wiped, the eyelids touched, ready to sleep; ready to sleep, the border flashed by, the clock struck midnight, the sentence had already reached its end.

■ □ ■ □ ■

CHAPTER THIRTEEN

"OH, YOU'RE LOVELY, JERZY, IN THIS SUN," ANNA SAID TO MARCEL, TO the pastoral melody of "Laura and Philon." It was the end of August, and they were sitting on a bench next to the little church in Wola, exposing their faces to the sun. In the morning, Anna had come for Marcel in Ulrychów, still before their first tea, and she smelled of lilacs. With their tea they munched at a little cake, and Mama was very pleased when, saying nothing, they sat staring at each other. Anna had on a beige shirt with delicate embroidery above the waist and a cream jacket to go with her pleated skirt. She wore neat, somewhat thick makeup, and her hands, perhaps a bit too cold for that time of year, were on Marcel's torso. She snuggled up next to Marcel and cuddled, and spoke again, and the gravel her foot shifted under the bench crunched into her words like a percussive, brush-tapped backbeat.

"Oh, you're lovely, Jerzy, in this sun, when around us lilacs grow; again you have a delightful smile, as belongs to only you. Do not leave me thus, my love, and now forever be with me; time's a price most consummate, and moment fast from moment flees; let us go tomorrow, then, they say there is a hotel there; where diamonds or just money buys back a life without a care. They'll take us far away from here, to Switzerland, where tears will dry; and there we'll find those happy days, which now await both you and I; and there we'll find our happy days, which now await both you and I."

That rustle on the bench was Marcel stroking Anna's hair and kissing her eyes, and these sentences, spoken to the tune of "Little House on the Hill," were by Doubting Marcel: "Your quiet words most lovely seem. Your lips are thirsty, your eyes do gleam. The problem, wife, for us it's late; it is not Switzerland, but ovens we await."

Anna quickly picked up the tune, laying her head on Marcel's shoulder: "As well you know, my love, a life like this we can't; for you might here remain, but as for me, I shan't."

Marcel leaned over Anna's mouth and sank both his hands into her hair: "You're oh so lovely in this sun, and I would like to kiss you; I'll go with you where you might choose, for I'm enamored of you; I'll go with you where you might choose, for I'm enamored of you."

And then they strolled for a long time through the streets of Ulrychów, ate the sandwiches Anna brought and one hard, green pear, which they took turns sinking their teeth into, this one crunching more quietly, that one more loudly. At the pond in the park they stared into the duckweed, and where there was a bit more water Marcel skipped the flat stones that Anna sought out on the shore, and their splashing softly performed a single, repeated note. Shortly before curfew, Anna got on her tram, and in the quieting dusk Marcel returned to Mama and again received tea with cake.

■ □ ■ □ ■

CHAPTER FOURTEEN

ALL OF AUGUST JUREK BATTLE-OF-MARSTON-MOOR-EK THOUGHT gratefully about the former Marcel, or even Marcelek, about beloved Marcelek, bed for a bed, tooth for a tooth, about his eyes as blue as his mustache is black, and about his discretion bordering on eternal silence, until Kaltz put twice the normal load of work on his desk, plus a heap of receipts for God knows what. But given the first opportunity, Jurek took his now spacious room in hand and converted it into a two-star guest house, and Marcel was cast to Mama. Jurek calculated how much would come into the kitty and counted how much would go out, still cursing that which makes the world go 'round and consulting every Sunday his better—though not quite so Aryan—self about a sequence of numbers worthy of a master bookkeeper. Helpless in the face of the balances, but especially helpless in the face of simple questions: like the biggest idiot in Tworki, like Newton and Rubens together and individually, he shrugged his shoulders and smiled like a moron, baring all his teeth, whenever he was asked where Marcel resided—*Wo* is *er* now, *bitte?*—or about where that son of a bitch has gotten off to, because they've got business, goddammit.

Yet the days passed, and Marcel was already here and there. Here he was still drinking tea and Mama's compote—so much better than the stuff in Tworki; here he was still wiping the dust off Jurek's books, and he read the one about the cinnamon shop in one go until five in the morning, when all the birds were chirping over Ulrychów;

and here he fixed the oil lamp and scrubbed the oaken floor, and Mama removed his splinter with a burning-hot needle. But in his thoughts he was already knocking, over there, on the door indicated to him; there he was already placing his miserable valise with Jurek's pajamas and a pair of his own underpants in the corner; and there he was already squeezing Anna's hand and cuddling Anna's head in the locked train car in air that was not so fresh, not like it is when you're snug as a bug. For had his words, written in itty bits, not spoken of it, as if they wanted to take up as little room as possible on Jurek's correspondence paper from before the war?

"Where's Marcel?" Jurek asked Mama on what was already a September Sunday, when he'd arrived, as always, at ten with a file filled with papers. Mama said nothing. "Where the fuck has he gotten off to?" he whispered to himself. "After all, we have to correct that balance today, or else Kaltz is going to make mincemeat, or rather, lay me waste."

"Where's Marcel?" he asked a second time. "Dammit, he knew I was coming with these documents, and Witek will be here any minute, so what about bridge? Don't you know where he's marched off to, Mama? Even though it's Sunday, and on top of that, it's raining?"

"Ania was here on Thursday," Mama said, and she croaked something crudely, despite it being a holy day, "and he left yesterday. When I wasn't here, because I went to Irena's. He disappeared. With all his things. He forgot his pajamas. But maybe he took yours, the ones with the dots. And he left you a letter. Would you like some soup?"

"Yes, I would."

"All last week Ania's sister was living here because she had nowhere else."

"Here?"

"Sure. They were talking about something until morning, night after night. And on Thursday Ania came herself, and he left yesterday. While I was out, because Irena's in poor health again, and I had to help her with the sewing and the coal."

It was carrot soup, wanting for salt but tasty; the salt shaker was on the left and came in handy, the letter lay to the right and, a second later, already had a grease stain by the heading.

Dear Jerzy,

I thank you and your most wonderful mother for everything. You have done so much for me and my family. You are really great people, and your mother is the kindest person in the world. I am well aware that what I am doing is a mistake and a trap, but it can no longer be helped. Give my regards to everyone, especially Sonia and Janka. I will be thinking about you all, and about you. I wish you much happiness. That things will work out for you. Ania, her sister, and I have gathered all our valuables and are going today to the Hotel Polski. It's already dawn. Be well, and write your poems.

Yours,

Jerzy

"I don't understand," Jerzy pronounced, and he broke up a carrot in his soup. "Dear Mama, might you know why the Hotel Polski? What the hell happened? Where the devil has he gone off to?"

That's right, Marcel—or should we say Jerzy—Brochwicz: Where have you gone off to? Where the fuck have you gone? *Wo bist du gegangen, gekommen, und kaputt?* And why at dusk, after everything's already become clear? Did you have a good trip, were you not too jolted and tossed, did the pajamas come in handy? Which side does the moss really grow on, what's hidden at the bottom of oceans, do they have white whales there, and where, in actual fact, does coal come from? Where do colors come from, does the Don really flow all that quietly, how does the nettle really feel about its sting? Precisely how many planets are there in the solar system, moral laws on our heads, yeah, and what's the real deal with that Bermuda Triangle?

I see you slowly leaving the house in Ulrychów with a valise in your right hand. Perhaps you've had a shave, because your cheeks are a little shiny, and where else could that waft of cologne be coming from? You have a cowlick from the back on the left side, you definitely washed your thick hair this morning, but it's a good thing the wind is blowing it down for you. You're already passing the Sowiński trenches; a young couple is standing over there behind a tree, and the priest himself is gracing that path by the little church. You're swinging the valise rhythmically, back and forth, it's warm, sunny, but you're in no hurry, and you're kicking stones again. The bottom button of your jacket must have been pinching you; you've unbuttoned it, all the better, no need to be pinched. Now, behind the church in Wola, you step onto that lovely path, and because you don't want to go even a few stops by tram, you have an easy road straight ahead, and it's a fine thing that this is a green patch. I'm not going to go any farther—Wola's a good place for me—so I see you only from the back. You're holding your back straight, you're still walking slowly, the valise is still dangling, but more loosely. I've forgotten whether you put on a tie, and now I can't see. You have a lovely silhouette, one could envy you for it, and that cream-colored coat hanging over your left arm as well. Now you're just a bright spot on the distant vista, now just a dot on the path, which is leading you and pulling you into its depths, and then you'll be gone, and I'll light myself a cigarette and take a deep drag.

Marcel Jerzy Brochwicz, take all that I have: what's left of the cigarette already burnt out in the tin ashtray, that bottle of whiskey with the red label there on the table in the corner, at least four of the shirts from the cabinet under the window—I especially recommend the green silk one because the red one hasn't been ironed—take the Swedish pen, it writes really well, maybe this aspirin and a couple of paper clips, and a monthly train pass, and from the kitchen the transistor radio, at least one of the two forks, the knife, the salt and pepper. And over here, from this little bench, take this computer with the Polish keyboard—as in Polski, goddammit, and why exactly was your hotel the Polski?—just so that I might watch your hands as you take it and pack it up, and your eyes, and your teeth as you smile at me.

To Marcel Jerzy Brochwicz, to Marcel Jerzy Brochwicz, my fingers and mouth—glory and honor.

■ □ ■ □ ■

CHAPTER FIFTEEN

"WHY THE DAMN POLSKI?" JUREK ANGRY-CUR-EK MUTTERED TO himself, waiting for the tram. "A hell of a way from here, and on a weekend, no less." He jumped off the second tram while it was still moving, and luckily today he got through the city fast, because Sundays in the park, the sacrament of quitting time, and the sun coming out after the rain do not exist for the cobbled street and Aryan sidewalks to be so packed with a populace in too good a mood. "Why the damn Polski?" Jurek repeated, as he stood finally before the hotel's cream façade and semicircular, silver-gleamed signboard, though we find the same krauts and guttural chitchat here, the same very large rifles next to the entrance, those very silent mouths and very knowing gestures.

"Vhere?" muttered this one fellow, perhaps the most important guy there because he had a long coat and black boots made from real leather, and he barred Jurek's way.

"I'm on business."

"You? Really? And vhere your suitcases? To Svitzerland vithout suitcases? *Papieren, bitte!*"

Jurek took out his ID and already had regrets.

"How are you called? Vhere do you live?"

"It's written here."

"How are you called? Truly? You are from Wola? You vill get no visa. There is no visa for Wola. Not everyvone can go to Svitzerlands or to Vittel. Better you go home."

"Someone in there owes me money," Jurek said, swallowing hard. "A lot of money. I would like to speak with him."

"Moneys? Ha, ha, of course, of course, vit them alvays moneys. Sorry, sorry, moneys today in Svitzerland, and then maybe for America or Palestine, train comes soon. *Ist gibt* no coming in today, could have come in earlier."

Dark silhouettes were flickering behind the door, and the dogs occasionally howled at the gold-plated chandeliers. Despite further attempts, Jurek did not succeed in getting in, and thus he stood on the other side of the street—there is such a street in Warsaw—and he looked up over the signboard at the windows, where the little valise and the spotted pajamas might be. He stood and watched for an hour, but nothing appeared up there in the curtained windows or pressed its nose to the pane, and he stood there watching until his eyes went dry, until his feet, with what we already know to be their fallen arches still quite flat, started to hurt from standing. But what is life if not the exchange of one position for another, for this evening Jurek, just now on the sidewalk, and a moment ago standing on the tram, and a bit further back on the train, will lie down and stretch out with his heels in the air because how should he behave, what should he, the man in him, do, when at his own door, propped against the banister on the stairs, a woman is waiting, waiting with a cherry beret on her head, nineteen and a half years old, long legs, neck draped in a silver chain, and red fingernails digging hard into her handbag?

First of all, one should keep up appearances. Shake, rattle, clang, curse under one's breath, and quickly open the door, glance furtively out the window, not turn on the lights, and say, "Truly, what a surprise! Perhaps you'd like a little compote? It would do you good before a stroll."

Danusia sat down on the edge of the bed, hard to say if it was Jurek's or Marcel's, obediently accepted the glass offered to her, and started to drink, just in case. Even if it tasted fine, it looked weird. Because the beret could fall off, the handbag fall open, the lipstick smear, and all that youth be befouled and annulled. Thus with her right hand she safeguarded that whole self enclosed in the handbag, where there was a pocket mirror, a perfume bottle, and cotton, and she stretched her neck out so straight that the Swan Princess would have had to fly away, and Jurek had to swallow hard and smell the air from the oak, and she brought her lips so high up on the glass that it was as though the glass was drinking from Danusia, modestly taking something from her and swallowing it noiselessly, transparently.

They were silent for as many words as they'd written to each other and read from each other. In the dusk two breaths wrestled with their faces, two hemispheres were spinning with no map in common. Finally Danusia said, "I receive such beautiful letters from you, Jurek. With such lovely poems. I even know them by heart."

"Really?"

"Yes."

"Really?"

"Yes, yes."

Australia was again drawing closer to Africa, Tierra del Fuego to the Cape of Good Hope.

"Come on, I'll show you something," Jurek said, and he took Danka by the hand. "My favorite place in Tworki."

Danusia nodded and, tightly gripping her handbag, waited until Jurek locked the door. They stole quickly over the path between the pavilions, and as Jurek was looking around to his sides, Danka's high heels pecked ellipses of haste into the gravel, signs of their brief passage and the quiet shush of their vanishing. The swing was already waiting and swaying lightly, as if it knew who would sit on it and get it going before they'd said anything. Actually, Jurek shot into the air with the daring of a habitué, and when he had already reached the upper limit, he let drop to the birch, staring at him with handbag pressed to her trunk, "You know, I don't know what to ascribe this to, but for a long time now I've had a hard time managing to write even a few decent, sensible words. Could it be because I've gotten lazy, or is it that each day resembles the next, gray, covered in a cobweb, a cobweb . . ."

"Of sadness," the birch said, with a sparkle. "Don't talk that way. Now I'm opening the envelope, and I take out the pages of your letter. You hear how they rustle? I drive away the black specter of melancholy, which follows me around like a shadow. Just then a trail of sunlight falls on the pages of your letter. The patch of gold grows, dwindles again in a spirited dance. 'All blackness and sadness drains from my eyes . . .' That's what you wrote to me not long ago, you remember? I will always write to you, Jurek, and my words will not let you fall asleep, freeze up in the black amber of melancholy, in the gloomy cocoon of the day."

Jurek was still swishing from one edge of the world to the other, from the east to the west of Tworki, enveloped in the dark shell of night. Nevertheless, he made a not-bad show of himself as he soared over the earth like a bomber-man, like a turbojet carrying letters. In the dark his bright shirt described a Milky Way of pure wool, his legs hung blithely and proudly, as appropriate of levitation, for which his elegant, wide cuffs were an unnecessary ornament, though full of sensuous charm.

The swing finally came to a halt; Jurek wanted something more. "Perhaps you'd like to get on?"

The handbag hesitated, receded into the abyss of the night, into the depths of Danusia, to the island of her still-pure self, but after a moment it moved forward, leading the girl to the place that had been made for her, stretching her arm toward the line of the swing so that there would be something to lean on as the entire body jumped up and perched on the plank board.

Jurek shoved off the ground with both feet, leaned out hard, forward and back, and the ship started pitching and picking up speed. "Maybe we're not a ship on calm seas at all," he said thoughtfully. "Nor Lindbergh's plane over the Atlantic. We're the Swing in Flight for Just One Night . . ."

"For just one night?"

"Yes . . . the Flying Carpet of Carpe Diem. And down below, already far away, we see the agitated river of existence."

"Each one of us knows that lust for repose; everyone, as he strives, thinks of stopping," Danusia said quietly. "He wants not to go, but to get there, and when the stormy wave sweeps him off of some small island, his arms, frantic from the pain, grasp after a clump of grass so as not to be caught in the current of the menacing, mysterious river of existence."

"Do you see the fleeting city lights below?" Jurek asked. "The flashing train lines, the tiny white needles of mountains? That chimney smoke, those vast little strips of beach? That's where our earth goes on, that's where governments rise and fall, that's where everything is born and everything dies. How strange it is to be a person. How difficult, how enormous a task: humanity."

"You remember," Danka said, "you once wondered in a letter how little room there is for goodness in this big world. You encounter so little of it that it's simply become a luxury. I also hold firmly to your assertion that among people a person is a rare phenomenon. A person who might have a soul. And a soul—that's the head and the heart. Especially the heart."

The swing glided so high that the handbag suddenly slipped out of Danka's hands; fortunately, Jurek caught it by the strap at the last second, and he slung it over his shoulder.

"Look, Danusia, we've already passed the first clouds, and the stars are shining brighter and brighter. We're alone among the galaxies of the cosmic night. Every touch of our hands is a new constellation, our every word is a new planet. There's planet Good, over there is planet Faith, and now planet Love and planet Hope."

"Oh, shine on, planets, words like bright stars that fade in the morning light and sink away into a boundlessness invisible to the eye. Having coursed along the distant and unknown tracks that are destined for you, will you yet return to shine brightly over the land again?"

"Over our Polish land," Jurek added.

"Over our Polish land. Which way do your secret roads lead, that thought would reach it again and might be heartened by your sweetness? Where does your road go, planet Good, planet Faith . . ."

"Planet Love . . ."

"Planet Hope?"

Jurek pressed the handbag to his chest, and Danka put her hand on his shoulder. They kept swinging in silence, in starless darkness again, under thicker and thicker clouds. A warm rain started to fall, and together they lifted their faces up toward the drops that were falling from somewhere above the trees. Their cheeks were already very wet, their eyelids awash, their lips moistened when they jumped down from the swing, which then froze in place like an ark, finally obsolete. They ran from the garden plot holding hands, and the handbag was hitting Jurek in the side. Jurek had never taken a key from his pocket so quickly, never opened a door so quickly, never kissed so hard with a wet shirt and a woman's handbag on his shoulder. What they lay themselves down on, those were pillows, what they covered themselves with, that was a blanket, that sweat was straight from Jurek's back, that cry from Danusia's throat.

They kept whispering to each other, weaker and weaker, and fell asleep. Now there's plenty of time till morning to putter around the room, to be snug as a bug once again, by that bed from which comes the light snoring of Jurek On-Tour-ek, next to that wardrobe and the desk. Here, right on the floor, the white shirt had a red-beret heart, and Jurek's shoes had snuggled down into the skirt, one on a gray, the other on a beige diamond, and the pink bra swelled solitarily in the corner. Under the chair the handbag, tossed hastily, opened like a treasure trove in the free world of things. One must tread carefully so as not to upset its form and order. Here lies the pocket mirror, face down, and on its obverse a landscape with a river flying by among spruces, it's just bounded away from the cascade; here's the perfume bottle with the faded label in the shape of a Greek vase, here's the hard horsehair brush facing up, here's the wooly cotton, and here are the keys with the amber pendant, and the lipstick in its shiny tube; and here's a scattered spread of envelopes addressed in lovely calligraphy on top, with an impression on the stamp that says GENERALGOUVERNEMENTPOST, envelopes carefully opened with a thin blade, envelopes with a number written in pencil on the corner, the numbers increasing, grayish-brown envelopes because that's the kind Jurek had at home from before the war.

"She leaned over me, kissed me, and ran out of the room. She leaned, kissed, and ran out," Jurek repeated to himself when he was fully awake and had stopped yawning. "Such verbs, just right for the lord of the manor or a viscount." Be that as it may, she'd risen at dawn, bid him a silent farewell from above while he was still sleeping and, God help him, not snoring, and then she put on her beret, gathered her things, grabbed her handbag, and was gone.

He took the shirt hung carefully on the back of the chair, sought out his shoes, which stood evenly at the foot of the bed, and avoiding the sight of the penguin, he looked out the window at the oak, already bathed in sunlight at its crown. Two white lab coats crossed the path, and a cat ran behind them, and a bird, frightened by something, darted from a branch, and a piece of paper was lying on the desk.

Beloved Jurek,

The heart must soar on, toward its own happiness and destiny. Now I know that one night has to be enough for our whole lives. Hold it within you, carry it with you. And when you cannot sleep, may you always hear my whisper whispering you a fairy tale, humming you an Eastern tune until you finally fall asleep, deeply and contentedly. In the lily-colored mysteriousness of our evening, among our silvery silk shadows, a warm goodness came to us, it spoke to us, and entwined our hands and joined our hearts and minds within one soul. Thank you so much for all your letters. Farewell, my viscount.

Your Danka

"Farewell," Jurek muttered. "Farewell," he barely whispered, and he turned sad. He walked helplessly around the room for a moment, lay down, and immediately got up. Again he looked through the window and felt a trembling in his veins, despair mixed with joy. He looked voraciously straight ahead until he got vertigo, as though he were plotting his course with his eyes, and he felt that the blue sky was pulling him toward it along the handrail of his gaze and that that blueness was preplanned and unreal, and for a moment it seemed to him that he'd seen the edge of his life, a blue-and-yellow band over that horizon that one could brush, touch, cross. Then something in him froze, faded, bent his head down. The path was empty again, sunnier and sunnier on the left side, gray on the right, but only by the first pavilions. Seen from below, raising one's eyes to the second floor, it became a trickle reflected in Jurek's glasses, a trail in the darkness of his pupils. Like the glow from a little searchlight, it shifted its circle of gold from corner to corner, it sought a place for its brightness in Jurek's eyes.

The first leaves had already fallen a few days before and had begun to color the dark gravel. Jurek leaned out toward the pavilions. Over the black-and-yellow earth two clear and increasingly distinct silhouettes passed: they were already heading to work by the yellowed path in Tworki. It was Monday, and Janka and Sonia were already heading to work with their handbags in their hands.

■ □ ■ □ ■

CHAPTER SIXTEEN

"YOU'RE ALL I HAVE LEFT," JUREK SIGHED, AND HE PLACED HIS LEFT hand on Sonia's hand, his right on Janka's hand. "Sonia and Janka. The two most beautiful names in the whole world. And both are right here next to me. Such beautiful names, such beautiful people. If only Marcel were still here to have his name said alongside theirs. Sonia and Janka."

Right after work they sat down on the warmest bench and watched the pajamas passing by. Though it was Monday, something sublime was happening in the warmed air, the purging of the day into an almost solemn, excruciating void. "They're not even putting their robes on. It's warm, like at the beach. Sonia, Janka, a beautiful, truly Polish September has begun."

Sonia positively broke into laughter. "Antiplato, as always, in sandals. And in yellow socks. His legs are truly never cold."

"Maybe the world came into being on a day like today," Jurek sighed again. "Warmth and anticipation. Curious what else will happen. Marcel would tell us for sure."

Sonia raised her arm straight ahead. "Look, Dürer has a hat today. But Rubens has something new on his head, too. A lovely cap, yes? Jeez, he's pretending not to see us."

They laughed with her; Rubens shrugged his shoulders, and Janka turned back toward Jurek and said, "I don't really understand all of this. Where did they go, and why? Why to a hotel? What kind of hotel is that, anyway? Why couldn't you come to tell us last night?"

"The Hotel Polski. That's what it's called. Next to the Old Town. Hotel Polski on Long Street, number twenty-nine. Totally decent. I stood there all day, but they didn't want to let me in. A mysterious business. I'll tell you in a minute, just let's not have Goethe and Bismarck stand there like that: we don't even smoke, and none of us has cigarettes."

The space beside the bench cleared out, and the day was like a thousand unyielding years of immobility, an interloper in the short term, and Jurek began:

"Don't go, my dears, don't go along that fateful street,
The hotel there is friendly but didn't let me in.
Their Jerry mugs amassed for service so discreet,
Marcel and his dear wife have disappeared therein.
It started on a Thursday, when Ania came to chat,
Deciding of a sudden, adieu, Warsaw, good-bye!
They sped off to the hotel, and sadly that was that.
They took the suitcase with them, and left us all to cry!

And so it was. That's it."

Antiplato appeared on the path once again, passed around the bench, but didn't even look at it, occupied as he was by the hole in his sock, through which he saw the Aegean Sea, the first caves, and the expedition of the Argonauts. Newton and Cleopatra ran briskly behind them, holding hands and giggling ecstatically, scolded by Bismarck, who was fishing butts out of the gravel.

"That's great, but did you manage to find out anything? What sort of thing is going on in that hotel? What's it all about?" Janka asked, still shaking her head.

"I didn't find out anything. They have them there to exchange for German POWs. Somebody reports to them and supposedly gets a visa to Switzerland or to Vittel on a special train, and then maybe to America or Palestine."

Something moved behind the bench, and Sonia whispered quickly to Janka, "Look out. Schiller's creeping around again with the gloves."

And in fact two rotten, dirty gloves fell from above and onto their dresses, and they heard the patter of feet running away.

"What do you mean 'supposedly'?" Janka persisted.

"Marcel left me a letter. He wrote that it might be a trap. That that's how it seemed to him. That maybe they were making a mistake. He always was suspicious. A trap in Marcel's lap as he's taking a nap."

"But come on, Jurek." You could hear the annoyance in Janka's voice. "You can't tell us exactly what he wrote in that letter?"

"But that's what I'm doing. That's it, I swear. That he doesn't really believe in that whole Switzerland thing. But he's going. Because it seems it's what Anna wanted. He went with Anna and her sister—you know, Joasia. And that's everything. What do you make of it?"

The sun finally shifted to the right, so perhaps a new millennium had begun. Sonia waved to Schiller, who blew her kisses from a distance, and she looked at her watch. "We won't see him again."

The amblers appeared on the path again. Dürer went up to the solitary Schiller, explained something to him at length, slapped him on the back, and Schiller finally agreed to play the fourth. Together they approached the neighboring bench, to which Goethe and Bismarck had already added another bench. They sat in a circle, Goethe and Dürer as a team, and Dürer dealt the cards so quickly and nimbly that Jurek turned his head in disbelief.

"I don't know," Janka spoke up. "He was always right. He always counted so well and knew all the regulations. He never made a mistake."

"It would have been better if he had stayed here with us. We have it good. So warm and so homey, so . . . so . . . so bright." Sonia sought out the word and looked toward the gate. "Someone's coming."

Coming, or rather running and flying by, he bowed to Cleopatra, he patted Newton on the shoulder. At a distance he was a wispy cumulus, the snows of Kilimanjaro over the warmer plain, and halfway down the road he was an apple tree blooming over the heads of common loonies, a wheaten giant, a bright titan for every mythology, and now, next to our bench, Olek, blond, first smiling, then hugging and kissing these blushes of ours, these hands of ours, this strawberry-blond hair, these lips now less red. Sonia snuggled up against Olek, and then, as if embarrassed, she sat down and straightened out her skirt. Olek squeezed in between her and Jurek and threw his arms over the seat back with satisfaction. Again they spoke of Marcel, but Olek didn't know anything new, all the more so for his just having spent a couple of days in the Kampinos Forest with certain individuals. It started to get dark, history had reached the edge of day, so they moved over to Jurek's room, and, with hopes no greater than they'd been, they taught Janka how to bid as well as to count points according to the Polish system. Then, after the first test round, which was known from the get-go to be the last, Sonia and Olek left for Pavilion B and Janka brewed Jurek one more tea. Soon the last train whistled from Podkowa, and at the station in Zurich, before midnight in the here and now, the clock was ticking steadily on, and the place was quiet and deserted.

■ □ ■ □ ■

CHAPTER SEVENTEEN

ALL ROADS HAD NOW LED TO THE END OF THE YEAR, BY WINGS ABOVE, by corridors below, their moles already sleepy, and first of all, to be sure, by streets. First by Marszałkowska, then Polna, Nowogrodzka, Krucza to Wilcza, and from Wilcza back to Marszałkowska. A week later, also on a Saturday afternoon, along Piękna to Krucza, Krucza to Redeemer Square, and farther on, as always, to Marszałkowska. Olek kept doggedly quiet, and Jurek's good deeds would not go unpunished. "We'll never buy them their presents. You don't like the little jewel chest, you don't like the belt, you don't like the earrings. So let's go get them both neckties."

"It has to be beautiful, Bookkeeper. It's our first Christmas Eve, get it? It's a really important present."

So they went farther up the Warsaw streets from store to store, and they took objects in their hands, looked at each other, and put them down until finally, at the end of the day, they stumbled upon Kozioł and Company on Hoża. It was dark inside, only the lamps along the walls were on, and for a long time they stood there motionless, having a hard time distinguishing the contours of the countertop and the several display cases. Though the bell on the door had rung, no one had yet come out to them, and Jurek asked, "So what does she really mean to you?"

Olek kept his silence, so much so that Jurek figured out what the "dead" part meant, and what a dumb question. He saw such lovely things, small and shiny, in the display case, and he gazed curiously through the glass. "Hey, Olek, look, maybe that brooch. It's nice," he said. "Must be pricey."

"I love her, Bookkeeper," he heard.

"Maybe it's silver. I wonder how much it costs," he sighed.

"I love her. Really. She means everything to me."

A thin figure in a white dress shirt and an enormous polka-dot bow tie appeared from behind the curtain and said, "How may I help you, gentlemen? You, sir, are entirely correct, to be sure. Pure silver, an original design."

The brooch shone in Jurek's hand like the eye of a lake against a dark desert, like a different time on a mundane day. Indeed, it was perhaps of a material other than that of our bodies, strangely concave and much better rounded. As smooth to the touch as an alchemist's dream, the brooch presented a shape ex nihilo, quivering but solid. Like a little leaf after a flood, it carried within itself both the modesty of a beginning and memory squeezed into the same base, and from there it unfurled with freshness and confidence. It would go great with Janka's coffee-and-milk dress, if only he were to pin it there above the heart, to offer his best New Year's wishes, and, when the party begins, to permit himself to follow her glow toward the dance floor.

"You only live once. I'll take it," Jurek said, and he raised his hand to his throat excitedly. "If you'll lend me the difference, Olek. I'll pay you back right after the New Year. I think Janka will like it."

Olek nodded.

"A very fine choice, I must say," the owner responded. "Very fine and auspicious. And for your friend, sir, I might also have something tasteful and worthy of serious attention."

He plunged into the depths of the store, and Jurek was looking at Olek. He hadn't moved till now. He was standing up straight, he had the persistence and attitude of a soldier on guard, as well as the beauty, strength, and will of those who were not.

"You remember how you shot the last goal against Cracovia? Diving straight by that center, Ciszewski, right before halftime? I never saw anything like it. And I don't think I will," Jurek said, smiling and nodding with excitement.

A watch now lay on the counter before Olek. Kozioł and Company straightened his bow tie, brought the polka dots even with his Adam's apple, and watched with satisfaction as Olek took it in his hand, raised it to his ear, listened closely, and then held it in his palm and stared at it for a long time. No matter that it was round and golden—such watches can be found in every shop and on every other arm. What was more important was that it somehow ticked differently, less compulsively, without taking a breath before each subsequent second. Its face was truly a playground for the little second hand, and though the needle pointed at each number in sequence, they all seemed accidental and interchangeable, subject to the one law of *ex aequo.* All the more so because the space they encircled was equally unstable and quite volatile. And that was enough for Olek to nod his head, pulling Jurek—who was sort of leaning on him—off to the side to look from the left side so that the watch's white surface suddenly started to shimmer and reveal something. Olek now saw what Jurek had seen, so now we all see it: an emerald sea with menacing breakers and a ship on the horizon. But it was enough for Olek to shift his head to the right, pushing Jurek, for another landscape and other bright hues to emerge. A great forest of firs divided by a straight, sandy road, and when seen from low down, still shoving Jurek, snow-capped peaks, and when seen from above, there's a river with bridges and an old town with a cathedral. It struck three. No, it wasn't the large clock over the door or the chime on the counter that rang out. Something had rung from within the little watch, or rather, it played the tune of a music box: thin, silvery notes emerged that were no less ancient for having come from nearby.

"It plays a minuet at noon," said the owner with the rumpled bow tie, which seemed to be glowering solemnly at Olek.

Olek covered the watch with his other hand and held it in the warmth of his intertwined fingers, just like he would a captive cricket or a coin after the toss.

"It's three o'clock here, two o'clock in Paris," the owner whispered after a moment's silence.

Olek leaned over the watch again. Truly, in the tiny notch at the bottom of its face he spotted the number that had been whispered and a name written in microscopic letters. And when he'd done a half turn with one flick of the pin, the number five showed up in the frame with the notation "Moscow," and then, after another half turn, the number nine and "Tokyo."

"I'll take it," he said in a husky voice.

"Sonia already has a watch," Jurek noted.

The polka dots swayed, and a bow tie–like fly made a sonorous buzz. "Young man! Allow me to note that wherever we are, that's what we have. By buying this Swiss watch from the firm Omega—for such is its noble, prewar origin—you, dear sir, will be placing on this honorable young woman's arm the most beautiful gold casing in all of Warsaw and the most original dial."

"I'll definitely take it," Olek repeated, and the owner nodded seriously, straightening his bow tie, set aslant by too long a speech. From his pocket Olek removed a wad of money held together by a rubber band. He counted out the sum, and they left with their bags in hand. They cut across Krucza and then took Hoża to Marszałkowska.

Meanwhile, the roads still led to the end of the year, on its own legs, by twists and turns and even by ruts and the trucks in them. Around the tenth of December, right after lunch, a Mercedes Camionnette pulled into the Tworki courtyard, and Johann arched his back to attention like a cat of the Nibelung. Nutcases ran in from all directions and silently encircled the vehicle. Goethe even encouraged them loudly to peer inside, but at the sight of a screaming Kaltz, and especially of Honnette, who had dragged his potbelly out of the administration building, everyone bolted behind the long-leafless trees so as to look from behind the oaks and maples at the things already brought, but not yet distributed. But what's with those cans standing evenly in the cardboard box, what's that weird stuff in the shape of a bottle packed in eights, and then what's with those closed cases with that mysterious rattling and buzzing inside? For among the simple objects three elegant pigskin suitcases had appeared, and beside the suitcases the pinnacle of evolution—a German woman. She looked fashionable and none too old in her pelisse, her quite shapely calves rooted in brown pumps on French heels, but oh, that hat. Honnette kissed the woman on the hand and then, feeling the gaze of the trees upon him, on the cheek; Kaltz bowed low to his superior, said something quietly, his arm describing a wide circle, and reached for the suitcases joyfully and lightly resting on her bent knees. They were already walking in the direction of the office, among the amazed oaks and maples, when the wife suddenly remembered something, went back to the Camionnette, and carefully removed a gramophone from the backseat. Oh yes, dear Newton, yes indeed, my sweet Goethe behind the maple, she removed, and now was herself carrying, hugging it gently to her pelisse and not handing it over to the men to carry, a real gramophone with a crank to wind it, to enjoy it and want more when the festive holidays arrive, and especially the *Ruhe* and the *heilige Nacht.*

Let there be no doubt, all roads were leading to the end of the year, with boots, thick gloves, pelisses, and even with fur hats. On the first Tuesday in December, Sonia had shown up on the central path with something splendid on her head, and Rubens, as soon as he'd seen her, took his own shapeless sack off his skull and didn't leave her side all the way up to the accounting office, observing from the side how a tail had been tacked onto Sonia's profile. A tail—nay, a bushy tail it was—made from a gray pelt, and the gray, fleecy pillbox hat rested on Sonia's head. The bushy tail swung joyfully, the pillbox hat was tilted perfectly as Sonia walked and dipped graciously to one and all as she stopped to exchange a few words and courtesies with Caesar, Nero, and Alexander. It was their good fortune that right after breakfast they saw before them, in their own imperial eyes, content and form both signifying and constituent in complete symbiosis. They were fortunate that, having now sat down for an afternoon of nine-plus poker, they didn't see Sonia's eyes and the furry tail bedewed from her cheek and the pillbox hat slightly aslant, as Sonia, together with the ringing of a chime, ran out onto the path and went straight ahead, wherever her eyes, wherever those eyes might carry her.

Why were they sorrowful, and why were they wet? Where were these tears from, these hunched shoulders, where did these quickly placed paces lead? She flitted among the trees, deviating suddenly from the trail by the wall, and she stumbled, scraping her winter coat on a birch, her pillbox hat brushing a branch. She straightened the hat, flipped the tail back, and ran between two maples as though through an open door. No place for us: farther on it grew more desolate and white, where the first snow had made some denser patches, and as Sonia disappeared into the depth of the glade she grew smaller and smaller, like a dark bird bounding away somewhere in the snow, frolicking beyond the wheat visible on the horizon, beyond the mystery of one's own gaze. What did she see, where had she gone, where had she disappeared? These questions want answers, but will they have them? Can we? Do we know how?

The last rays of December sun fell on the edges of the tables in Tworki. Time to return to the road among the maples; Sonia is still pacing the horizon there, whereas before us there is the birch, the still-moving branch, the wooden benches again and the path between them, and dinner already on the table.

■ □ ■ □ ■

CHAPTER EIGHTEEN

IF YOU'RE GOING TO MEET UP, THEN YOU MEET UP ON A CERTAIN DAY and at a given time. On the morning of December 24, the presents were already lying safe in the cabinet under Jurek's sweater, where they gleamed and ticked by turns. In the largest administration hall, on a long table assembled by bringing desks together, various Germanic items were waiting, and on the other side, Frau Honnette herself was attaching the horn to the gramophone she'd placed on a tablecloth she herself had brought. It was still cold in the hall because the oven had not yet been lit, and eight in the morning was still a long way off. Janka, in her winter coat, along with Sonia, with her pillbox hat on her head and gloves on her hands, were helping Bronka and Jabłkowska set up the plates and glasses, bring in the last Christmas balls, and separate the knives from the forks.

The workday was to end at twelve. The clock by the door cuckooed twelve times, twelve times the little head popped out, and over the desks, with their pencils and abacuses already neatly laid down, the heads of the employees, still full of numbers, looked up, their bodies rose heavily, called to general attendance, what with the subsequent births and new pages of the calendar. Herr Director the Humanitarian had expanded the hospital budget and invited the entire administration and the rest of the personnel for a modest snack so as to embrace the holiday, play some music, and even feed all the employees under his dignified command.

What a strange scene, if one were to take a view of the whole and draw all those gazes toward oneself. The round clock on the right-hand wall showed 12:07. Between the wall and the row of interlinked desks stood four columns supporting a high ceiling. Before them, toward the middle, the slightly lower ceiling proper began, freshly painted and punctuated with flat, round lampshades. They weren't yet shining, these out-of-work stars in the finished sky, patient Fortinbras over the flickering Christmas tree, now lit, now not. So now a real fir tree from the Helenów Forest glowed with candle-shaped light bulbs, sparkled with angelic, Aryan hair like all verbs about light, silver, and gold. Gleam, glisten, glow, and sparkle, thus Jurek had already lifted the magnesium in his left hand and leaned over the camera, gleam and glisten, and then finally to distribute the prizes and awards, but first keep smiling.

Before the Christmas tree sat two little chairs, and on the chairs sat the exalted, the beneficent ones. Honnette placed his hand on his belly, and he drew up his legs, with one little shoe atop the other, and shifted them to the left so comically that any old grandfather could grab him by the shoulder and, like an infant, carry him off to a warm playpen in Alsace; he smiled vaguely in his uniform, minus the insignia because it's not appropriate, but perhaps is necessary, in light of the fact that the lens doesn't lie, nor do those lights behind his neck, nor does the wife next to him in the white blouse. Honestly, it's fine, Jurek—he was looking at this scene—who cares about the quilted blouse with elbow-length sleeves, and who cares about that rather open smile, who cares even about those hands arranged on those knees, where the black skirt falls on stockings before—and this is really weird and delays the picture—the left foot, which, as the right foot is basically pressing its heel to the floor, moves back under the chair, where it quite playfully rises up on its toes, knocking the heel upward, and all of this has some kind of meaning when it is fixed this way in the frame, like maybe it means that the leg, or even the entire person, would like to frolic about, to leap up and, at least once, to tick like a single second.

But the real smiling begins behind the long table of desks, where the lowly employees are standing. Unfortunately the frame will not omit the closed mouths and wide-open eyes of Kaltz, Quick, and Jabłkowska, backs arched and eyes fixed on the lens as ordered, but the closer they are to him, the more the disciplined line goes soft and melts: Bronka's discreet smile, Janka smiling pretty clearly, as though to herself, and now the whitest teeth, the most radiant face above a white, quilted blouse with only elbow-length sleeves, so it's great to see the bulbous watch on her wrist, Sonia's beaming face, Sonia's mouth and her laugh, which, facing the lens and Jurek under the black rag like an old lady in mourning, cannot get itself under control. No one can say what or whom she's laughing at, but there's no time to think about it, and he also has to get the focus right on those piles on the desks, on that useful scrap metal, because enameled pots are standing there evenly, and pans with lids, and a few pitchers and cups, and there's even one big golden skillet, and beside it cartons of cigarettes, little day planners, not so many blocks of chocolate, combs and scissors in cases, and, now quite close, real sandwiches with egg, a few with kielbasa, while next to the drinking glasses, set out with their stems in the air, a bottle of pure schnapps, we won't say from where.

Jurek finally took the picture and assumed his place in the line. White coveralls and work clothes, from which Kaltz formed a second line, flowed into the hall. When the doors had already closed, he went up to the gramophone and, at Frau Honnette's nod, turned the crank. The heel under the chair rose up even higher, and everyone heard the echo of a chorus of Rhinelander angels from before they were mobilized. The record creaked a bit, but the words resounded clearly as they repeated "son," "tiny," "holy," and "happy." Finally, after a couple of carols, silence returned, and the objects on the table seemed for a moment more present than the people. Perhaps Honnette sensed this, because he stood up from his seat so quickly, straightened his uniform as though in apology, with a slightly embarrassed movement, and said, "On this festive day, may the personnel—all the doctors, nurses, and administrative staff—accept our best holiday wishes, and *grüss Gott.* As the director of the Hospital for Psychiatric and Nervous Disorders in Tworki, I am especially pleased that our medical institution enjoys the high esteem of our German authorities and carries out the tasks set before it with great diligence. As a token of recognition for the work of our staff at the institution, all employees will receive a calendar for the year 1944, as well as Christmas presents, which will be distributed by my assistant, Herr Kaltz. Next, all of you gathered here are invited to enjoy a modest refreshment prepared from our supplementary fund. And once again, *grüss Gott.*"

Timid applause rang out, and the objects came sort of closer, now almost familiar and named. Janka received a pair of scissors and a metal comb in a most suitable color and a cup painted with flowers; Kaltz handed Jurek the very same mug, checking his name off on the list, as well as a white pitcher with the identical pattern; and now they were waiting to see what Sonia would receive. Kaltz was somehow dawdling for a long time, circling around, summoning each lab coat in turn and handing him or her a mug; Quick and Jabłkowska got their hands on two pans with lids, and when the recipients had already started to move toward the sandwiches, Kaltz's body swayed strangely, he snatched the golden skillet from the table and, with a sudden movement, gave it to Sonia. She froze, amazed, like an Egyptian pharaoh with the sun in his hands, and she held it clumsily by one ray and drew the gazes of all her subjects into it, even with the first sandwiches now in their mouths. They had good reason to be surprised: the value of the present, its extraordinary workmanship, its usefulness in times of war, its priority among the wonders of this world and, especially, of this hall. It became clear right away that she had found herself the queen of this most honored birthday, the local patron saint of the Adoration, the master of ceremonies in the manger. And also the orator for this lofty occasion: one had to say something—their expressions and gazes were saying things. Let Sonia offer thanks with the first glass. Sonia turned her head; she pointed to Jurek with the skillet, but when Kaltz cleared his throat and poured out little vodkas, the staff line simply pushed her out front.

Sonia hid the skillet behind her back, raised her glass, and took a breath. "On behalf of the administration and the medical staff of the Tworki Psychiatric Hospital," she said, "I would like most sincerely to thank you. We thank you, Herr Director and Frau Director, for preparing this holiday refreshment and for rewarding us with such precious gifts. We would like, Herr Director and Frau Director, to offer you our best holiday wishes. God bless, *grüss Gott.*"

Honnette nodded benevolently, clearly pleased, and Kaltz folded his hands meaningfully, and behind Sonia's back a timid, though soon quite sonorous, applause broke out. Frau Honnette put on a new record with her own hands, and the next toast, to the health and success of all those present, was done to the sounds of a cantata. A still-life came into being: next to the cups and pans more and more empty plates with crumbs started to appear, more and more cutlery and wrinkled napkins were set down, but the cantatas, and then the sonatas, and finally the first marches held the picture over the table, where, in the glow of the Christmas tree lights, widened eyes looked into the distance, up to the first images of salvation. On Honnette's order, Jurek took another picture and, when such a thing was possible, the clock on the wall indicating exactly 2:20, he pulled Sonia and Janka out of the hall. The cups clunked on the way out, the skillet reflected the little lights of the Christmas tree with a golden gleam, and our friends were now free, now on the path, now in Jurek's room.

Olek had arrived right before five because earlier he'd taken both mamas, his own and Jurek's, to Aunt Irena's, and now he was lugging a bag full of cake, jars of cabbage and plum compote, and a side of spruce branches. Jurek had already long since been looking out for the first star. He even opened the window and leaned out so far that Janka came up and grabbed him by the belt, but finally he gave it a rest because there were more and more clouds and his glasses were getting steamy. When the rest was being set about the table, he drew a Christmas wafer from his book and circled around impatiently, correcting whatever was laid out unevenly and imparting advice. "More cabbage on this platter," he said ponderously, like the lord of the manor. "And please remove those pits from the compote." Until finally Sonia flung a napkin at his nose and giggled at his stupid expression.

She was still laughing as he was breaking off a piece of the wafer and, with such consternation, scrunching up his face and furrowing his brow in the hope that the wafer would be evenly and attractively divided; she was still laughing as he stood up, removed his glasses, and fluttered his eyes comically before launching into a solemn speech, waiting for everyone else to stand as well; she even laughed when he berated her with a glance, goggling theatrically, but now she was listening as he said, "Beloved guests, dearest friends! In the not-too-distant past, hardly two thousand years ago, the star of Bethlehem glimmered over the world. Since those days in which Jesus started to roam the valleys and hills of the Holy Land, love has been marching through the centuries. It has not yet taken over the world, has not uprooted egoism and selfishness from the hearts of men. Too often the history of the world has been an arena for violence and war. And this year the Christmas holiday does not pass joyfully by. The church bells summoning us to Midnight Mass merge with the sounds of a war still underway." Jurek paused and lowered his head, as though figuring out what to say next. "O Poland, Poland!" he whispered suddenly. "If man only had strength enough to press you to his bosom, O Poland, great and holy martyr." He paused again and lifted his eyes to the faces of Janka, Olek, and finally Sonia. "Christmas Eve. A day like any other, and yet everything this Christmas Eve speaks the language of extraordinary people. A day with an odd and mysterious power to lead hearts to harmony and peace. A day when we are better, purer, closer to the eternal, most beautiful truths. We wish each other all the very best."

He picked up a piece of the wafer, and everyone else followed suit. They sat at the table and for a short while, in deafening silence, ate fish refried on the golden skillet, but to their good fortune, Olek remembered something: "You remember, Jerzy, how in the first grade, for the whole school, we put on that . . . well . . . nativity scene? In the first part you and me and Heniek were the three wise men, and your beard slipped off because you leaned too far over the crib, remember?"

"Not really," Jerzy mumbled.

"And in the second part, when you were Herod, your beard slipped off again because you shook your scepter too hard. I thought I would die, remember?"

"Through a haze," Jerzy mumbled, and Sonia snorted with laughter. Everyone started laughing, and they joked more than they consumed until the exchange of gifts, and then they were simply curious as they sought something in a handbag or under a sweater and clumsily concealed it behind their backs. No point in writing about it—it's better to get to the fun: from Janka, Jurek received striped socks, the short kind, a little short on the ankle, quite lovely, and he decided to try them on right away. He took off his shoes, and Sonia started giggling because he had one sock on that had surely been inside-out since morning, and for a moment he stared helplessly at the threads sticking out from the stripes. Finally, as though nothing had happened, he took off his socks, scrunched up his feet a bit—because you don't always know how those toenails will look—and he pulled on his new stripes, the color of the sea at dusk. They fit unexpectedly well, and Jurek paraded around the room and did not at all want to put on his shoes, but a new present was already writhing colorfully in Sonia's fingers, fawning up to her hand. It was enormously generous on one end, perhaps too much so, and there, on the other, it was tight-fisted, returning to its narrow corridor. Olek lowered his head quite strangely, as softly as a bird that wants to sleep, and with a few deft movements Sonia untangled the knot of Olek's tie—thin, a dark garnet—and with one tug she pulled it out from under his white collar. She cast the new tie around the liberated space and watched as Olek tied it. The knot should have been of the English Windsor type, but Olek's measurement was off, and the thin end stuck out, and Sonia was laughing at Jurek's joyous expression. After a second try he succeeded, and just as Jurek had expected, the blond looked good in this new fashion, where the discreet Bordeaux mixed with the garnet and the flecks of cream and little stars of ripe orange, and the abundance of material contrasted well with the height of the man.

"I've never had anything like it," Olek pronounced, and he straightened his collar ceremoniously. "It's really lovely . . . extraordinary."

"The latest American fashion," Jurek said. "As wide as from one kidney to the other. The Brooklyn Bridge, from bank to bank."

Sonia started laughing and seemed to be waiting for something. Jurek checked out of the corner of his eye whether everyone had gotten his jibe and, satisfied, took his closed hand out of his pocket. One could already see the corners of a tiny little bag and the tip of a pink ribbon, and even before the open sesame Janka had turned red. And rightly so—once the bag was so awkwardly torn asunder, she received something silver and twisted like a shell, and even prickly. She received an expression of terror—will she like it or not?—and, behind the glasses, eyes round with dread and expectation. "It's really nice," Janka said. "Very original. It's truly . . . extraordinary."

Sonia nudged Jurek, who had been readying himself for the ceremonious pinning for too long, shuffling his socks, and showed him precisely where the brooch should be situated. It glistened with a new shine, like Poland's wedding to the sea, like a stigma on otherwise smooth matter. Janka took a breath, the brooch rose and fell, and in Olek's hand it already ticked, in Olek's open hand it was already ticking: the watch. And a moment later it played, for it was eight o'clock. It played a Mozart minuet and, in the silence that ensued, strung glass beads of sound on an invisible thread. They were arranged over four bars, and they were like a sweet knocking on a door, and the thread became increasingly more visible, tangible, beautiful, and ruthless. The final drops were still sounding when Olek transferred the watch wordlessly to Jurek, walked up to Sonia, and with a forceful, decisive gesture, removed the bulbous watch from her wrist, with its already quite rotten leather strap and its slightly cracked face. Jurek was standing behind Olek as solemnly and eagerly as a nurse with a scalpel, and Sonia giggled, but when Olek took the watch from Jurek's hands and carefully placed it on her proffered wrist, she turned serious and squinted her eyes. Now it was set on her arm, and everyone stared at its handsome hands, which said that 8:03 had just passed, and now 04 and 05.

Sonia looked at Olek, kissed him on the cheek, and said quite loudly, as though she'd wanted to let everyone know: "It's . . . really lovely. I've never seen anything so beautiful . . . It's absolutely extraordinary. Really, I'm speechless."

Olek showed Sonia and Janka all the landscapes, placing Sonia's wrist at various angles, and inquired what time it was in Paris, then indicated the answer himself, winding the little pin, and then took a long time explaining the mechanics of the operation. Sonia attentively followed Olek's movements, the care with which he explicated every technical detail, and she learned perhaps more about Olek than about the watch, because when it fell to her to show what time it was in New York, she threw her fingers helplessly over the dial. Olek patiently repeated his explanations, and finally all the presents, variously proffered and accepted, blended into these festive bodies. They moved toward the dessert and every so often, from over their cake and compote, they kept casting glances at their newly acquired things, now incorporated into this life, and it seemed to Olek that he did in fact look handsome in that tie, and Janka supposed that the brooch was rather expensive and worth the price, for it really did go well with her dress, only Jurek's socks itched a bit at his flat feet.

"What time is it?" he asked Sonia at nine o'clock and at ten minutes after nine. "Do we know what time it is?" he asked after ten and a couple more times before eleven. "I wonder what time it is," he repeated, smiling aggressively, before midnight.

"Sixteen minutes to twelve," Sonia answered, fixing her eyes attentively on the hands of the watch as she had after each time he'd asked, "and now it's a quarter to twelve."

"Midnight Mass!" Jurek shouted, and he tore himself hastily from his seat, knocking what was left in the vodka bottle onto Olek's trousers. Sonia giggled and was still laughing as they walked the path in the direction of the Tworki chapel, and Olek had such a funny gait. "Is it midnight yet?" Jurek asked her just as they were blending into the crowd of pajamas with coats thrown on. She looked at the watch face and tilted her head slightly, and the words rang out from over the altar: "The people that walked in darkness have seen a great light. They that dwell in the land of the shadow of death, upon them hath the light shined."

"Amen," the congregants whispered, and the Mass rolled swiftly through the minutes, right until the turn of the minute hand, right up to the last *have mercy upon us.*

And shine, like the stars shine, like the stars shone as the friends were leaving the chapel together with the silent crowd. The clouds dispersed, and one could see a few constellations, so that one still felt like there was something to long for in the fresh air. They strolled the paths from wall to wall; before the boiler room Jurek chatted briefly with Virtuoso, for whom the day had gone well enough, so that Sonia laughed her head off, and then, around two o'clock, when they'd frozen a bit, Olek proposed that they drop in to the administration building to see if something was up.

Sonia opened the door with her staff key, and they went in hesitantly, as if entering a spa during the off-season. The Christmas tree was lit, and they were met by the crowded shadows of abandoned things, of forsaken places. The two interior columns issued dark borderlines upon whose crossing they found themselves in the square of a feast. The plates had grown dusky around the edges, beneath the bright scales of their eyes; the forks splayed their fingers. Olek found an unfinished bottle, distributed its contents, and they drank in silence, solemnly, staring at the flickering lights and the dance of their glare on the wall. One suddenly illuminated the corner where, on a desk, the gramophone rested with its horn, which now projected its own tinny gleam. Sonia ran up to it and grabbed the first disk that caught her eye. The sonata didn't find its way out, and now Sonia's hand was placing the next disk and turning the crank so that songs of a winter journey might ring out all the sooner. But they didn't last long; Sonia pulled the last of the disks, in a colorful cover, out of the pile. Colorful names, colorful sounds, a deep blue waltz, a silvery Boston, a pink foxtrot. "It's not really appropriate," Jurek muttered over his glass, tapping his fingers on the tabletop. "No, not today." He shook his head, but he managed to drag Sonia into the center of the hall. "We could dance in about two days," he said in a firm tone, but he managed to take her by the arm and lead her two steps forward, then two steps back, and eventually three. Sonia glanced down several times at Olek, still sitting, and there was nothing to be done about it—he had to obey at least one of these two commandments, to take Janka by the hand and to follow Jurek's waddling and Sonia's steps, which were now four forward and four back. They stamped their feet harder and harder, when suddenly a shaft of light from behind tumbled onto their dance floor. Someone was standing in the open door; in the wide-open door Frau Honnette was standing and, with her bright blue eyes, was looking at them intently from the office. They froze in place, and only Sonia giggled softly. The newcomer hadn't changed her clothes, as if she'd spent that night all alone, and she still had on her white blouse and black skirt and her high-heeled shoes, which seemed to bounce lightly. She looked at Sonia, who was laughing, and for a moment their gazes crossed paths. Jurek ran up to the gramophone, but Frau Honnette shook her head that no, there was no need to turn it off. For a few more seconds she stared at Sonia, who was leaning awkwardly, in an almost perverse manner, on Olek, and her gaze was like two blue telescopes, now focusing in, now focusing out, aiming precisely on the constellation of faces with Olek's torso in the background, after which she extended her hand strangely, pensively before her, so as to give something or take it away, gave a slight smile, turned around, and left without hurrying down the bright hallway.

The clock in the room and Sonia's watch said that it was already four o'clock. In Paris it was three, in Tokyo ten, but here snow had started to fall. It turned Janka's hair silver and collected on Sonia's pillbox hat as they were returning along the path to the girls' room. They said good-night, and Jurek, laughing, asked what time it was for the last time, and at 4:15, Christmas Eve came to an end. Olek shaved in Jurek's room—Jurek didn't yet have to—and they changed clothes quickly and took the morning train to Warsaw to enjoy a holiday breakfast with both their mothers.

▪ ▫ ▪ ▫ ▪

CHAPTER NINETEEN

IF IT'S TO TWORKI, IT MUST BE TUESDAY. JUREK CAME EARLY IN THE morning in a new shirt—a Christmas gift from his good mother—already prepared for a visit to the girls, for whom he brought his own gramophone and disks with such music, O Janka and Sonia, that today even Olek is superfluous if one has legs of one's own, weak as they may be, though they're tapping out the waltz well enough. *A shame,* Jurek thought as he hummed the tango milonga and opened the door to his room in the familiar manner. *A real shame that I didn't bring the gramophone earlier.* A piece of paper, which had surely been slipped underneath, lay on the floor.

Just as he reached the doorstep, a breathless Janka threw herself into his arms. There was a thaw outside, and his shoes were wet from his having taken a shortcut.

"Look, look what I found on the floor in my room," he said. "Everyone writes me letters."

He read aloud from the piece of paper. Janka was trembling, and Jurek noticed that the bones and knuckles of his hands were turning white, and he suddenly understood that this was all connected, that it had to do with some distance in which everything was melting and fading away and casting a strange light. In the picture above Sonia's bed, the sea smothered its waves on the sand, and the yellow-blue strip blurred Jurek's vision, softened the contours before him, right down to their very color. He sat down heavily on the bed.

"What's happened?" he asked quietly.

"I'm scared. I'm scared," Janka said, and the first tears fell from her eyes.

"What's happened? Do you know what happened?"

"She left very early this morning."

"What time?"

"I don't know. She had such a strange expression."

"Sad?"

"I don't know. She gave me a kiss while I was still in bed, and she came back from the door and stroked me on the cheek, really strange."

"Where did she go?" Jurek asked, standing up. He looked out the window, and again he saw the clean line of the forest, the trees standing firmly in place, and their penumbras reflected in the puddles. "Where the hell did she go off to? Why is she saying good-bye to me, and like this?"

Janka ran up to him and clung to his back. "I'm scared," she whispered. "I'm really scared. She's from Berdichev."

"What? What do you mean? You're kidding, right?"

"That's where she was born. Then she left with her parents."

"How's that? What do you mean?" Jurek wanted to turn around, but Janka held him in a tight embrace, and a moment later he just gave a heavy sigh. There were so many molecules of oxygen in the air, such a mix of pluses and minuses.

"What's this garbage you're talking? Where did she go?" he repeated. "Where? Where?"

Where did you go, Sonia? You put on your pillbox hat, your coat, warm knee-high stockings under your skirt, and you left the room, not whistling at all; you didn't run down the stairs this time, you put one foot in front of the other so you were trudging along holding onto the railing, and then the foyer, and, suddenly, the still-cold morning air, with the sun somewhere in the east. Where did you go when you'd finished writing by the windowsill, when you'd slipped the piece of paper under Jurek's door and then stood there for a long time, as though waiting for the door suddenly to open and someone to take you, anaesthetized, by the arms, and lead you to the golden sands, where there are as yet no footprints to be seen? Where did you go, paying no heed to your love or others' love for you, not caring that you had a name to repeat and to whisper, his eyes and mouth to kiss, his torso like an ark of certainty and the sinewy cords of his hands, that whatever there was in him desired you and invariably, always, ever wanted you? Where did you go? Was it to the desert, where the bushes are aflame and the dunes are like waves, or to a place where the ferns are wintering amidst the moss, though there aren't so many tracks on the earth, not so many paths in Tworki, and there's nothing strange in your having gone into the administration building and sat down in front of Honnette's office, waiting for him to appear with a cigar and a book because this is where he's spent every day? Like always, he arrived early, and upon seeing you, he smiled awkwardly, and the wood of the little bench underneath you became all the more biting. You over-sweetened the real coffee he gave you in his office, not asking you to sit down, and you stood before him, you drank in tiny sips, as if you didn't know whether you were allowed, and you were silent, just as he was, after you'd had your say. He tapped the coffee spoon on the desktop a while, stood up ponderously, went out, came back with Kaltz, and the rest of the coffee in your glass soaked into the undissolved real sugar and froze in dark craters. They *sprechened* amongst themselves in the corner for a long time, the azalea in the flowerpot was green, and that hurt you. Kaltz's fist was clenched tight, and his eyes closed as Honnette went up to you, as he avoided your eyes and spoke, and his Adam's apple flew high up and down, like the scales of one's conscience, from evil to good: "You've lost your mind, miss! You've completely lost your mind! In a moment I'll bring in Dr. Okonowski. You must calm down and go to the isolation ward. You must lie down and relax. I repeat, you are ill, mentally, very ill. *Geistesnervenkrank.*"

Where, then, did you go, Sonia, by which path, by which trail exactly, as you repeated that nothing would change the fact that you're from where you're from, and you shook your head, no, definitely not, you're definitely not joking? Where did you go when Kaltz wanted to take you by the hand, and Honnette looked you in the eyes for the first time and gasped, with terrible difficulty: "I'm begging you, miss, you'll take a vacation, a medical leave on account of your health. You're ill, miss; no one will believe you, not even our patients utter such nonsense." So where did you go, what river did you float down beyond the sixth mountain, or was it the seventh, when they then ordered you to get back to work and to forget about the whole thing because he and his assistant, Kaltz, don't recall a bit of it, but you were shouting, "No, no, please do what you must, Herr Director." The office grew brighter, and the lamp on the desk burned like an unnecessary bonfire, like a reality from another world in which you were stuck, and you stared into the lamp as Honnette and Kaltz went out so that you could think it over, go away, or simply go to the pavilion as they were coming back from a two- or three-hour walk. It was quiet in the hall, and it was enough to turn the doorknob to find oneself on the parquets made from local oaks, to pass around the wall made from our domestic brick, to stroke with one's hand the coarse bark on this side, then that side of the poplars. But you didn't go that way, on your side of the door, on the bemossed north of your existence, and you haven't yet gotten to name the things in the office. You didn't see what those slender, sharpened sticks are lying next to the white square, what is that there, transparent, filled with water, and when Honnette came back, you said, "Please call them in, yes, that's what I want."

"I'll take you myself, miss," he said, and his eyes were like two buttons torn out, and he took you by the hand with a stiff but gentle movement. Kaltz waddled behind you to the car, whispering something voicelessly, and at the last moment, when the car was already moving, he jumped in and sat next to you, and he closed his eyes again, and suddenly he grabbed your hand. Johann, standing in front of the guard booth and feeding the pigeons, straightened up and saluted. There was no one on the platform, and through the window you saw the rails fleeing to the side, toward Warsaw and Podkowa, toward Podkowa and Warsaw. The road was straight, cobbled, and after a moment, along the right side, there appeared a dirty, rusty sign that said PRUSZKÓW, because that's where you were going, Sonia, that's precisely where you were off to.

They were standing helplessly by the gate as Johann was now telling them about the car, and the pigeons had stopped crowding around, and they all stared into the road, which, across the tracks, ran straight up to the first buildings. "Let us pray. Let's pray for a bit," Jurek said to Janka. She wore such a distant, vacant expression that it made him uneasy. She was visibly trembling again, and he held her fast. "Maybe Fatty'll be right back, and I'll try to find something out. Maybe nothing's happened yet. Maybe he'll bring her back."

They crossed over to the chapel behind the administrative building and knelt before the altar. It was dark, and Jurek turned his eyes toward the single lamp illuminating the monstrance. The shadow of Virtuoso, who'd been disturbed, passed among the pews; the smell of wax reached them from the altar. "Our Father, who art in heaven . . ." Jurek said under his breath.

"Our Father, who art in heaven . . ." Janka repeated very loudly, shaking more and more.

"Hallowed be thy name . . ."

"Hallowed be thy name . . ." Janka said, so resonantly that Jurek actually shuddered and started. "Let's pray more quietly," he asked.

"Your kingdom come," Janka said, more and more quickly and loudly. "Hail Mary, Mother of God, who shines in the gate of dawn kyrie eleison Lamb of God who guards the castle keep with your faithful people forgive us our trespasses as you takest away the sins of the world for I long for you . . ."

"Janka, what's with you? What's this babble?" Jurek asked, taking her by the hand.

Janka broke down in tears, huddled on the floor, and whispered as though to herself, "Hallowed be thy name, hallowed be thy name, hallowed be thy name . . ."

Jurek leaned over her and ordered her to stand up. "Please calm down. Maybe she'll come back, maybe she'll be back. Perhaps you have a fever."

In fact, her body was on fire beneath his hand, and he led her to her room. She laid down, pulled the blanket all the way up to her nose, poor little red thing, so that Jurek brewed her some tea and watched for a moment as she slurped it hot and unsweetened and finally, without a peep, fell asleep. He came back through the gate and sat on the bench in front of the administrative building. The sun was shining more and more, and the last clumps of snow disappeared in a flash, cleansing their sins, like whiteness ashamed of itself.

Someone was crying out in the distance; the screams were reaching closer to Jurek's back and were increasingly dreadful. They finally pierced his ear. "Where is she? Where has she gone? Sir, my lord, Mr. Bookkeeper, you have to tell me!" Antiplato, noticeably unwashed, sitting sadly on the bench, sought Jurek's eyes with an absent gaze.

He was in scruffy pajamas without a coat; his socks were on inside-out, one sandal was unclasped, and his nose was running.

"You have to quiet down," Jurek said, putting his finger over his mouth as though explaining it to a child. "What were you screaming like that for?"

"Where is she?" Antiplato bellowed even louder, and the veins popped out on his forehead. "Why did she leave so early? Where'd he take my Sonia? Where'd he take my sweetie, my tweetie? Where'd they go? You have to tell me, Mr. Official Man, you have to tell me. Bookkeeper, I'm begging you."

"Calm down!" Jurek growled. "The nurses will be here in a minute, and they'll lock you up. And they'll never let you out."

Antiplato hunched over, grabbed Jurek's hand, and started kissing it with abandon. "I'm afraid, sir, I'm so afraid, you have to do something, O Father, I don't want to be without Sonia, you have to do something, I'm so terribly afraid, O Father . . ."

Jurek tore his hand away angrily, but Antiplato slid even closer and tried to get on his lap. "I want my dad," he said, sobbing. "Pencil-Pusher, I want my dad." He threw both arms around Jurek. "I want my dad!" he shouted again with all his might.

"Please calm yourself this instant," Jurek said, hissing, and he pushed Antiplato away forcefully. "Please go to the pavilion this instant, or else there will be trouble. The guard's already looking at us, and in a minute they'll put you in a straitjacket. So get going, go lie down, I'll keep you posted, maybe something will come to light soon. Maybe Sonia will be right back. Now get to your room and don't come out."

Antiplato stood up timidly and returned along the path, staggering from grief. In the distance some pajamas grabbed him by the hand and led him quickly to the pavilion, casting glances to the side.

The car with Honnette and Kaltz had not yet arrived, and Jurek drew the note from Sonia out of his pocket. It must have been torn from a notebook in a hurry, for it had traces of ink from the previous page on its obverse; it was delicately rounded at the corners, and its edge was coated in a red thread of paint, like anything with any hope of lasting. It was just at that instant, in this conglomeration, that he saw Sonia's handwriting for the first time. It was not as pretty as his own: the letters suffocated in the narrow words, and there was hardly any bowing where there should have been, and no flourish, a sign of faith in oneself. Jurek touched them with his fingertips as though he wanted to check whether they were permanent or just black spots before his eyes, and then he started to read.

All I get is a "fare thee well," he thought at first, before feeling ashamed. *Again with the viscount, goddammit. Again, no kisses—abandoned and consoled—and Olek like a god, a young, nameless god, as if she didn't want to say his name or was afraid, "he was everything to me," a pure, incorporeal being, perhaps loved too much to be named in so common a fashion . . .*

He read out the sentences yet again, stared into them as though into a mirror, repeated them like aphorisms, last words, and their black luster seeped into his belly, permeated his skin once more through the strange osmosis of foreboding. As though something in Jurek had suddenly made itself known, but what, which veins, what cartilage, as if it had become clear that Jurek might have to—from now on, until the Last Supper, until the first dawn, which he will not see—might have to turn these sentences over in his dreams like a millstone, to chew them like an acrid vitamin, like his own tears upon waking. Therefore let us, too, accept their grace and instruction, let us learn them by heart, scratch them into our voluminous scrolls, learn them now, even if the grass is lovely and green today and Indian summer is raising its baton in the air. Let us all—the sad and the happy, countrymen and citizens—let us learn them now, so as not to die in bad humor under canopies of sheets, so as not to live without meaning, without tingling in our hands and a tickle in our throats, let us learn them, for I assure you, though I know as much as you do, like you I get up every day and go to sleep every evening, I assure you that that piece of paper is the best thing that's been done for us, that's been thought about our life here and the road laid out before us, that it's the best of the optional prayers that have been written down for us. Let us learn them with Jurek Pay-Per-ek from *A* to *Z,* from *A* to *Z:*

Dear Jurek!

Be good to Janka, and don't think ill of me. I loved you very much. You're a really great guy.

Strange how things work out! Seems like it's the way it had to be! Say hi to everybody I got to know and love through you, especially to your mother. And give *him* another kiss from me: he was everything to me. Fare thee well.

S.

P.S. Be happy!

S.

Why, in this final moment, was S., formerly known as Sonia, as she was choking on the words under her ballpoint, as the crooks of her hand crawled as though with ants and her mouth trembled like disturbed water, thinking of her signature, why was her signature on her mind? Why did she double it as though she were breathing twice onto a mirror, why did she leave two mists in that transparence, two strokes in nothingness? And why did she limit it to the very beginning, to the first letter, why did she roll up her full rug on the floor of our existence, why did she leave a grain from the delicate stalk? I pledge that I will answer these questions as best I can; when it comes down to it, I'm nearly out of alibis, since I take the commuter train here every Tuesday, sit on the little benches, and feel the attentive gazes of those white hospital jackets. In my heart I am begging them with puppy-dog eyes not to tie my hands just yet, not to bind my sentences, for I still have a few letters to tap out, a few more words to impart; a few more letters, a few more words, and perhaps I'll make it yet.

"Perhaps I'll make it yet," Jurek said quietly as he hopped onto the train, as he ran down Jeruzalemski Boulevard, and then Marszałkowski, Krucza, and Wilcza. "Perhaps I'll make it yet," he repeated hopefully, because Kaltz whispered to him right after he'd come back with Honnette that money could get you somewhere with the Gestapo in Pruszków. For now, Herr Jerzy, the folk back in Germany have greater and greater needs—as they often say around here—given the circumstance, but today in Pruszków they're stuffed from the holidays and they don't need much of anything. Perhaps we can still make it before they take her off somewhere, lock her up in Warsaw or something. "If only Olek were here and had some cash on him," Jerzy said to himself, running with what remained of his strength across Piękna and passing through the gate by Myśliwiecka, where Olek was supposed to be at the appointed hour.

They'd taken separate rickshaws to the station so as to get there faster, and before him Jurek saw the cheeks of the rickshaw driver, wet with perspiration: with every push of the pedals he tilted first to the left, then to the right, and pressed now his left hand, now his right into the handlebars, his entire body worked and strained so terribly that it steamed and rippled under his jacket, it tightened up so under his pants that each moment seemed full of that moving mass, of that straining presence, of that evidence of being on a narrow leather seat.

They jumped out of the commuter train, running all-out; only Jurek stumbled a little, but he caught his glasses in his hand, and it was Olek who, on leaving the house, first said, "Run." They ran a bit along the tracks, took a shortcut through a few gardens, and then pressed straight along the main road. Dusk had already fallen, the stars were already pulsing according to their own relativity, Jurek and Olek's steps beat several meters ahead of them with an increasingly dark echo.

Yes, time had already forked like a river at its mouth. Here on Grodziska Street the houses huddled together, flickering their bright windows, and there, in the Kopry district, in the glow of the stars, the poplars grew straight into the sky and the stones in the furrows formed their own constellations; here, at number sixteen, the Gestapo building, behind two motorcycles and a truck, two men of lower rank were smoking cigarettes, and there, a ways out of town, the eye of the glade followed the moon's finger. Here Jurek and Olek were offering real American smokes, trying to learn something, here they went inside, now they were talking with someone in a dark storeroom, they waited for somebody else, gave someone something and chipped more in, and there the juniper bushes hadn't grown as high as the soles of little shoes; here they told Olek and Jurek to come back tomorrow afternoon, around two would be best because then they'd definitely be able to set it all straight, and here, on the sly, with the rest of their hope, they took Grodziska back to Tworki; there, night and day no longer existed, neither the hours nor the minutes followed from one to the next, and there, high above the juniper bushes on a thick bough on a thin poplar, high above the ground, there hung, there swung, Sonia, hanged.

The starry sky above Sonia, the old dress on Sonia. Its blue and yellow spots blew about in the light gusts of air, and, as though compelled, Sonia dangled and swayed with them. Death had come, and Sonia rocked from left to right, from right to left, she shifted over the earth like a metronome for humanity, like the pendulum of existence, like steps in the last dance. Sonia's arms were fast beside her, they guarded Sonia's sides, but Sonia's head was slightly tilted, placed sleepily in the noose, for death had come. The pillbox hat lay upside-down on a stone, it had bedded down softly on the earth. Death had come, and Sonia's hair, unpinned, with no band, fell over her face, whispered something into her mouth, looked into her eyes. And the soles of her little shoes, because death had come, were touching at their tips. With each swing of the rope they turned quietly in a single, fluent harmony, following her knees, slightly parted, filling out her gray stockings, pulled a bit down, for death had come. Nothing had lasted, and nothing had passed. Sonia was dead, they'd hanged Sonia out of town, in Kopry, Sonia hung from a poplar, and death had come.

When they returned, breathless, Janka was lying in the dark room. Their mouths were dry, and they threw themselves on what was left of the holiday compote in the liter jar. Janka got up to make them tea, and only now did Jurek turn the light on, anxiously, as though he were touching his own eye. They didn't look at each other, and they drank, wanting the tea to last forever, a sea of respite. Jurek had to lie down for a while because he was feeling weak, and when he moved Sonia's pillow he saw the watch on the sheet. It was no longer ticking, no longer clicking, it wasn't wound, and it rested at its leisure in those white depths like a mechanical brandy bottle. With an obstinacy that was difficult to resist, it indicated that it was five o'clock, and that in New York the eleventh hour of the evening had descended forever.

At the eleventh hour of the evening the rays of the morning sun reached in through the window and woke them. They'd slept so sloppily, Olek on an overcoat on Sonia's bed, Jurek in his clothes next to Janka, who was naturally curled up in a ball so that there would be as little of her as possible, and they didn't say a word to each other until after they'd each finished their third tea. They led Janka off to the office, and as they were hurrying along the path, they had to loosen the scarves around their constricted necks, so warm had they become, so hot did they feel under the oppressive blue sky. Jurek waited for Kaltz, spoke with him off to the side, and now they could go, though two o'clock was still a long way off. But that's said too easily, stated too effortlessly, for they were now pressing forward toward Pruszków, and now they were in Pruszków, now they were milling helplessly around the Gestapo, going in, coming out, and still waiting because two o'clock was yet a long way off. Maybe they'd better save what it would cost them, but then why not, such a trifle means little in the bulk of the day, just dollars and zlotys in the face of all those zeroes. "I don't have anything left; I've given away my last grosz," Olek openly admitted, and his honesty was met with honesty.

"*Erledigt.*" Olek and Jurek detected a guttural *hochdeutsch* accent. "*Exekutivmassnahme, Zugrunde gehen. Entschuldigen Sie, bitte.*" But, of course, as you'd expect, then it was "Get out, *raus, raus,*" because the fellow had only just dozed off in the olive grove.

"I'll kill them," Olek screamed as soon as he'd run out of the Gestapo. "I'll kill every German I see. I've killed too few of them so far. I'll crush every kraut who comes my way. I'll keep killing them as long as I live. God, I hate them! I'm going to kill every last German I find!" Then he suddenly started to sob, sat down on the curb, and Jurek took him by the elbow and gave him a clumsy hug. They stood a while among the passersby, who stopped out of curiosity with their parcels and their mesh bags in their hands, and Jurek felt how, somewhere deep under his hands, Olek was leaving himself and turning into a great big dead tree.

They wandered around for a long time, and finally they came to the Kopry district. "They brought her right at noon," said the boy from the last shack. "And strung her up right away. They left fast. She hung there all night. In the morning, as soon as it got light, we buried her by the woods so that there'd be a burial because, you know, that's how it can be done."

A small cross made from two branches nailed together stood on the mound, and the clay was still moist after a full day of sunshine. Jurek knelt right down in the mud and cried into his folded hands, and Olek didn't even go up to the grave, but turned around; though someone was calling after him, he ran like a deaf striker toward the village. Jurek wanted to chase him down, but how? So he tried to concentrate on his praying. But as he was reciting the "Our Father," he heard "Dear Jurek," and he saw before his eyes the cramped, black letters of Sonia's letter. The rumbling steps indicated that Olek was back, the clang of metal that the ground beneath them was hard and deep.

Still silent, Olek gave one spade to Jurek, and he swung the other into the mound.

"Olek, please stop," Jurek said. "Stop, please. What are you doing?"

"Dig," Olek mumbled, and he took another swing. "Dig, Jerzy. It'll go faster."

"I can't. You've lost it. We can't do this," Jurek said, setting the spade aside.

"Dig, Jerzy. We have to."

Jurek turned up a few clumps, then a few more. It was still a long way to Sonia; Olek scooped up whole shovelfuls of sand and clay. There where Jurek's tears fell, where the sharp spades were breaking through, where everything was settled and buried, that's where all the shades and colorful threads were slumming, where the dress hid nothing, where the blood had no drainage, where rhyme found no rhyme. Jurek's sobs grew louder and louder, and he sank his face heavily, with all his strength, into his hands, the clay caking on his eyelids.

It was still a little farther to Sonia when Olek put the spade aside, knelt down, and now carefully removed the sand from the folds of her dress, from between her shins, from shoes that were squeezed together. Her face finally revealed itself in its vanishing, in the farthest distance, and in the negative column one would have to turn life and everything inside-out—to call birth death, emptiness an eye, a crack a mouth—to describe this face, to take it in one's hand and name it, for it to have a name. Olek took a couple of steps, as if he wanted to run again, but then he leaned over the grave, removed the chain from around Sonia's neck, and placed it in his pocket without wiping it off. He noticed a protuberance in the stocking on her left foot. He gently removed the material and pulled out a paper bag. From the bag he took her ID, two pictures of people he did not know—an older man and a woman—a pocket calendar, and a drawing of a house with a garden. He placed them back in the bag, and he slipped the bag into her stocking a bit higher so that it would never fall out. He quickly filled in the grave and lifted Jurek from the ground. They turned back toward the village, and every so often Jurek would stop suddenly, as though he couldn't cry unless he were standing still, and Olek pulled him by the arm. They arrived at the Tworki station in silence.

"Did you know?" Jurek asked, and Olek indicated that he did not.

"I'm going," he said a moment later, and Jurek nodded.

"I'll never get this. Even though she knew that someone loved her. Even though you loved her. Why did she leave you? How could she?"

The sun had already faded behind the poplars, and between the dusk and the earth what remained of the light froze like water after the frost. They stood in an icy circle of quiet, and Jurek felt that Olek's gaze was forcing its way through his pupils and into his body, filling it with the cold, unbearable, white silence of death.

The distant whistle reached them from Milanówek and Podkowa. "She never called me by my name," Olek suddenly said toward the sky. "But she always knew which door I was coming out of. She was always standing in the right place, even though I came in a different car each time. I walked right out to her. I have no more reason to live, Jerzy."

When the train rolled up to the platform, Jurek felt like he wanted to get on and ride to the end of who-knows-what, and after it disappeared around the bend, he stared for a long time at the bare tracks, along which flowed the blood from its chilly, two-track metal veins. Then he noticed Janka at the gate and quickly approached her. Again he slept in Sonia's bed, and when he woke up it took him a long time to realize what room he was in.

■ □ ■ □ ■

CHAPTER TWENTY

FOR THE EARLY EASTER THAT YEAR THEY WERE INVITED TO HIS mother's house. Janka didn't much want to go anywhere, and when, at five o'clock, Jurek triumphantly brought a few eggs obtained from a certain someone so that they could paint them together before services, she looked at him in a sort of daze and wanted to gobble them up as soon as they were boiled. In the end she agreed to go, wearing the coffee-with-cream dress, for Jurek had emphasized the need for suitable attire. She looked curiously around the commuter train, to the left and right.

"Are you looking for someone?" Jurek asked.

She blushed. "It's the first time you're taking me to Warsaw," she said. "So many new faces."

"Maybe you'll find your man on the tram," Jurek grunted, satisfied when she blushed even more. "Your chances are also good on the street."

It was a Saturday afternoon, the sun was shining, and Jurek wanted to show Janka Ulrychów before the curfew. They went to the pond, but the Indians and the bandits somehow weren't able to surface from his memory, and he went quiet. He just waved his hand, and they cut across the park. Mama was already waiting at the window, and she greeted them with a freshly baked cake.

"A very fine mazurka," Janka said after the second slice, gathering the last crumbs meticulously from the plate.

"Mazurek," Jerzy mumbled through a full mouth. "We say, 'a

very fine mazurek.' Or even better, 'a delicious mazurek.' Or, 'what an exquisite mazurek.' It really is an excellent mazurek, mmm, mmm."

Janka's face flushed, and she quickly washed the compote glasses. But one broke so that Jurek just said again aloud that it's good luck, though maybe not his. In the evening, Witek—the insult added to injury, the last hole in the bridge of Janka's life—came over to play bridge, and the round stretched into eternity, contrary to the law of gravity, that sinking of one's usual shame into the ground. What's with the clubs already, Janka always seeing black? It's like mourning, no other color, and Jurek bridled and Janka turned crimson and pale in turn, the rainbow before the next storm. Fortunately, Mama took pity on them: she gathered the fortune-telling cards, and Janka could relax, cover herself under a blanket on the couch, turn her head away from the world of this Warsaw family in the fifth year of the war, in what was the first millennium of this nation, give or take a few years, which Mama was just now enumerating from the future and which were forced out under the lightbulb before the last good-night.

"Good day, good day," Jurek twittered on Monday morning, and he drizzled a thin, ever-so-thin trickle of water on the sleeping Janka, on Janka quite distinctly asleep, from the liter bottle. She woke up screaming, and splash, he poured all the rest on her and then, with an upraised arm, calmly waited until the last drop fell from the bottle. Janka broke down crying.

"Why did you soak me?" she asked, catching her breath between one sob and the next. "What did I do to you?"

"It's the Easter custom: Soaking Monday," Jurek announced triumphantly, but Janka kept crying.

"What did I do to you?" she asked, burying her face in her hands.

"But it's a custom," Jurek said, a little disconcerted. "I'm about to soak Witek—he's still snoring in the kitchen." He looked at her suspiciously, and he took out the second bottle from behind his back.

"A custom? What custom?" Janka muttered, and she didn't talk to him for a couple of hours, though a moment later Witek was wringing out his pajamas over the sink, and a vase of water had fallen across the shirt of Jurek's very good mother and didn't hold back a single drop.

Jurek was also quiet, quite like he'd been yesterday, when he hadn't made a peep except at Mama's insistence, but only picked at his egg and mumbled, "Happy holiday."

Janka didn't want to go on the holiday stroll, and when Jurek came back with pussy willows in hand, Mama placed her finger over her mouth and dragged him into the kitchen. "She's been sitting at your desk since two o'clock," she whispered to him. "She may be crying. She's packed her things. Take care of her. It's in the cards."

Actually, she was leaning over a leaf of the best prewar paper and holding his pencil in her mouth, the same one he'd been chewing for a couple of months now. He tiptoed up to her; the paper was blank, and Janka was somewhere else. "What are you doing?" he asked. "Are you writing something?"

Janka flinched and turned her face toward him. "Jurek, I'm from Berdichev," she said.

"I'm sorry? What was that?"

"I'm telling you that I'm from Berdichev."

Someone laughed—Jurek, probably; someone cackled—that was maybe Jurek; someone was laughing, at first hard, and then was giggling shrilly with his hand on his head, and that was definitely Jurek Mazurek, just now by the desk, now on the couch, still cracking up, now losing it: "Hold me back, people! I'm losing my mind. It would seem, ha ha, that I've lost my mind. A nutcase, nutcase, not right in the head. Very, yes, quite ill mentally. Hey everybody, yoo hoo, quite sick. Tworki, Tworki everywhere, Tworki in my room, Tworki in my home, Tworki in the whole country." Jurek lay down on his back and kicked his legs joyfully about. "Tworki, Tworki, it's Tworki everywhere. King Mieszko the First Tworki. King Jan Sobieski Tworki. The victorious Battle of Tworki, ha ha, the Third Partition of Tworki, the Tworki Uprising, in March and April, in December and February. People, people, hold me back, for I am from Tworki! What's your name? Tworki Tame. What's your other? Tworki butter!" Jurek turned onto his stomach and rolled onto the floor. "I'm from Tworki!" he screamed again.

Janka pressed her hands against her ears, and the pencil was against her temple, ready to fire. When Jurek settled down, she lay her head down on the blank page like onto a small sheet so that it might envelop and wrap her up, albeit from below. Jurek stood up and leaned over her back. He wanted to pluck the pencil out from her fingers, but Janka held it fast. "Leave it."

"Let me have it," he said quietly, and Janka unclenched her hand. He put the pencil into the little jar with the other pencils, pulled the slightly damp paper from under Janka's head, and folded it carefully. He pulled Janka's hands away from her ears, leaned over once again, and whispered something, but who knows what, because at just that moment, outside the window, the tram rolled by on its two rails, and one raven cawed to another on the tree.

They had to be back at work the following day, on Tuesday at eight o'clock, no exceptions, in boundless longing, to where there stood an empty desk and a chair pressed too closely behind it. Mama looked at the tram stop outside the window, and Jurek hugged Janka so that Mama could go on fussing and wringing her hands, clinging to her strange hope. From the tram they ran straight to the commuter train, they made it at the last second, and they sat in the last car. Jurek held Janka's hand and looked around discreetly to the left and right. It emptied out after Włochy, and Jurek asked Janka, who was staring out at the garden plots passing by, at the disciplined rows of shrubs: "Do you know why she did it? I can't stop thinking about it."

" 'You can live,' " she said to the shrubs. "That's what she whispered to me. Back then, in the morning. 'You can live.' "

"That's what she said?"

" 'You can live.' "

"Exactly that?"

"That's it. 'You can live.' "

"She could have, too. In Paradise, in Tworki. Snug as a bug."

" 'You can live.' That's what she said to me. But she couldn't anymore. Understand?"

"No. Where was she going, to whom?" Jurek asked the paths abutting the rails. "What was she looking for? Do you know where she was going? You should know, anyway, you saw her going somewhere."

Janka said nothing.

"Was she going to see someone? Did she have to go? Did someone want something from her?"

Janka said nothing, and the trees outside the window passed like the syllables of an inhuman silence.

"Was she visiting someone?" Jurek asked a cluster of clouds in the sky. "Was she working for someone? Did she know something we don't know? Had she figured something out?"

There were fewer little houses by the tracks now, and they would have been strange to live in.

"Was something wrong with her? Was she running from something? Couldn't she just be in love with Olek, and that's it? You should know. Someone should know."

"We're here," Janka said to the bicycle by the fence.

"I feel awful," Jurek told Janka. "I really don't think I'll make it. Something's not right with me. Help me."

The train came to a screeching halt; Jurek jumped out first and gave Janka his hand. From the direction of Milanówek and Podkowa twilight was setting in, and Tworki's modest little lights pulsed warmly, tenderly. Huddled together, they passed through the gate as if through the door of a plush bedroom.

■ □ ■ □ ■

CHAPTER TWENTY-ONE

THE KEYS UNPRESSED, THE MOMENTS UNOCCUPIED. AND FINE, THE days passed half baked, swallowed down flavorlessly. Jurek spoke less and less, and it happened that he spent whole evenings with Janka in silence, playing Battleship, drinking tea, and waiting to fall asleep. He'd arranged it with Kaltz so that he wouldn't go to Pruszków, wouldn't go there for anything in the world, Herr Director. And when Jurek and Janka had just a bit of time for themselves, they took a walk. His feet, too flat and poorly shod for silent marches, for blazing trails in the walled-in space, continued to ache. Path after path, oaks and poplars like kilometer posts, another lap around the equator, another year in Tworki, a whole life on one's feet. One can already see the first buds on the bushes, the cats sniffing at each other's tails. *But how many more steps, and what's it to anybody?* Jurek said to himself. *And who needs more days?*

It was Sunday, so he'd been walking since morning, since leaving the chapel, and now he finally sat down, tired out, on the bench by the main path, his face to the sun. He got so warm that he dozed off. When he opened his eyes, he saw that Antiplato was sitting next to him. Perhaps he was dozing as well: his eyes were closed, his face sunken, emaciated. He hadn't buttoned his coat over his pajamas, and it happened that he'd put on a second pair of socks under his sandals, for stripes of a different color showed through the holes. When Jurek moved, Antiplato opened his eyes and said quietly, "Beautiful weather this time of year. Soon spring will be in full bloom."

Jurek kept quiet; he wanted to sleep, to walk, to sit and sleep, so that another day would pass.

"What happened?" Antiplato asked.

"What's that?"

"Tell me, Mr. Bookkeeper."

"What am I supposed to tell you?" Jurek asked, bristling.

"About Sonia," Antiplato said, smiling slightly.

"What about her?"

"Everything."

"Why about her? Anyway, you know. She's gone. She's dead. She died. She's met her maker. She's kicked the bucket. She departed this world near the end of December, in the year of our Lord nineteen hundred forty-three." Jurek bristled again, fell silent, and Antiplato's gaze sank grimly into his socks, as he raised his left buttock slightly. After a moment he looked at Jurek with sudden excitement.

"Hungry for a week. All it takes is for you, Mr. Delivery Man, not to go with Kaltz, and we have zilch on our plates. Mr. Supply Man, you'll take care of it!"

Jurek smiled weakly and shook his head, lost in thought, *The soul's crazy, life's crazy, dreams are crazy, dread is dread.* He was seized by such sadness that he hunched over and grabbed his belly.

"Tell me," he heard over him, and he felt a hand in his hair. "Tell me, Mr. Office Man, tell me what happened."

"What? What?" he asked, casting the hand from his mop. "What the hell am I supposed to say? Don't you have anyone else to pester today? Did you have to come to me? Don't you see I'm resting? Go ask Goethe to tell you something; he's standing right there behind the oak, and he's bored. I'm sleeping. I'm having a really good sleep."

"Tell me about Sonia," Antiplato said, and he stuck his hand into his coat pocket. "About Sonia, and about Sonia's death."

Jurek said nothing.

"I'm asking you, Mr. Employee Man."

Jurek kept his mouth stubbornly shut.

"I'm begging you, Mr. Accountant Man."

"Why should I tell you?"

"You have to tell me. You have to."

Jurek was as quiet as a rock.

"Say it, Mr. Bookkeeper: Sonia, Sonia, Sonia, Sonia."

Jurek bit his lips.

"Say it, Mr. Bookkeeper."

"I'm not saying anything," Jurek screamed, and again he leaned over.

"Say it, Mr. Bookkeeper: human being." Antiplato gave Jurek a glove that had fallen off the bench, and he pulled the other back from the edge.

"Say it, Mr. Bookkeeper: humanity."

"I won't say it . . ." Jurek screamed, and he started to sob.

Antiplato touched his shoulder lightly and whispered conspiratorially, as though someone else were listening in: "I'll help you, Mr. Calculation Man. You have to start at the beginning. For instance: 'Sonia, a bonny lass was she . . .' And now a new line . . . 'I met her . . . I met her long ago . . .' " Antiplato stammered, and then he said timidly, "It should be a kind of rhyme to Sonia."

"What rhyme? Where's the rhyme? Why a rhyme? There is no rhyme! And now there won't be any. Anyway, you know," Jurek whispered, crying.

Antiplato remembered something, and he started to feel about himself nervously. "For you, Mr. Accounts, I have here . . . I wrote especially for you . . . it took me three days to put it together . . . oh, here it is." He removed a crumpled piece of paper from his pajama pocket, stood before the bench, pulled up his pants, raised the piece of paper right up to his eyes, and started to read in a solemn tone:

"The gramophone's playing,
Couple glides by couple,
The record is baying,
Scraped by an ancient needle.

Our Jurek glides with Janka,
They've left the ground behind,
A dance their *lingua franca,*
A language so refined.

Our Sonia's lost in dancing,
Her eyes scrunch up with joy,
Her kisser's red enhancing,
Her hair is Olek's toy.

The lamp, though it's a-shining
(With Sonia's features dark),
And now the light is waning,
For love is on the make.

But then we're dancing further,
There's room enough for all,
But soon the fun is over,
The scratchy disk appalls."

Before the ultimate stanza Antiplato took a deep breath and stood there gravely, heels in:

"Misfortunate machine,
Commanding all our woes!
You've cut short her routine
By flicking up your nose."

"Well?" Antiplato asked, after a moment's silence, biting his lips and sitting back down next to Jurek. "How do you find it, Mr. Surplus?"

"How do I find what?" Jurek whispered with some effort, still balled up. "Oh, yes, I think it needs a little more work."

"And how's that?" Antiplato muttered, with a slight flush on his cheeks.

"You could tweak it here and there."

"Tweak what, then? What's this tweaking?" Antiplato spoke angrily, and he was tapping his fingers nervously against the bench, slightly raising his left buttock.

"Well, a few formulations. And besides, the ending is not too clear. And you should check the scansion." Jurek lifted his head and looked furtively at his neighbor. "But on the whole it's on a very respectable level," he added quickly.

"Truly?" Antiplato brightened up. "Truly? And now it's your turn, Mr. Enumerator. For starters, a rhyme for Sonia."

Jurek was again looking at his own belly and had tears in his throat. "I can't, I can't," he whispered from his very entrails.

"You must, Jerzy, you must."

"The first rhyme to Miss Sonia . . ."

"You must, son, you must . . ."

"Green leaves and petals of begonias," Jerzy groaned with great difficulty through his tears.

Antiplato actually jumped for joy and heaved a deep sigh. "You see, Mr. Bookkeeper, you see?"

Jurek leaned on the bench and looked straight ahead. In the distance, over the Helenów Forest, the blue of the sky was emerging from space and breaking off toward its own path.

"So what else was there?" Antiplato said quietly, and he slid closer to Jerzy, but not too close.

"What else was there?" Jerzy repeated pensively, and he wiped his tears with the back of his hand. "What else was there? What did it look like?"

For a minute he whispered something under his breath and passed the index finger of his right hand over each of the fingers of his left, calculating something. Finally he announced in a quiet, weary tone, "In Tworki, then, the accountant Sonia worked around the clock, hired in '40, of Berdichev stock, barely had I met her before I wrote . . . I wrote . . ." Jurek stammered and thought it out.

"A road . . ." Antiplato said.

"Why a road? That makes no sense."

"An ode, then . . . I wrote an ode."

"Barely had I met her before I wrote an ode, praising her in worthy lines, because she was sublime. That's how it went . . . in the beginning."

Antiplato leapt up joyfully again, fell back, careful of his left buttock, and patted his belly. "But we're going strong." He looked Jurek in the eye. "We should write it together. A little by Mr. Accounts Man, a little by Antiplato. We could do the whole thing. About how the town was built, about summer vacations, about reaching the heights and new customs." He was clearly getting carried away in his daydreams, and he put one sandal over the other. "But we could do it together! About voyages by ocean and sea, finite and infinite, about workers leaving their factories, about cops and robbers, about poor pensioners, about shepherding, about the national spirit, about spies yet to be found out, about our mundane day from eight to four, about gothic castles and the return of heroes, how they are always victorious in battle." He fell silent, and for a moment he stroked his scruffy beard in thought. "Oh yes . . . but first we have to wrap this up . . . so what was next, Mr. Chair Master? Maybe something like: bookkeeper Sonia loved . . . loved"—he was stammering again—"loved the patients . . ."

"We've already said that she was an accountant."

"So what? The repetition's good. It should be repeated."

Jurek was again looking into the distance. An otherworldly flag had been unfurled: the golden orb of the sun stood in the very center of the sky. He inhaled all the way down to his diaphragm and recited:

"Our S., the fair accountant, she loved me till the end;
her neck will be in stripes, her body hanging in the light.
I got from her a letter, which could not time suspend.
But where to send my answer: to Berdichev I write?"

"Okay," Antiplato gasped with relief. "Now we're getting somewhere. Only more detail, and in order. You promise, Mr. Bookkeeper?"

"I don't know."

"Promise me, Mr. Accounts Man."

Jurek drew the letter from his pocket. "You see, she signed up to die." He sighed deeply. "And now I have to sign up, too. To die. To end my life. Evidently it's my fate. That's what's written for me. To write my whole life up to Berdichev."

Antiplato nodded. Jurek turned to face him and, pointing at his own chest and trying to smile as if it were a joke, said in a voice not his own: "Here's where Poland will write."

Antiplato nodded and straightened out his sandal, which had slipped off his foot.

"But, but," he said, stirring violently after a long silence, "do you happen to know, Mr. Figures, what time it is?"

"It's past twelve. Twelve-o-nine."

"I have to run," Antiplato said. "At quarter past twelve I'm getting a shot from Dr. Okonowski. Already my seventh this week."

He tore himself from the bench, pulled his pajama shirttails down underneath his buttoned coat, and moved hastily toward Pavilion J, muttering something under his breath. The flag of the universe fluttered in the light, warm air above the Helenów Forest, and Jurek felt a weariness and an irresistible, sweet sleepiness. He pulled his legs up onto the bench and in a moment was asleep with his head in the collar of his coat and his hands folded across his belly, which rose rhythmically, as if something there didn't have enough room and wanted to fly out toward Tworki's main path.

■ □ ■ □ ■

CHAPTER TWENTY-TWO

YOU WOULD HAVE ALLOWED THE MAN HIS REST, HIS SLEEP, LET HIS yap-yappety mouth take a breather, his fingers stop knocking, such a comfortable bench, such lovely weather, but not here, always someone's footsteps on the path, voices over his collar, the rumble of the train into each stop, and then continuing on its way to the last station, to the end of the line, to Warsaw. I find it hard, when I'm primed for the telling, to wrap this story up, I get a bit protracted, and if you'll permit me, I'll leave out the yawning and lower the legs back to gravel.

For where might one seek material for what comes next, where, if not under our very feet, in the depths of the very earth, in a quaking stomach where minerals glitter, cluster together, and are joined into clumps, into clods, hardening in bands of ruddy iron? It suffices to dig them out, take them to the foundries; it suffices to blow the dust from them, to chip at them with hammers and toss them into the open-hearth furnace. Then the pig-iron pours out, a river of hot flame, but what we and history need is the solid alloy, the refined steel, the metal for sharpening, to be filled with powder and sent out among the privateers, among the groups armed and ready for combat, among the assault units. The bullet has a caliber, it stings on one end. Mama's cooking up the first soup of August. Today in Starówka, Olek a.k.a. Lula blew away at least four krauts, one such führer point blank in the stomach, the rest from an attic on Freta Street. The bullet flies along its trajectory, smashes the wall on Freta, a wardrobe crashed out of the sky, Olek was lurking briefly by the entrance. Smoke, smoke over the town, not so far from Ulrychów, though here the birds are singing. The magazine is full of bullets. Have to bring wood into the kitchen, Mama is panting and wiping the sweat from her brow. The wind has died down over Warsaw, iron streams are swelling in the ground, Olek is running along the wall, a shell hits the red brick. Mama mixes the soup, suddenly a tank rolls into the yard, such alien houses, untamed since they're not shot up, the magazine's empty, a bullet cuts the world in two. A whistle, the whistle of the flying bullet, the ground is shaking from the direction of Warsaw, air greets you in the window, not far from here to Mama. Olek was firing again, the kraut fell on his back, now the whole brigade is after Olek, both quickly around that corner. Now Mama's turned around, the soup is hot, a bullet flies over the table and hits Mama in the heart. Mama's on the floor, lying there, her dress red, the soup made from cucumbers. The magazine is full again, the unit wants to hold the house, and Olek yells something to the Magnificents and keeps pulling the trigger. On the other side, the Germans, Olek covers from the flank, everyone's run in through the gate, only he's stayed back. Some commotion behind the house, another mortar's landed, chips of paving in the air, Olek risks it. Olek skirts the gunfire, Olek risks it, he gets another German, he takes no cover. The next bullet flies, it's marked for someone of twenty-two years, Freta Street, number sixteen, the thirteenth of August. Olek is dead, Olek is gone, the trunk of his body split, the wood of his bones, the wood of his bones shattered at the base of the cross. His temple touches the ground, his calf-high boots are weirdly lowered and muted, cut short, and his legs drawn up, so sad without a ball. A river of blood encircles the corpse, on its bank lies the former Olek, striker, representative, leader, and sometime blond boy in love. The bullets whistle without interruption, they're still smacking into the nothingness that is Olek, the bright down of his hair flutters lightly in the breeze. Olek's not breathing, the air's stifling on Freta Street and in Ulrychów. Witek, Stefek, and Heniek, crouched in the gate, are looking at Olek, who's been fouled once and for all, mowed down evenly with the ground, and they're yelling something awful before them, for they too will die the day after tomorrow from three and four bursts of machine-gun fire. Olek's not breathing, there's black smoke over Warsaw, a distant dark cloud over Warsaw when one is looking from the platform in Tworki, from the very tracks among the poplars because the train's no longer running.

It's still burning, Jurek thought between the rails, taking big steps from one tie to the next, breaking the shadows of the poplars on the tracks with the contour of his body, which was still preserved, or rather saved. The earth is still shaking, as though something were going on inside it, swelling and bursting, and the city was still burning, and one could walk those tracks all the way to one's death, from paradisiacal Tworki to the first tongues of fire, to the very depths of hell, where Olek was, with Witek, Mama, and our whole existence in sudden focus, in the machine gun of the moment. Anyway, he'd very nearly been there himself, as soon as quitting time came one got on the train, the one at five after four, though it was more reliable and prudent to get on the one before that and go barely three kilometers, where the train had stopped for the eternity of August, and maybe for the coming months, and instead, at five, he was heading back to the gate of the verdant grounds and to paths thirsty for our flat feet. He'd nearly been there himself, nearly had a rifle in his hand, assuming they'd have given him one, because he shot quite wide, because in training exercises before the war, from ten meters, he could hit as many points as there were diopters in his glasses, and there were a lot, and at forty meters he'd confuse a person with a post, which some posts did not merit, and he could have easily become a topsy-turvy soldier, the prodigal son of Our Mother the War and Our Lady of Ammunition, an astigmatic casualty in the euphoria of liberation.

Sixty laps, forward and back along the tracks, from quitting time till dinner with Janka, now waiting with tea and slices of bread, four for him, the bookkeeper foot soldier, only two for her, your average accountant. With the start of October, his legs no longer wanted to walk, the tracks no longer had anywhere to lead him, and the smoke over the city stopped luring him with its mysterious shadow. The following autumn started like a premature end to the year, the penultimate section of the ultimate settling of accounts.

■ □ ■ □ ■

CHAPTER TWENTY-THREE

THE JERRIES WERE GONE BY THE END OF DECEMBER. THE NUTCASES, having tossed their robes on in a hurry, crowded behind the trees and stared goggle-eyed in the morning mist as Honnette supervised the property being loaded onto a truck. When all the heavy trunks had been checked off by Jabłkowska and rested neatly next to one another, like the little heads of grandchildren in sleeping bags from Schwarzwald, Frau Honnette came out of the administrative building and, paying no mind to the white of her fur coat, carried the gramophone right up to the truck bed. She showed Johann where to put it, cast a glance at Jurek, and, for a moment that lasted longer than the whole war, fixed her eyes on Janka, who was standing next to Jurek by the gate; finally, without waiting for the obsequious opening of the door, she climbed into the back seat of the black Mercedes.

Anyway, who was there to open the doors courteously, to sanctify with crossed fingers as one should the first dawning of a promotion, the harbinger of a raise, because Kaltz had already vanished from among the living, the jabbering, and retreating. Kaltz, absent, excused, humbly buried, had lain somewhere in the sands of Tworki for some two weeks, had seen snow from the cleaner side, had given all of himself to the ground. Back then, going to Pruszków every day, even when there was nothing there to buy, sometimes even roaming there without a car, traipsing about the fields and side streets God knows where, and what for, going so far as to ask, we should add, for a knife, anything steel.

"*Banditen* on the road," Honnette had muttered to Jerzy, when he himself had brought the body back from the Gestapo one November evening. "You are now in charge of all the accounts because Quick is these days too stupid—no change in salary." Yes, the *Banditen* sliced Kaltz's throat in one stroke, all for a golden signet ring and some loose change in his back pocket, and with a single blow they put Jurek on the job. The *über*-bookkeeper thus did what he could; every two hours he walked among the desks, half of which were already empty, and looked menacingly at Jabłkowska; once he stopped as close before Quick as the front was to the Vistula; menacing and nonchalant, he cast down his own balance confidently, aggressively before Quick's irrelevant figures, just as he now leaned against the gate with dignity and modesty next to the best living woman accountant in a coffee-and-cream dress in the morning, waiting coldly, patiently to seize the whole thing, recovered like memory, from the gate to the wall, from pavilion to pavilion.

The truck had already rolled out through the gate, and Honnette went up to the Mercedes. Behind the trunks of the trees, bright spots started to shimmer and suddenly moved forward like paint squeezed from tubes. Honnette swept over the administrative building with his eyes, the sky concentrated over Tworki, and beckoned toward Jurek. When Jurek had taken three steps forward, Honnette tossed out, now from his seat, an *auf Wiedersehen* so loudly that he might as well have been saying good-bye to all the poplars, to the pavilions and paths, and he slammed the door without waiting for an answer. The car moved, the spots stood in a row before Jurek, grins on their increasingly distinct faces, yet still quiet, unsure of whether they were allowed to laugh.

"Lunch at the usual time," Jurek said amidst the first titters. "Please break up and return to your buildings."

Cackling and chatting animatedly among themselves, the robes went back along the main path and ran in groups to their rooms. Jurek went up to Janka, who was pressing her cheeks through the bars of the gate and staring at the tracks. "What now?" she asked when he'd thrown his face in, too.

"Nothing. It's over. We've survived the war. Nothing else can happen to us now."

They went for a walk. They took the trail that bordered the

grounds to the forest, and they stood for a moment by the river, which was covered in a couple of spots by thick ice on the bank; they went back through the birches near the garden plot, and their whiteness was still cold, and each time they later came here after finishing work, they checked the encrustation of spring on the lower branches. At the end of March it had gotten unusually warm, and the white of the bark already had a kind of seaside sheen. They started to pack up when the first leaves came out; they got up early on the first Tuesday in May, drank their glasses of compote, winked at the penguin, and took their suitcases out onto the path. The sun broke nimbly through the treetops, and the shadows made a patchwork of shapes on a background of gravel. All a-yawn, Virtuoso dragged himself out from under a bench. The radiant expanse of Tworki was slowly coming to life, it was still empty and quiet, the soft, indistinct, but altogether good moment just before a very early breakfast. In the flower bed, crimson roses were gearing up to bloom, perfectly befitting the coffee-colored dress, and they smiled to one another like two matching colors. They went out through the gate, and Wacek, the security guard, saluted them in jest; they put their suitcases on the platform, and Jurek Unsure-ek, Jurek Obscure-ek Manure-ek, embraced Janka in what seemed a long good-bye.

From the direction of Milanówek and Podkowa there came a drawn-out whistle, happy and sad, the first and the last. If it's a Tuesday, then we're leaving Tworki, time to get on, close the door, buy two tickets; time to give Janka the suitcases and leap quickly onto the last step, holding on to your glasses. They pressed their faces to the window pane. The gate nestled back around the bend, the poplars remained on alert, and at the end of the platform the rusty sign with the station name appeared one more time. "Tworki," Jurek read in a whisper. "Tworki."

Yes, there is now a great quiet over Tworki. Everyone's gone off somewhere, left, disappeared, still some time until breakfast. A light wind is stirring the dust on the platform, the paths lead no one anywhere, the benches all around are unoccupied just now. There, behind the trees, a few pajamas will leave their timeless, striped imprint on the wind, a vertical pattern in matter and time, from collars to shoes, from alpha to omega. A good time to offer the justification as promised, once again to give an incomplete answer, a partial alibi.

A few sentences, a paragraph, beautiful exclamation points like tears welling up in the eyes, a signature. S., Sonia, the name of Sonia, Sonia by the name of Sonia. Sonia, Sonia, S. like two interlocked horseshoes, Sonia signed in absentia. Signed Sonia, who's dead, who consents to die. Sonia, now gone from her signature, who no longer wishes to be her signature and knows that that name does not mean her, Sonia, who would like to sign, if only not to live thereafter. It was six in the morning, and Sonia was by the windowsill trembling from the cold; she signed, she shortened her name to a modest initial in order to distance herself, such as she was, from this place, to subtract herself timidly, so as to leave barely a sign of herself, something minimal, minimally significant. But her signature remained, the sign remained, S. remained, yes, a modest logo curled out from two sides, as if it were standing against itself and folding closed before the next step, but it was inevitably obliged to signify. Because, after all, the two horseshoes of this one letter, hard as they may be, much as they may weaken superhuman hands with each passing day, allow us to write them out, to draw them out, stretch them out in one line from *S* to *A.* Whatever might be lacking arises in these strange but familiar letters; S. is again called Sonia, the one called Sonia, who is now not Sonia, a few days ago enjoyed cabbage washed down with plum compote, and she really, really liked the vodka. The repeated initial brought us back to the beginning, for there was no Sonia anymore, she no longer sufficed. And yet, wasn't it she who accepted, sensed, reinforced, and suffered this repetition with the sort of lost breath that hovered in her copy pencil? She wrote S., she finished the S. and suddenly, once again—the sill was as cold as stone, clouds were rolling by outside the window—and once again, as though all of existence, the question of being, and the history of the world flared up in that trembling body, she repeated the *S* two lines lower, she appended her name to the postscript in a resonance, in a quiet, quiet echo. Ta-da, ta-da, ta-diddy-da, Sonia's here and Sonia's there, ta-da, there Sonia's dead, here the sound carries on, here Sonia, who's not Sonia, the letter of her name is signed, it's calling and calling, it's constantly transmitting something.

And so I come as called, I receive the transmission, on so many pages I sign for this unwelcome, unaddressed gift and call on you, because perhaps one of you will come, one of you will arrive permanently at my bench, yes, I'm calling you, all of you, come at any old time you can, come from all corners by whatever train you can from morning to night and read, please read, and hallowed be your names, and sign for receipt, Jacek, Ilona, Roman! Certify receipt, Krysia, Ewa, Robert! Sign your names, Darek, Agnieszka, Ania, Karol, Gustaw, Maria! All of you whose names might be called today, sign again, confirm it, certify it, check off that you've received it, throw in your own post-postscript.

Beyond the window the fields and little houses, the motley fences flew by, the stops multiplied into infinity. Malichy and Reguły have already gone, Michałowice and Opacz have flown past, and soon thereafter Salomea, Raków, Reduta, and Włochy, just as if God had mixed it up after leaving Paradise, just as if God, on leaving Paradise, had really scrambled the languages and from one name he had made many. Janka and Jurek stood at the exit, sliding their suitcases close to the door; the train started to slow down, and in the distance they beheld the name Warsaw.

■ □ ■ □ ■

CHAPTER TWENTY-FOUR

HOW WELL THAT MAY MORNING TOOK ROOT IN MEMORY. THEY'D LEFT the room while the sun was still stuck beyond the Helenów Forest and the remnants of night were tangled in the shadowy treetops. Long streaks of pink adorned the sky more and more, and patches of fog sipped at themselves. Jurek and Janka went in front; behind them Ania, Asia, and Bronka were talking with some boys, and one could hear bursts of laughter. At the tail of the procession Marcel was telling Mama about a nightclub in Adria. As they were passing through the gate, next to a sleepy Johann, Sonia and Olek ran up to them, a little out of breath. Sonia always wore that same dress, now a bit wrinkled, differently radiant in the dawn colors than it had been yesterday afternoon; Olek didn't let go of Sonia's hand, and he looked everyone so deeply, though cheerfully, in the eye. They said their hellos, and the procession turned left past the gate. That same trail as always, through the nettles and ferns, took them to the Utrata. A bit of light now took the middle current toward Pruszków, and by the dark banks one could see the bright spots of flowers. The mist on the birthday meadow managed to lift, and the bonfire gave off its last warm breaths. They stood in a circle around it and recalled the evening's fun. Soon the sun started to reach their faces, and they continued walking along the river all the way to its beginning, in the direction of its not-too-distant sources, just a few kilometers away. The current was getting weaker and weaker, and the banks were coming closer together like eyelids toward the pupil. It was getting quieter and warmer, and they went slowly, majestically, savoring each step. At a certain point Sonia jumped lower down, right down beside the water, and she gathered a few marigolds and forget-me-nots. Whistling, she bunched them into a small bouquet, and then she ran tiptoe up to Jurek. He stopped when she touched his back with her hand and, surprised, turned his head toward her.

The river glistened at their feet, the river meandered, the trees cast their first, still-long shadows, the river was shining; and smiling, without a word, without a word, Sonia gave Jurek the flowers.

NOTES

Chapter Two

8 *New Courier* The *Nowy Kurier Warszawski* was a Polish-language newspaper introduced by the Nazis in October 1939 and was generally known as a propaganda rag. There was a strict ban on any independent press during the occupation.

10 *"Your mouth, young lady, is ravenous for kisses, / It dreams of nymphs afeared of their own cares."* This poem, "On the Day Before" ("W przededniu"), is by Leopold Staff (1878–1957), one of the most important poets to come out of the Young Poland movement at the turn of the last century.

14 *Her sea, as she immediately explained, was at one time also our sea* Between 1920 and 1939, the port city of Gdańsk (in German, Danzig) was a free, autonomous, and primarily German-speaking zone, though it was entirely surrounded by independent Poland.

Chapter Four

22 *Krupp and Daimler be damned* Krupp was a major German steel producer from the eighteenth century through World War II, when the company became famous as an arms manufacturer for the Third Reich. Much of their workforce in the early 1940s

consisted of slave labor from concentration camps, including Auschwitz. Today Krupp belongs to ThyssenKrupp AG, a major producer of industrial steel. Daimler-Benz AG produced automobiles, aircraft, and other machinery, most notably Mercedes-Benz, from 1926 to 1998, when it became DaimlerChrysler.

23 *Battle of Warsaw, the "Miracle on the Vistula"* Following World War I and the call for Polish independence at Versailles, the Bolshevik Army fought to preserve Russian dominion over lands formerly held by the Russian Empire. The Battle of Warsaw (August 12–15, 1920) marked Poland's decisive victory over Russian forces.

31 *Maginot Line* The string of French fortifications constructed along the border with Germany between World War I and World War II, the Maginot Line became emblematic of ineffectual defensive planning following the successful Nazi invasion in 1940.

Chapter Five

34 *if Poland hadn't depended so much on its corridor* The Polish Corridor was the large strip of Polish land that stretched to the Baltic Sea, separating greater Germany from the German-speaking free city of Gdańsk (Danzig) and East Prussia. Adolf Hitler initially argued that an invasion of Poland was necessary to reintegrate a splintered Germany.

Chapter Six

45 *Professor Wilczur movies* In popular Polish films directed by Michał Waszyński in the late 1930s, Kazimierz Junosza-Stępowski played Professor Wilczur. The screenplays were written by Anatol Stern (1899–1968), a major poet and critic, and were based on highly successful novels by Tadeusz Dołęga-Mostowicz.

45 *the mysteries of Paris* *The Mysteries of Paris* was a sensational multivolume serial novel from the mid-nineteenth century. Its French author, Eugène Sue (1804–57), was particularly interested in the lives of Paris's underclass.

48 *Operation Arsenal* Meksyk II, or Operation Arsenal, was a successful 1943 mission of the Polish underground. The objective was to free Officer Jan Bytnar and other Polish military personnel from Nazi custody. Part of the operation was staged in front of Warsaw's Arsenal building, where Resistance fighters liberated the prisoners as they were being transferred to Gestapo headquarters.

Chapter Seven

57 *Mickiewicz's* Forefather's Eve From 1820 until his death, Adam Mickiewicz (1798–1855), Poland's national poet, wrote four interconnected plays known collectively as *Forefather's Eve* (*Dziady*). Standard texts in the Polish canon, these plays can be confusing for students, in part because the protagonist's name changes from one play to the next.

57 *Fredro's* Revenge Aleksander Fredro (1793–1876), a major Polish playwright, wrote the comedy *Revenge* (*Zemsta*) in 1834. The play centers on the convoluted love interests of two families feuding over an estate they share.

58 *"It's supposed to be Tarnowski"* Stanisław Tarnowski (1837–1917) was an important teacher of literature and a cultural historian. Among his major works is a book devoted to the comedies of Aleksander Fredro.

60 *Old Shatterhand* German writer Karl May (1842–1912) wrote sixteen novels for young boys featuring the adventures of Old Shatterhand, the European friend of an Apache chief on the American frontier. Old Shatterhand was allegedly based on May himself.

Chapter Eight

65 *an idyll on Szucha Boulevard* During the Nazi occupation, Szucha Boulevard was the location of the Gestapo's Warsaw headquarters.

66 *Campo dei Fiori* Campo dei Fiori is a piazza in Rome used as an open-air marketplace and, historically, as a space for public execu-

tions. Most notably, sixteenth-century philosopher Giordano Bruno was burned alive there in 1600 for the heresy of declaring that Earth orbited the sun. In a famous 1943 poem titled "Campo dei Fiori," Nobel laureate Czesław Miłosz (1911–2004) fused Bruno's execution on the Roman piazza with the Nazi suppression of the Warsaw Ghetto Uprising, which took place just over the wall from a popular carousel.

Chapter Nine

88 *Adenoid Hynkel* The character Adenoid Hynkel was Charlie Chaplin's parody of Adolf Hitler in *The Great Dictator* (1940).

Chapter Eleven

96 *Berdichev* Berdichev (in Polish, Berdyczów) is a city dating back to the fifteenth century; historically part of Poland, it is now located in northern Ukraine. The Jews of Berdichev, more than thirty thousand people constituting more than half the city's population, were murdered by the Nazis in 1941.

Chapter Thirteen

106 *"Laura and Philon"* A pastoral song, "Laura and Philon" is based on a text by the sentimentalist poet Franciszek Karpiński (1741–1825).

Chapter Fourteen

108 *the one about the cinnamon shop* The short-story collection *Cinnamon Shops,* by the Polish-Jewish writer Bruno Schulz (1892–1942), is credited with revitalizing Polish literary language in the interwar period. Schulz was shot by a Gestapo officer on the street in his hometown.

Chapter Sixteen

122 *Kampinos Forest* An ancient forest outside of Warsaw, Kampinos was the site of much combat during both world wars. During World War II, the Nazis used the forest to carry out mass executions.

Chapter Eighteen

133 *drew a Christmas wafer from his book* In Central and Eastern Europe, Roman Catholics often celebrate Christmas with a thin wafer made from wheat flour and imprinted with a religious image, generally that of the Virgin Mary holding the infant Jesus. Celebrants at a family gathering break off pieces of the wafer while exchanging blessings.

136 *like Poland's wedding to the sea* When Poland was partitioned in the late eighteenth century, it lost access to the Baltic Sea, which was necessary for the military and economic stability of the then-defunct state. When Poland regained its statehood following World War I, the reacquisition of access to the Baltic was regarded as a major event, and it was marked by a military ceremony called the Marriage to the Sea, complete with the casting of a wedding ring into the water.

Chapter Nineteen

143 *rusty sign that said PRUSZKÓW* An industrial suburb of Warsaw bordering the village of Tworki, Pruszków had a significant Jewish population before the Nazi invasion. During World War II, the Nazis established a transit camp there, from which most detainees were deported to concentration camps.

150 *"Erledigt." . . . "Exekutivmassnahme, Zugrunde gehen. Entschuldigen Sie, bitte."* The German speech, in its *hochdeutsch,* or standard, non-dialect accent, translates as: "It's done. Executive order: terminated. Regrets."

■ □ ■ □ ■

ABOUT THE AUTHOR

MAREK BIEŃCZYK is the critically acclaimed author of the novel *Terminal* and of several collections of essays and literary criticism, including *On Transparency* and *The Eyes of Dürer: On Romantic Melancholy.* A noted wine critic and expert on French culture, he is also a prolific translator of Milan Kundera and Roland Barthes, among others. He teaches at the Institute of Literary Studies of the Polish Academy of Sciences and lives in Warsaw.

■ □ ■ □ ■

WRITINGS FROM AN UNBOUND EUROPE

For a complete list of titles, see the Writings from an Unbound Europe Web site at www.nupress.northwestern.edu/ue.

Words Are Something Else
DAVID ALBAHARI

Perverzion
YURI ANDRUKHOVYCH

The Second Book
MUHAREM BAZDULJ

The Grand Prize and Other Stories
DANIELA CRĂSNARU

Peltse and Pentameron
VOLODYMYR DIBROVA

The Tango Player
CHRISTOPH HEIN

Mocking Desire
DRAGO JANČAR

A Land the Size of Binoculars
IGOR KLEKH

Balkan Blues: Writing Out of Yugoslavia
EDITED BY JOANNA LABON

The Loss
VLADIMIR MAKANIN

Compulsory Happiness
NORMAN MANEA

Border State
TÕNU ÕNNEPALU

How to Quiet a Vampire: A Sotie
BORISLAV PEKIĆ

A Voice: Selected Poems
ANZHELINA POLONSKAYA

Estonian Short Stories
EDITED BY KAJAR PRUUL AND DARLENE REDDAWAY

The Third Shore: Women's Fiction from East Central Europe
EDITED BY AGATA SCHWARTZ AND LUISE VON FLOTOW

Death and the Dervish
The Fortress
MEŠA SELIMOVIĆ

The Last Journey of Ago Ymeri
BASHKIM SHEHU

Conversation with Spinoza: A Cobweb Novel
GOCE SMILEVSKI

House of Day, House of Night
OLGA TOKARCZUK

Materada
FULVIO TOMIZZA

Shamara and Other Stories
SVETLANA VASILENKO

Lodgers
NENAD VELIČKOVIĆ

And Other Stories
GEORGI GOSPODINOV

In-House Weddings
BOHUMIL HRABAL

Tworki
MAREK BIEŃCZYK